Dracula Hearts of Glory

Dracula Hearts, Volume 3

A. J. Gallant

Published by A. J. Gallant, 2024.

Also by A. J. Gallant

Braeden the Barbarian
Forbidden City: Braeden the Barbarian
King of the Castle

Dracula Hearts
Dracula: Hearts of Stone
Dracula Hearts of Fire
Dracula Hearts of Glory

of Kingdoms and Magic
A Dragon Named Koontz

"of Knights and Wizards"
Knights of the Dragon
Knights of the Wizard

Olivia Brown Mysteries

I Was Murdered Last Night
Five minutes after Midnight
Dead Man Talking
Murdered Last Night

Paranormal Detective
Killer Detective

Young Adorok
Young Adorok

Standalone
A Christmas Carol A New Version
Garden Star The Awakening
Moon Diamond The Cat Detective

Dracula

Hearts of Glory

Book three

(DRACULA HEARTS)

A. J. Gallant

Dracula: Hearts of Glory

✕

THIS IS BOOK 3 OF THE series. Dracula: Hearts of Stone is the first, and Dracula: Hearts of Fire is the second.

✕

"I like a man who grins when he fights."
WINSTON CHURCHILL

"All men are brothers, like the seas throughout the world; so why do winds and waves clash so fiercely everywhere?"

Emperor Hirohito

"Love is an irresistible desire to be irresistibly desired."
Robert Frost

CHAPTER ONE

THE MORNING SEEMED splendid, with the sun casting a warm glow on the delicate, rose-colored clouds, but looks could be deceiving. Life had more tricks up its sleeve than a wizard. The crescent moon was changing into its daytime attire, an attractive silver outfit. With summer in bloom, a blue jay was gathering peanuts from a nearby bird feeder, flying back to its nest at the top of a pine tree. Nothing made it happier than peanuts in the shell, returning to his mate to show how he was such an excellent provider. Life should be so simple for everyone.

Only the occasional car went by at such an early hour in Moncton. The wind was light. The scents of flowers were on the air, and magical properties changed the DNA of vampires. However, some appeared to be immune to its altering forces and were imperceptible madness for a few, distinctive darkness for others. It was a thing that could twist the souls of some. Nasty magic that could unquestionably alter the world.

Jenny was smiling in her parents' bedroom, giving them both looks of what have you *done?* It was a surprise that had taken them all off guard. Even Dracula himself had not considered it. Once was a freak of nature, but twice? The look on Jenny's face was exquisite, scolding, and yet perplexed. She wanted to hate the news, but wasn't sure if she did. "Mother, you're pregnant? I'm gonna have a little brother or sister? Oh, I hope it's a girl. It would be so much fun to have a little sister. Holy crap, does that mean she's going to be a wizard because of bozo here?"

"Jenny!"

Dracula nodded. "It would be nice if it were a girl."

"Dracula!" What was he thinking? Allison knew the vampire already had the knowledge it was a male. Why would he allow Jenny to hope it was a girl? Men! She guessed they were full of testosterone and baloney in equal proportions. She felt like throwing him out of bed as if there hadn't been enough thorns recently. Telling Jenny that it was a boy was not likely to be pleasant. There would be no proper time for that revelation. Perhaps it would be best just to spill it.

The doorbell rang again.

Jenny didn't want to answer it because she was preoccupied with the conversation about having a sibling. The chatter was irresistible. Different imaginary scenarios were developing between her and her kid sister and everything she could teach her. She considered they could end up being quite the duo. Vampires better beware of Jenny and her sister. Maybe she could be the one to pick her name? What joy would there be in watching her grow up? How fun would it be to make clothes for her sister? Her mind was swirling at the thought of it. "Who could be at the door so early?"

The Master spoke, happy that Jenny was taking the news of the pregnancy better than he had expected. The house could crumble if the girl had exploded in anger. "It's Jareth. He's here to guide you to that tainted wizard."

Jenny thought about what might be in store for her. Her journey had only begun as a wizard, yet she had already faced many dangers. Being Dracula's daughter came with responsibility, and she wasn't sure if she liked it. Being responsible was one thing, but being expected to step up and help save the world was something else. The scale was unbalanced, and it did not lean to her side. Her life would never be all sunny days and starry nights. If she died fighting that evil wizard, she would return as a ghost, kick Dracula's ass, or hang out with Zacharia. "Don't you think that evil is such a stupid word? Nobody's completely evil. Everyone has some good traits. A serial killer might give money to the poor, saving some while he kills others."

"That might be true, but some have the Grand Canyon full of bad traits, with only a knapsack full of good. Helping an old woman across the street will not make up for burning her house down."

"You're weird."

Allison felt scared for her daughter, knowing that it might be the last time she would see her. She hated having to think of such things. Her life would have been so different if she had had an ordinary child, but she wouldn't give up Jenny and all she was for the world. The girl was complex, and even her mother wasn't sure of all her abilities. The worst part was her doing things no child could accomplish. She turned to Dracula. "I'm sure you can get someone else to face him beside Jenny. You must know plenty of wizards with experience who can care for him. I don't want her going after a wizard at her age. She needs time to develop her skills."

The vampire hesitated. What should he say, and how should he say it? How was he to proceed? Dracula knew she would be in danger. He had to select his words carefully lest her mother forbids her to go. He had gone from depressive to excessive in such a short time. Though they had discussed it all before, important things would come back like boomerangs. It was a difficult situation. "Allison, I know you don't want to hear this, but Jenny is the King of the Castle, so to speak, when it comes to wizards. Because I am her father, she has a significant role in the upcoming battle. I wish it weren't so, but I fear the outcome would be disastrous if she neglected her duties. Imagine a world run by miscreant vampires?"

"But she's only a child."

"A child, yes, but she's far from ordinary. Why must we engage in the same conversation over and over?"

"Why can't you just kill the stupid wizard yourself?"

Jenny savored the conversation. It was fun to see the mighty Dracula struggle with the right words. She continued to labor because he was her father. Perhaps she always would. Having kept it from her for so long might irritate her forever. But a word of praise from him was worth more than compliments from anyone else.

Dracula thought Jenny would likely be a big part of the battle. There was a high risk that the world would sink into the pits of hell without being able to extricate itself from an unbearable fate. There would be pockets of good amongst a sea of evil, a sea of sin ready with the most ferocious waves to pummel any that dared to surface. Misery would flourish as hope diminished to a mere speck of light. She didn't want her child to be placed in jeopardy, nor did her father. However, he was aware of the larger picture that would break over humanity's head if his daughter took a passive role. She needed the experience and to be battle-tested. "Just because she's supposed to be a major player doesn't mean she has to play, but I fear the future is dim without her. Remember the Blood Book? She desperately needs it. More importantly, the world needs her to get it."

Allison didn't want to think about what he said. But no matter how much Allison hoped, some realities were unchangeable. "I don't want her to be important. That's not what I mean. Oh, you know what I'm saying. I don't like the sound of any of this. I'd bury my head so deep if I were an ostrich."

The lion rose from the hall, entered the room, and swatted at the air. Everyone watched the cat's strange antics. Sarah was pursuing Zacharia's ghost as he floated around. It leaped and batted at him awkwardly, following him as he moved around the room. She sprang into the air, trying to bite the ghost.

Jenny waved at the space where the cat now gazed. "Hi, Zacharia."

Annoyance filled Allison's voice. "That's just what we need, a ghost in the room."

Dracula entered the mind of the lion so that he could watch his friend as he drifted around. Zacharia was bored, so he figured he might as well be nosy. He wasn't accustomed to being a spirit and had trouble moving his soul around. Outside, he could see the white light in the distance that beckoned him with relatives in silhouettes awaiting his arrival, but he refused to go for the present. He figured there would be no turning back if he entered that light.

Allison smiled at Jenny. "Did that lion really tell you I was pregnant?"

"She did. And how long would it have been before you told me if she hadn't? My sister would have been two, I suspect."

"Jenny, it's going to be a boy." Allison watched Jenny's smiling face change. If Jenny had been a canine, she would have growled. She imagined the gears, where they were humming joyfully only moments ago and now were grinding to a halt.

Disappointment washed over Jenny. "What? No, how can you know that?"

Allison gestured toward Dracula, who looked away.

"Aw, not a boy. Tell me it's a sick joke. It's really a boy? It's a freaking little brat? I'd rather have a monkey. I suppose I could always lose him in the forest. Father, I'm unfamiliar with this area. Are there any cliffs nearby?"

"Fundy has some nice cliffs."

Allison shook her head. "Don't encourage her."

"Jenny."

"What?"

"I met a fish that couldn't swim, so I refused to throw him in." Dracula smiled at his daughter.

"Okaaay."

Again, the doorbell sounded.

Allison didn't know what to think. If the boy was a wizard, what trouble would he get in? Perhaps she would luck out, and he would be an ordinary child, but since Dracula's genes were probably dominant, it was unlikely. Jenny had been tricky enough to parent, but a boy with testosterone. Girls would sit on the sofa and play with dolls. Boys would jump off the couch on their heads, cry, and do it again. Sibling rivalry could destroy the house. One thing was the age difference. Jenny would be a lot older. Perhaps Jenny's magic could keep him in check, or perhaps she would tie him up with a spell. "Whoever is ringing that doorbell at this hour of the morning, I should sic Sarah on him and make her eat him."

The lion turned and ran downstairs. Jenny blurred to save Jareth from being eaten, making it down just in time. There would be few opportunities to be bored in this madhouse.

"Jenny, don't you leave without telling us!"

Dracula grinned regally. "I believe she's gone to save Jareth."

"Oh, my goodness. Are you telling me that Sarah understood what I said? She was going down there to eat him?"

"Indeed." Dracula slowly nodded.

Dracula gave Allison a tender kiss. They watched the doorway in silence as they waited for Jenny to return. Even with all the trouble in the world, Dracula enjoyed life as he hadn't been able to do in a long time. A degree of all the carnage was exciting, although unfortunate. Boredom couldn't stand up to a good fight. Hundreds simultaneously engaged in battle were like fireworks.

"What are we going to do about the baby?"

Allison turned and gave him a look that could cut diamonds. "What is that supposed to mean?"

"My mind is troubled."

"My fist will trouble your nose if you bring that up again."

"That's not what I meant."

Jenny and the lion ran up the stairs and back into the bedroom. "Jareth will meet me at noon tomorrow at the Bell Tower on Main Street, and then I'm off to either flatten or get flattened."

Dracula met his daughter's eyes, and she returned his gaze, both refusing to break off. Nobody could stare long into those eyes except Jenny. He liked that fact more than he thought possible because it was like one of life's little surprises to the vampire. "Have you been paying attention to your dreams?"

"Yes, *Father*. I've been eating three meals daily and even washing behind my ears." She sighed. "I admit my dreams are bizarre lately. Evil vampires control New York City. It's just terrible. It's such a dark atmosphere that I can't even describe it. Strange-looking eyes were everywhere. I sure hope I didn't see the future."

"Will you two stop that!" Allison was becoming aggravated by their antics of staring one another down.

"Stop what?" they said simultaneously.

"Stop staring at one another as if you're enemies."

Both Dracula and Jenny had to laugh. It was just a game to both, the early stages of bonding. They enjoyed doing it, so it wasn't likely to stop. It was going to be one of their father-and-daughter things.

"It's a boy, for sure?"

Her father tried to look disappointed, but she didn't believe it. "Yes, it's a boy."

Jenny thought about it as she showed a mischievous smile. "Let me touch your stomach. I'll see if I can change it into a girl. I'll bet there's a spell for that."

"Jenny, that is not the least bit funny."

"But what if there *was* a spell to change him into a girl?"

"Stop it."

Jenny stood akimbo. "I'm going back to bed even though I won't be able to sleep. I'll just stare at the ceiling until my eyes bugged out. That book better be worth it. It better tell me how to enchant objects to keep the vampires a hundred miles away and show me how to change a boy to a girl."

She went back into her bedroom with the lion following. Allison and Dracula stared at one another, and when he tried to caress her leg, she slapped his hand. She gently guided his hand to her face, feeling the warmth of his touch against her skin.

CHAPTER TWO

THE SKELETON WAS AN IMPOSING SIGHT. It was now burning with red, blue, and yellow flames. The crackling sound consumed oxygen, sending black smoke into the air; small red skulls of long-lost souls floated inside its chest cavity, occasionally bumping into one another with a loud *tok*. It was developing and getting stronger, taking some energy from the nasty enchantment particles that circled the globe. It spat flames into the sky to warn anyone who would dare approach; they went up almost a hundred feet before dissipating. It had a developing mind that changed with every wizard it killed. So, it knew it was infinitely better to be the vanquisher than the vanquished. The devourer stared down at its two victims, a sinister grin spreading across its face. It considered its next move, whether to see if it could pick up another wizard's trail or finish its enemies in front of him.

The flames consumed Alexander's vampire dog. She squealed as she lay on the grass burning up; the blaze ravaging her, going deeper and deeper. The fire had reached Tessy's organs and began to engulf them. She had never felt such pain, but just in time, her system finally got the upper hand. She was now healing faster than her body was being destroyed. When the fire and her healing properties were almost in balance, it prolonged the agony because the flames had the slight upper hand. But the enchantment had weakened just enough for the healing to overtake the hurting. Her restorative properties extinguished the fire gradually. Finally, the dog could stand, but it felt strange. Most of her fur had been burnt away, with two tufts remaining and both near the end of her tail. She looked so peculiar, as strange as a hairless cat. The air felt foreign to her bare skin. It tickled and made her scratch, but a minute after extinguishing the fire, her fur grew back.

Alexander lay nearby, also being consumed by the flames. The sheriff's skin turned as black as charcoal because of the severe burns. He had stopped screaming and was motionless as his fire continued to rage, unable to move even an inch. He had lapsed into a coma. Death was coming. Although invisible to most, the spirits of his relatives waited patiently for his soul to depart, and two males apparently arguing about something.

Tessy produced several distressed barks as she circled him, not knowing what to do. It wasn't a situation that her aggression could solve. It was the worst she had ever felt, the desperation and hopelessness hitting her as hard as any blow. What could she do to save her master?

The skeleton approached the sheriff, preparing to rip his head off. It would be a satisfying conclusion to the battle, and it had plenty of strength. It was curious how much energy would leave the sheriff, sensing he was special. Tessy attacked with barks and mighty snaps from her powerful jaws, showing her nasty side. She circled it, leading the monster away from Alexander, which she had intended.

Again, the skeleton attacked the dog, but she got out of its way this time. It chased the animal around on the lawn, but the shepherd was faster. It shot balls of fire at her, but she dodged them all. The dog's tenacity and courage annoyed it because it so wanted to stand over her dead carcass, knowing it had vanquished it. Not understanding why it was so persistent in defense of another. The dog blurred off, and the skeleton was glad to see it go as it again headed to finish Alexander, laughing at the prospect.

Tessy zoomed back with a large branch, knocking the monster off its feet. It jumped back up to a standing position, furious, launching spheres of fire at her, one the size of a basketball; Tessy dodged all of them. The shepherd flung the limb, catching it in the ribs and it stuck there. The ungodly thing staggered around awkwardly, tried to remove the now burning branch but couldn't quite manage it. It was a graceless ballet of jumps and turns. Most of the branch was sticking out from its back as it attempted to extricate it. It would have been a funny sight had there not been so much riding on the outcome. It stopped and glared at the dog, rushing it and spitting flames, but the branch caught on the lawn, causing it to fall again.

This time, standing like a bug turned upside down wasn't easy. It had never been so enraged in its young life and would relish killing the dog. Finally, it got up and tried to catch the dog again, but she was too fast. It paused as it attempted to conceive a surefire method to tag the animal with its deadly flames, deciding that more fire was better. It saturated the area with many fireballs, hoping she would run into one, but she didn't.

Tessy wanted to bite the thing so much that she could barely contain herself. Even though she knew it might mean death, resisting was difficult. She was desperate to snap one of those damn tibias. She was a red sheriff, an attack dog that needed to attack but couldn't. Tessy relentlessly attacked and then pulled back, with the heat from its fire being an excellent reminder of Tessy's excruciating pain, like trying to defeat a forest fire with a broom. Wherever it walked, large sections of grass perished from its radiating flames. Unbeknownst to Achak, the formidable monster was now in control, and progressing rapidly.

"Bark, bark, bark!" Tessy backed up, then ran and jumped several feet over the monstrosity, simultaneously urinating on it, with the urine sizzling as it hit the fire. The thing shook at the indignity as a drop touched its skull. It launched a barrage of fiery embers at the dog in retaliation, but none of them hit their mark, with one burning a deep hole in the grass. The skeleton thought the dog was somehow a match for its might, but wasn't sure how that was possible. It believed it was king of the world and had been correct to this point.

"Bad dog!" said the skeleton. Disappointed in itself, it felt a pang of frustration for its inability to take down the animal. The fiery monstrosity felt like it was evolving, but did not know the end result. It had even grown two inches taller. It got more intelligent as it developed and was getting views of the world. Would it soon be able to make its own plans? Perhaps it would be Achak's master? It could imagine controlling that wizard and making him fetch.

While running, a beautiful blond jogger with her ponytail dancing in the air encountered the skeleton and was attacked with no prior knowledge of its presence. As she was running, fire headed directly towards her, but she was pushed by the dog and sent flying just in time. The flames just missed her. It knocked the wind out of her, and it hurt. She got up and ran away as fast as possible, in pain from the impact, but she survived the encounter.

It stood still for a time, and its skull turned 360 degrees around and back to its original position. The beast appeared to be concentrating hard on something as strange sensations went through it. It felt cold, then hot, and it felt the wind for the first time. Something was going on, but what? It held its bony hand out in front of it, jarring it forward as if attempting to get something to manifest. It repeated the actions several times until a bright red blob of molten lava finally appeared, transforming into a flaming sword in the skeleton's right hand.

Wielding complicated magic, it impressed itself with what it had accomplished. It loved the sword's weight and was captivated by its beauty, with skulls adorning the hilt. It attacked Tessy, and each time it swung, the weapon fire flew from it in multiple directions, some approaching the dog in such proximity it was a miracle that the flames missed. Chasing the dog around in a circle, swinging the blade vigorously, becoming more frustrated that it couldn't tag her with it. It hurled the sword at the dog, but she skillfully dodged it, and it lodged in the ground. The grass died several yards around it.

The magical corpse strolled toward the weapon and pondered as it did so. It retrieved the sword, turned, and stared at Alexander. It was more determined to cut his head off and end him. Perhaps that act would be enough of a distraction to end the dog. Yes, it decided that it was the best option that was available.

It blurred toward the sheriff with murder in every inch of its being, forcing Tessy to act. She grabbed the skeleton's femur and crunched down hard, breaking it, but in doing so, her head caught on fire. It fell, surprising it with what the animal had accomplished. The monster actually felt the pain of it. Sharp shepherd teeth grabbed it by its left leg and tossed it over a hundred feet across the grass. The thing fell to pieces as all its bones detached and came apart. It hollered in agony, but quickly pulled itself together as if it was new again. The dog squealed as the flames burned her head, but they extinguished.

The skeleton retrieved its weapon again, seeing the dog in a different light. Perhaps it was a danger to it in its early stages of development. Should it consider fleeing from the shepherd? In order to become so powerful that nothing could challenge it, it needed to survive. It halted and focused on another wizard, which would provide more power for it to absorb. Resistance was impossible, as that was its purpose for being. It turned, trying to fix on the magical emanations; they appeared to be on the wind from the southwest.

Those particles resembled green smoke to the supernatural creature, tasting as sweet as chocolate. It concentrated hard on whatever wizard it detected. And so it departed the area, rushing off in search of more power.

The dog grabbed Alexander and rushed to the 18-acre Central Park Lake, knowing that the flames would again consume her, but to her, there was nothing else she could think of that might work. She was prepared to accept that sacrifice, even if it meant it was the end of her. Tessy rushed the sheriff into the lake, and his flames burned underwater. But gradually, the fire diminished on both her and her master. Tessy pulled Alexander out of the water and onto the lawn; shaking the water out of her fur, she nudged him. He was lifeless and burnt to such a degree that no one would recognize him. The dog nudged him again and got his ashes on her nose. Tessy could sense that his soul had departed his body, and tilting her head up, she howled.

CHAPTER THREE

Michael and Lauren were looking at cribs and other baby-related items in a baby boutique. The place had a pink and blue motif, with a large pink baby girl and a blue baby boy crawling in diapers on the ceiling. They were happy and energetic. Michael had such a grin on his face that it looked permanent. He had accepted that he had gotten Lauren pregnant, but his mind continued to give him scenarios of life with a baby. Would he be a miniature Michael? Lauren, dressed in black with her swords on her back, looked exceptional. An associate was eyeing the couple and her blades, fearful of approaching her. She recognized she was a red sheriff, but the sales clerk was wary of all vampires.

"Michael, your mind is like a beehive stirred up with a stick."

Michael whispered in Lauren's ear. "Hey, you are not supposed to go in there. Stop reading me. Should we get a sign that says *Vampire Baby Onboard?*"

"Be quiet, you doofus."

Michael gazed at a tiny blue plastic tricycle. "You need to watch how you talk to me. I don't want the baby calling me Daddy Doofus."

"The baby will have you figured out by the time she's two."

"When *he is* two, we'll be playing baseball. I'm gonna get him one of those little plastic bats."

The sales associate finally approached the couple with a bit of trepidation. The last customer had left, so she figured there was no other choice. It sure didn't look like they were going to go away. Diane was trying to be brave as she cleared her throat. "Can I help you?"

Michael smiled. "We're having a baby. Even though it's supposed to be impossible, we are having a baby."

Lauren looked at him with her gray-blue eyes and gave him a look before she turned her attention to Diane. "We're going to take that crib and that stroller. And one of those baby carriers. Oh, and a car seat."

It had been a slow week, and Dianne was happy she would get many sales. She had just asked for a raise, which might help her get it. She thought they were a cute couple and attracted to Michael, but she wouldn't dare show it. Lauren, who had also been poking around in Diane's head, knew it, but she wouldn't tell Michael.

Michael thought about the baby carrier. "Lauren, you know you can't be wearing the baby while you're out battling vampires. You know that, right?"

She turned to Michael, a little annoyed. "I have seniority, big Daddy, so while fighting the vampires, you'll be home watching the baby. Just think of all those stinky diapers you're going to change." Then she talked baby talk to him. "Isn't that right?"

"But, but, I'm going to be a red sheriff. Couldn't we just get a babysitter?"

Lauren gave Michael a look that could stop a bullet. "You want to leave our baby, a product of two vampires, home with a babysitter? Is that what you want to do, Michael?"

His eyebrows tightened. Why did women always think they were right? And that they usually were was irritating. "Why, what would happen? Would he eat her?"

"Michael, what is wrong with you?"

Michael noticed Diane staring at him. "Lauren, this stuff is all new to me. I have no experience with vampire babies or any babies. Would he bite her or not?"

"Anyway, if I get killed, that makes you the Daddy and the Mommy."

Why would she say such a thing? Of course, he thought about it and knew that it could happen. "Oh no. Now I have to think about that. What is wrong with *you*? Reading my mind when you promised you wouldn't. That's a point for my side; make that two points for that insensitive remark."

"I don't think I'm gonna like changing diapers. In fact, I just might be allergic to it."

He didn't like where this conversation was going. "Well, somebody's gotta change him."

Lauren turned to him and showed him the biggest smile.

"Oh."

"That reminds me, Michael will take that changing table."

The sales associate smiled and nodded. "Would you like this delivered?"

"Yes, please."

"Hey Lauren, we could sell him on the black market and make a nice profit."

"I could sell you on the black market, except that no one would want you. Besides, you two will be inseparable when you see her cute little face. It'll be a bond that will last a lifetime. I insist. I'm kidding. We'll share everything equally except for the diaper changing. But you will have to watch her while I kill vampires."

"How is that sharing everything equally?"

All kidding aside, Michael didn't like the thought of changing diapers. "You have to change him on occasion. What if I sprain my wrist while changing him? I think my wrist sprained just now. Besides, where are you gonna be if not home changing diapers on your days off?"

"I'll be at the mall shopping."

"I'll be back with a total in just a minute." Diane headed to her cash with a smile on her face. She liked both of them.

Michael stooped and talked to Lauren's stomach. "Do you think you can learn to change your own diapers?"

"What did she say?"

"He just laughed and laughed."

CHAPTER FOUR

DRACULA AND PIERS ANTHONY sat on a bench near the Petitcodiac River in Moncton. Dressed in a black Armani suit with a crimson alizarin tie, the Master looked exceptional. Piers was wearing a black sports coat over a white striped shirt with black pants. Dracula brought his sword to get Piers accustomed to wearing his. It became one of their favorite locations to hang out and discuss things. He enjoyed discussing his daughter and other topics as well. They also appreciated walking the path along the river for miles, and the walkers, joggers, and bikers added to the atmosphere. Normalcy was quite a luxury for Dracula. He got a lot out of ordinary people doing everyday things.

"So, you haven't sunk your teeth into anyone yet?"

"No, and I don't intend to bite anyone."

"You're going to be a vampire that doesn't bite? Interesting concept. Like a singer that doesn't sing."

They had discussed some sights the Master had seen over the years. As an author, Piers was very interested. The best research was talking to the Master. Piers was like a hungry sponge that couldn't get enough information. If the world ever normalized, he considered asking Dracula if he could do his life story, but getting it all in one book wouldn't be easy. Obviously, it would be a series of books, and he got excited just thinking about it. Guaranteed to be bestsellers for years to come, it would give people a better understanding of the world of vampires. He hoped the Master had not read his mind just then. He would have to wait for the proper time to ask him, and if he refused, he would badger him.

"Let's go back to the subject of the great fire."

Dracula nodded as his memory drifted back in time. Dracula nodded and recalled as he explained. "The houses in England in 1666 were made of wood and tar, so you can imagine how that blaze consumed the city. That fire had a life of its own and went on for five days, destroying over 80 churches and some 13 000 houses. Around 80,000 people were evacuated. It looked as though the devil had come down to play at night. The sky was so red. The smoke and stench were quite something. It was a catastrophe, covering an area of over 400 acres. A horrible sight greeted us as over eighty percent of the city lay in ruins. I saved a few, but fire is quite the monster with a mind of its own and hurts like hell. Left when they began the reconstruction. I still remember them widening and improving the roads, horses everywhere. It started in a bakeshop on Pudding Lane, if I recall correctly. The city was battling another plague."

Piers Anthony nodded. "Sounds like a nightmare. How many people perished in the fire? Thousands, I would imagine?"

Dracula thought about it. "Supposedly, they recorded only ten deaths."

"Really. How many do you think you saved?"

Dracula shrugged. "It was too long ago to remember such details. Old memories have a way of blurring, like a wet painting dropped on a hard surface. The memory is there, but you can't quite get to it."

"Un-huh."

"I believe the high number of killed rats helped control the plague. I still dream about it occasionally, with the smells and the sights bringing me back there. Some things you just can't get out of your head."

"Where were you when it started?"

"In the Tower of London."

A young couple was kissing on a blanket on the lawn to the left of them when a woman vampire wearing a bright yellow dress attacked them. Dracula ran interference and knocked her across the yard. She attempted to blur, but he was too fast for her. He grabbed her and snapped her neck. Then pulled her head off, and she turned to bones, tossing her in the middle of the river. Several seagulls went by on the tidal bore, and it looked like they were surfing. He displayed more anger than usual while accomplishing the killing. Vampire against a vampire was one thing, but a vampire against a human was despicable.

Piers had stood up and watched the bones disappear into the chocolate water. Only moments ago, she had been alive, but her nastiness had cost her everything. "She was beautiful; too bad she had to be an asshole."

Dracula returned to the bench. He thought about Jenny and wondered what life had in store for her as his daughter. Life often rained on one's picnic. "Perhaps you'll tell someone what Moncton was like way back when. The Moncton area will one day be four cities near one another, with Dieppe, Riverview, and Shediac reaching that rank. Of course, Dieppe has city status now."

He nodded as he watched a butterfly land on Dracula's left shoulder. "Yes, this is an interesting part of the world in its own right."

A namuhwoork flew over in the form of a crow. It circled and then touched down in front of Dracula, transforming into a beautiful naked redhead. She nodded at Dracula as Piers Anthony's eyes widened significantly. Looking her up and down, the author noticed she had a blonde streak in her red hair.

Dracula nodded a greeting. "Summer, you look radiant as usual."

She sat beside them, and Piers tried hard not to stare. "And you look as formidable as ever. The power of your daughter vibrates throughout the land. Hello, Piers Anthony."

"Do I know you?"

"No. Dracula, I come with a message from our king. We will be on your side during the upcoming battle. Though our numbers are few, we will try our best to aid in what must be your victory."

"Thank your king and queen for me and tell him the gift he wanted will be forthcoming."

"I bid you both farewell."

Piers watched as Summer turned back into a crow and flew off. "I liked her better in human form."

"Yes, quite attractive."

"And perky."

Dracula suddenly got a strange look on his face, and it wasn't a happy one. He could feel their animosity approaching. "Piers, don't take this the wrong way, but you have to run. More than a dozen vampires are heading this way, wanting to fight. There's too many of them for me to keep you safe."

"You want me to run? Are you sure?"

"Run, now!" He pointed in the direction that the author should move.

Piers blurred off even though he didn't want to abandon his friend, but he knew Dracula was right. He knew he would distract him from the task at hand. With so many biters, one of them would surely take the author's head off, and he was fond of his head. They would probably kill him just to irritate Dracula. He took the long way around and headed toward Dracula's house on Martin Street.

Dracula pulled out his ancient sword adorned with bats and placed it on his lap. About ten seconds after Piers blurred off, thirteen vampires appeared before him. They were a rough-looking bunch, dressed to look tough, except for the fat fellow wearing a moo

moo. What in the hell was he thinking? They were rugged, looking like bikers, though they had no bikes, all carrying swords, with one having a 9 mm Beretta M9 shoved into his belt. Although he wasn't sure what was up with that, they were grimy and dirty. Had they come from digging in the garbage? It sure smelled like it.

"Is that him?"

"That's him. I recognize him from the photos."

The Master smirked and shook his head. So many wanted to kill Dracula that he thought he would get a complex. "Can I help you, gentlemen?"

"You are Dracula, right?"

"I am."

The big fellow with the scruffy beard stepped forward, and the Master supposed he was the gang leader as he was pushing the others out of the way. He was cocky, his smile crooked and unmistakable. "We're here to kill you, and when we're finished, we're going to take over this city. We're gonna be famous."

Dracula stood up with his sword, noticing that most of them took a step back. "Brave last words. Your skeletal remains will soon be scattered."

The leader went for Dracula's head, but the Master moved so fast it appeared as if his own head fell off; his blood ended up on the faces of three others, with one wiping it off and tasting it. He turned to dust, his skeletal remains fell, and the battle resumed. It didn't make a difference that their leader was deceased; they were out to kill Dracula to become legends. Ford pulled his pistol and emptied it. However, Dracula slapped every bullet out of the air.

When the muscular African guy pulled out a Hithroma dagger, he figured it wasn't a good sign when Dracula laughed at it. His eyebrows tightened as he said: "Un oh." Abasi discovered the dagger lodged in his own chest. It was excruciating when he removed it. His head fell off, and he collapsed.

As their numbers decreased, they emitted grunts and moans during the collision of blades. When their numbers were down to five, the short French fellow from Louisiana tried to make a run for it, blurring towards Main Street. He only got about six feet away in the opposite direction when Dracula took his head. The velocity of movement sent the severed head rolling across the lawn; as the skin turned to dust, the skull continued to roll.

Piers Anthony returned to engage in battle, and he had only been gone for about a minute, but he saw that most of the miscreants were now bones. He took the head off the fellow that turned to attack him, the overweight fellow wearing a green muumuu. Dracula dispatched the others and then returned to the bench.

"Have you ever visited the Great Barrier Reef in Australia?"

The author didn't think he would ever get used to such carnage. Piers had never been to there but had heard and read about it. "That's all you have to say? No thoughts on the battle? And no, I've never been there."

"It's a beautiful place to do battle."

"I see."

"You don't listen very well. You knew there was no danger for me with that bunch, yet you returned to risk your life. History has many dead heroes, but now we need them alive more than ever. Don't do it again."

"It seemed like an idea then, but now not so much."

CHAPTER FIVE

A THUNDERSTORM LIT UP THE FIELD, and the hail started beating hard on the small rural house. It bounced explosively off the small dwelling. Dorian disliked the rain as it only dulled his hearing abilities, which is why some vampires preferred to attack in it. The element of surprise was sometimes the deciding factor, with one vampire killing another. In such a confined space, the noise was excessive.

The hard rain had turned to hail, sounding like the place was under attack, disrupting his contemplative mood. He tried hard to stay the course, but it wasn't easy. A golf ball-sized piece of hail broke a part of the kitchen window that had been cracked, and Dorian turned as it hit the floor. As if it were a living being, he directed his words towards the chunk of hail, accusing it of intentionally breaking the window. "Oh, come on!"

Wave after wave hit the kitchen windows, sounding louder than he thought possible. His senses were attacked, and his concentration obliterated. It stopped and turned into moderate rain. He nodded as he appreciated that the noise had ebbed down.

"That hail was so loud it hurt my ears."

Lemuel lay inside the coffin with his arms crossed. He tried to remain patient, but it wasn't working. He so desperately wanted out that he was salivating. Lemuel kicked and punched in the confined space, but it accomplished nothing. At least the spider had survived it. Lemuel wanted to strangle Dorian. He wished the roles were reversed where his brother was in a box and he could take his good old time. Lemuel would tell *him* he was going outside to watch the birds or some such foolishness, and then he could squirm.

"Get me out of here!"

All the time he had spent under the sound-absorbing ground was beyond description. All that quiet had been exasperating. Lemuel believed he had gone insane and somehow had come back. He expected someone to release him when they discovered him, but now he had to suffer further indignity, feeling like a jack-in-the-box that no one would ever let out. To truly comprehend his suffering, one had to experience it with distorted time and endless minutes. He never thought that his own mind could be such a ruthless enemy. He had imagined the sound of someone digging him out many times. "What, I can't hear you?"

"There was loud hail a minute ago!"

"Fuck the hail. Get me out of here!"

Lemuel had been out of the ground for more than a day, but it felt longer. He scratched at the wood until his nails detached and his fingers bled. That single day had felt like a year. His brother felt sorry for him, but his pity accomplished nothing. All his screaming and belittling accomplished nothing. It was merely a distraction. The process of having him extricated was a complicated thing. The spell attached was vexing, and even centuries had not weakened it. He was both impressed and saddened by the enchantment. Dorian's Blood Book would not reveal a counterspell to get him out, which worried the wizard.

It appeared those painstaking wizards had thought of every eventuality all those years ago, including that he might be located and dug out. However, such potent magic that it interfered with his book was not something he ever thought possible. What if it destroyed it? No wizard could claim expertise in all aspects of magic because of the numerous uncertainties. Those who had the most years and knowledge behind them were the most feared.

Lemuel produced excessive expletives that would have impressed a pro hockey player. "Get me out of here! I'm tired of being in here." Then his voice had a sad tone that trailed off. "I want to get out." It was a definite improvement from being buried alive some twelve feet down because he could now have a conversation with his brother, but not having seen the outside world in three hundred years was too much to bear. All he could see was a tiny spider. How the hell did that stupid spider get in here? Although it sounded crazy, he didn't want to kill it because it was all he had for company. He could talk to his brother, but he got some comfort out of the fact that he could see the spider.

"Lemuel, it's strange, but the book won't show me any spells I can use to get you out. I'm not exactly sure what to do."

"Dorian, what the shit! Am I supposed to live here forever?"

"Of course not. I'll think of something. I'll have you out soon." Dorian didn't sound confident because he wasn't. He couldn't think of a damn thing, and the harder he tried, the further the solution seemed. Stress was making it a lot harder to think. Was the coffin's enchantment affecting him? What a sneaky spell that would make. He could feel the waves of the magic radiating outward. A Blood Book was what every wizard sought because it was bound with its owner, allowing them to make the most potent enchantments that they could weave. It read one's thoughts and always acquiesced in a timely fashion. It appeared to be balking, and all the spells had to be done manually, one at a time. Dorian was not yet prepared to tell his brother because, for all he knew, the book was concealing the proper spell from him.

Dorian stared down at the coffin and didn't look happy. What if he could never extricate his brother? Listening to him complain for the next century would be more than he could bear.

"Don't do that." The tone was like a father talking to his child; his voice made it out of the coffin to Dorian's ears.

A puzzled Dorian. "Don't do what?"

"I wasn't talking to you. I was talking to the spider."

Dorian's brow tightened as he looked both puzzled and concerned. That made Dorian wonder about the effects of being confined for so long. Nothing to do and no one to talk to would leave too much time to think. What if he was insane when he got out of there? Everyone needed social encounters; otherwise, the brain would change into something strange. If Lemuel had taken a spider for a friend, it didn't sound beneficial to what was perhaps now a warped mind. He considered bringing it up but decided against it; it was a topic too weird to tackle now.

Once he got him out of there, he would have to deal with it, but until then, there was no point. Although he might face death at the hands of his brother by letting him out, whatever the consequence, he would have to face it. He could just run away and leave him in there, as it was unlikely that anyone else would or could let him out. The situation was getting harder to deal with by the hour.

"What did I tell you? How many times have I told you not to crawl on my face! Get over there. I'll slap you so hard your legs will fall off."

Dorian couldn't help it and had to laugh, but he tried hard to muffle it.

Lemuel hit the coffin's side with his fist to get his brother's attention. "So, what the hell have you been doing for the last three hundred years?"

"I've been trying to find you."

"Not trying hard enough. What are you gonna do now?"

"I'm going to enchant an ax and break you out of there. I think it'll work."

"Don't hurt the spider."

"Shut the hell up with that stupid spider. Now be quiet and let me read this. *This spell will enchant any ax that will break down any door. Ground-up dust of the glowing light click beetle and three drops of wizard's blood are required. Yes,* Lemuel, I think this will work."

"Hurry the hell up, will ya?"

"That attitude is not helping anyone."

Dorian searched for the ax, knowing he had seen one somewhere but could not remember where. He wasn't even sure if it was inside or out. After a quick search of the interior, he went out and looked around. The small dwelling had been pushed some forty feet, so he returned to its original location to search for the ax. It took a few minutes, but he found it by stepping on it, near where the front door had been, with a small amount of soil on it from digging his brother out of his grave. It was solid, and he considered it useful for chopping necks. There was a little rust on it, but that would make no difference to the enchantment. He kissed the blade for luck.

"Here goes nothing."

He took the ax into the house and placed it on the table. Dorian pulled a small rectangular box out of his right pocket, much heavier than it looked. From the small box, he retrieved seven other boxes filled with magical ingredients. The box itself was enchanted, capable of holding over a hundred boxes, but at the moment, it contained only twenty-three. He located the one with the crushed beetle that he needed, and it was more than half full, plenty for the spell, as it only required two pinches. There was a pungent odor to the ingredient, but he liked it.

Lemuel began to impatiently strum his fingers on the bottom of the coffin. "What the hell are you doing up there?"

"Lemuel, I need you to be quiet while I cast this spell."

"Hurry."

Dorian adjusted the ax so it was facing south. He sprinkled the dust onto the blade, ensuring a line of the ground-up insect reached from one end to the other. Dorian rubbed his hands together, turning a bright yellow; he then uttered the words the book showed him. "Dontramos Dasha coretha." The ax took on a bright yellow, and he nodded. It appeared to increase its weight tenfold, a good sign.

"What's going on? Did the enchantment work?" Lemuel had no confidence that whatever spell his sibling was conjuring up would do anything, but he prayed he would be out of there soon. He closed his eyes and listened.

"I now have an enchanted ax that's supposed to cut through everything. I will chop it open near your feet, and it will be loud. Puncturing the spell on the coffin should cause it to dissipate. Are you ready?"

"Am I ready? Are you trying to be funny? Just get me out of here, and you better not kill my spider."

"What the hell is it with you and that spider? Here goes." He brought the ax over his head and got it down hard onto the coffin, but it was as if it hit the most rigid material ever. It slid off to the left, making him lose his balance. Dorian checked, but it didn't even leave a scratch on the wood. He couldn't believe it, and again, he came down hard on it. However, the result was identical. On the third swing, the handle broke off, and the head fell with a clunk on the floor and stuck itself about four inches into it. He picked up the head of the ax and stared at it, still glowing yellow. He threw it over his shoulder, and when it hit the base of the door, the door fell into the field outside.

"What the hell?"

"What happened? It didn't work? Don't tell me it didn't work!"

"It didn't work."

The silence was as painful as a bite to the neck.

CHAPTER SIX

ACHAK WATCHED THE FIERY SKELETON from inside his wigwam deep in the Quebec forest. He observed the vision in a few enchanted tears in the palm of his left hand; the image was sharp though small, a scene of the battle with Tessy and Alexander engaging his creation. It was fascinating to watch as he cheered, just as one would cheer for his favorite player in a football game, with his fist clenched. He thought he should have given it a name like Bones. The outcome disappointed him. Achak would have thought such a powerful creature could have easily handled the German Shepherd. But she was obviously no ordinary dog. She was a vampire transformed by the Master, and knowing that would have made the dog's death that much sweeter. If he could figure out how to turn animals into vampires, he would have an army of them.

The wizard thought seriously about rushing to the area and killing the dog, but it was too soon to show his hand. Seeing him fight alongside it might give away that he had created it. The time wasn't right to show his power and plans; however, he hoped it soon would be. A wizard had to have patience and diligence, and sitting back and waiting was difficult. His dreams were becoming more vivid; he knew that time, and his destiny was accelerating. He was unaware of the end result, but it felt like the universe was compressing, hastening things.

The native put the tears back into the small bottle with an eyedropper, as much as he could. Then placed it on his little French antique table, a smaller version of the one he had outside. He went over, lay on his cot, laced his hands behind his head, and thought about Jenny. The book told him that a confrontation was coming, and he felt his life might depend on the upgrade the flaming skeleton would give him. It also informed him she was Dracula's daughter, which made him apprehensive about the battle.

Would the Master show up with his daughter? If he killed her, it was likely that he would come, eventually. He wished he could rush his creation into its task, but all he could do was watch and wait. Although patience wasn't one of his better qualities, he had improved over the years.

Achak was bored and restless. The wizard spent part of his time walking circles around the wigwam. A crow cawed from high in a tree on a branch, moving with the wind. He wondered if it had been a warning. Achak had an enchantment that would make any bird that approached become one of his sentries. He sat up, listening, and then watched as the bird walked into the dwelling and let go with a loud caw.

"Someone's coming? Is it another wizard to do battle? Oh shit, is it the girl? I'm not ready."

"Caw!"

The crow informed him it wasn't Jenny, and he was relieved by that information. Achak stood up and went into a brief meditative trance. He brought his palms together, twisting with pressure. He summoned all his energy to the forefront in case he had to fight. It could be another wizard seeking his aid or someone to usurp his power. It was definitely an uninvited visitor. The necromancer hoped he didn't have to risk engaging in battle because a wizard rarely started a fight unless they were sure they could win.

Achak stepped out of the dwelling and met Dorian. He recognized him immediately. Although he was showing a cheerful face, he could sense that he wasn't at all happy. He knew of the brothers, how their powers fed off one another, and how they would threaten his life if the other were with him.

"Achak."

"Dorian. How are you? Did you find your brother after all these years?"

"I did."

Those words put fear into Achak. He wanted to hear anything but that. He scanned the area through his eyes and through the nearby birds as well. Achak was adept at concealing fear, as most wizards were. "Is he here?"

"No, he remains trapped in the coffin, sealed by an ancient spell that I can't break, and that's why I'm going to need to borrow your Blood Book."

"You talk gibberish. You know my book is bound to me and will do you no good. How the hell did you get past my perimeter spell?"

"It's an old one, and I recognized it immediately." Dorian wiggled his fingers as he prepared for battle. "Let me worry about the binding. I'll bring it back, I promise."

Achak took several steps back. Both wizards had protective spells to shield them in battle, but they almost never worked properly. One incantation depended upon the makeup of another, and weird things could happen when wizards were in proximity. "We both know that I can't let you do that."

Dorian shot blue lightning bolts out of his right hand, highlighted with razor-sharp black edges; they weren't shocking but deadly. Dozens of them hit Achak's protective shield, cutting through it in certain areas and striking his shoulder with blood flying from the impact. Magical properties slowed his healing. Their intention was to disable his right arm with the blow, but it missed its mark. Achak countered with balls of red fire that contained toxic smoke, but they deflected and dispersed into the trees, setting fires everywhere around him. Desperate to break Dorian's concentration and diminish the energy surging within him, he made an unsuccessful attempt to disrupt it.

"Give me the book, and you live."

Achak launched several balls of light that made Dorian's protective shield visible. A giant bubble surrounded him, and now he could see two holes in the protective sphere. He launched two small snakes inside the bubble. Once there, they struck Dorian several times before he grabbed them and killed them with fire. But it had weakened him to such a degree that his protection vanished. His shield split into several pieces and fell away from him.

Both wizards shot bolt lightning at one another, which resembled natural lightning but made of fragmented, broken glass. The shards sought one another and nullified what the damage would have been, deflecting, shredding trees and branches, and cutting into the wigwam. One hit the Blood Book, but it sustained no damage. The air crackled with enchanted particles, causing the atmosphere to heat up as animals fled the area for miles.

"Damn it!" Dorian felt the snake's poison weakening him; he would run out of energy before Achak. Although his system could vanquish the poison, it wouldn't be in time to enable him to survive the battle. He would surely be dead if he had not come with a complicated pull spell. "Dachandra!" Dorian vanished as his magic pulled him to within several feet of his brother. There he collapsed.

Lemuel heard the fall. "Dorian, did you get it?"

Silence.

"Dorian? Is that you?"

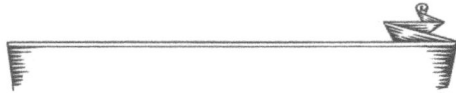

CHAPTER SEVEN

JARETH HAD GUIDED JENNY deep into the Quebec forest. He sensed the outer edges of Achak's evil magic, seeing its shimmering wave about fifty feet in front of him. He resembled an old man, but in prime condition, as solid as a mountain. His chest and shoulders were big, his hair and stubble white, with a wrinkled face, although he was ruggedly handsome. They were in a swamp, soft ground, with an old fallen tree covered in green moss. The trees had suffered scorching. Achak had walked these woods many times. The wizard liked to walk and think his impure thoughts, making plans to help no one except himself.

Not a sound broke the eerie stillness, creating a sense of unease. No birds sang, nor other animals heard. With the Sounds of the forest missing, it was as if they were in a vacuum. Even the wind felt peculiar, heavy, as if unseen hands pushed down on it. Were they already too close for comfort? Jareth looked sad as he stared down at the girl wizard. Although she looked like a small thing that needed protection, he knew she could flatten him if desired. It made him happy to know that the powerhouse was on their side. She would be a shield for justice, something extraordinary if she survived the journey to adulthood.

"What? What's wrong?" The girl had mixed feelings about her position; she didn't want to disappoint anyone, but it was all happening much too fast. She needed time to live and learn. Her father had told her that the world was running out of time, and she believed him. Jenny could also sense something untoward in the air but didn't know what it was. Negative feelings were now coming in waves, depressive in nature. It was best to fight them and move on.

"If he kills you, I'll be the last to see you alive. This moment will go down in history." He was talking to himself.

She looked up, showing him her disapproving face; he could have used better words. "Geese, that's a real confidence builder. You should be a professional speaker. I really needed that pep talk. Go, team."

Jareth liked her personality and appreciated her heart and fortitude. He remained fascinated because she was Dracula's daughter. She was intelligent and potent. He thought that Jenny would have made a good friend, not to mention the brownie points he would have earned from the Master. "Do you know why I said it?"

Jenny looked into his green eyes as she thought about it. Green eyes? "Hey, weren't your eyes blue a second ago?"

"They change. Emotions change them, stress, happiness."

She thought it might be fun for him to cross the border with different color eyes than on his passport. It was a strange thing to think about. His mind was all over the place. "I imagine you said what you said because you don't want me to be overconfident or some such thing, but there's no prospect of that. They have already pounded that into my head. Experience usually comes out on top. Blah, blah, blah." Jenny heard movement and turned her head to the left. She couldn't believe what she was seeing; her lion and Sarah had followed her all the way to Quebec, even though she had brought her back home three times. Nevertheless, she was there, prancing among the trees, her footsteps light and purposeful. "Sarah, no. You don't know how much danger you're in following me here. Didn't I tell you to stay home with Mother? What am I going to do with you?"

The lion lets go with a brief roar as if to say deal with it. The cat felt that her place was at Jenny's side, and nothing would stop her, neither vampire nor beast. Sarah was again eager to set eyes on her wizard girl. It felt as good as jumping on prey. The lion made Jareth uncomfortable as she stared at him as if he looked delectable.

Jareth shook his head. "You know he'll kill her just to mess with your concentration. Are you prepared to deal with that?"

That was one thing that she didn't want to consider. "No, I'm not."

"Then I suggest you repeatedly play that scene in your mind. How will you react? You must delay your emotions until after the battle lest you also perish. I guess your cat will not survive this. Nothing good will come of getting yourself killed as well."

She sat on the mossy tree, feeling defeated before the fight begun. She wasn't supposed to be emotional, even if he killed her lion? Many things were simple to say but not so easy to do. Genuine feelings would not be easy to block and perhaps impossible. Probably looked proper on the chalkboard of things not to do? *Don't cry, and whatever you don't get killed.* She could visualize it for a month, but if it happened, it might overwhelm her. Jenny loved that lion, and part of her would die with it. Sarah licked her face, and her tongue was so rough it made her laugh. "Sarah, stop."

"I need your permission to leave you."

Jenny stared up at him. "And if I tell you to stay?"

"Then I'll stay here, but I can go no closer."

"Go ahead; my lion will keep me company."

Despite being more than a mile away, the crack of a branch echoed through the stillness, reaching their ears. The atmosphere of the forest changed. It felt like they were deep in the jungle, and something big had set its eyes upon them. Something was making its way toward them. A fat red cardinal on the edge of Achak's influence sensed it and flew off in the opposite direction. It felt like midnight in the graveyard, full of eerie shadows.

"Do you feel that?"

Jenny showed him a knowing smile, which made her beautiful face much more so. "I know; he's increased his level of defense. I can feel the magic from here. If I'm dreaming about him, he's probably dreaming about me. He knows I'm coming."

"No, I mean, something is coming now."

"Yeah, I know that too. Some kind of magical thing."

"Then I bid you adieu. Be careful, Jenny, daughter of Dracula." Jareth blurred off into the trees, zigzagging as he went. He prayed he would see her again.

Jenny scratched both sides of Sarah's face and received another face lick. "It would save us a lot of trouble if you would eat Achak, and then I could just take the book. Are you hungry for a big steak named Achak?"

The lion flicked her tail several times; she hadn't transformed into a cub in a while. Sarah was also aware of the impending danger; she could smell it, but the scent was so unfamiliar that she couldn't identify it. It was a strange stink to her sensitive nose. Then Jenny saw it out of the corner of her eye, and it must have been seven feet tall. A man, but not really. It was an enormous shadow of a man, a walking silhouette, dark and menacing as it approached.

Jenny thought it walked like a Bigfoot, or how she thought a Bigfoot might walk. She noticed it didn't go through the trees, but around them, so there had to be some substance to it. The lion stood up, puzzled because she had never seen such a thing. It remained more than a hundred feet away, inching closer, observing, and judging.

"Only the shadow knows ..." She didn't finish it because the rising specter, part of Achak's defense, fascinated her. How do you fight a shadow? The light came to mind. Now it was about twenty feet away. It stopped and stared at the cat, surprised to see it there. Sarah hunched down, looking as though she was stalking it, and then she took off and took it down. She grabbed it by the neck, trying to suffocate it, but it hit her with both hands, affecting her, so she fell and couldn't stand. Sarah's head went back and forth as she tried hard to orient on the spinning forest.

Jenny pulled her sword as they both glanced at the cat. She attacked and was surprised at its speed. Why didn't it get out of Sarah's way? Perhaps it had never seen a lion before? That magical creation likely had never seen much of anything before. Jenny jumped and sliced several times at it, finally catching it in its abdomen. Blood flew from the wound. It didn't heal and continued to bleed. *If something bleeds, it can be killed.* It skillfully evaded several more attempts to cut its head off. The shadow pulled something off its back and threw it at her. It missed her, but when she glanced at the tree behind her, she saw it had split in two.

"That was so close. What the hell are you?" Both her hands tingled, glowing bright white. She aimed them at the creature and unleashed a bright and powerful light. The light had enveloped the area as a fast-moving shadow, knocking down almost a dozen trees, and then she couldn't see it. Had it been vanquished? The bright light diminished as the forest returned to normal.

Jenny observed movement from behind a tree. It stepped forward, still bleeding, but it had survived. It aimed an invisible bow at her and loosed several shadowy arrows. Jenny blurred and eluded most of them, but one caught her right through her left hand. The pain shot up her arm. Blood flew as Jenny screamed. She immediately felt peculiar. Jenny's hand and arm were so weak she could barely move them, and then through blurred vision, she could see that it was creeping up on her, and she had commenced turning to shadow.

"Un oh." Jenny fell to her knees. She wanted to create a ball of light, but she couldn't. Her left arm was almost entirely paralyzed. The shadow creature rushed up to the wizard and stared down at her, directing the bow towards her, pulling the string back as it aimed. Although she couldn't tell, she guessed it was probably smiling.

CHAPTER EIGHT

ANNIE GOT OUT OF BED AT FIVE IN THE MORNING. Seeing Alastair up surprised her. The vampire looked out the window, but the sun wasn't up yet. The sky got that here-I-come-glow. Annie could see the moon hanging up there. She wore a Fuchsia-colored dress and combed her white hair, staring at the location on the beautiful antique Victorian Bow Front Chest where she would have kept her rose. Had it only been an ordinary flower, she wouldn't have cared much, but then who would steal a common flower? She sure missed her butterflies. The boy who had taken her rose had surprised them, and the brat had been faster than both, enabling him to escape. Now she had nightmares about it as he taunted her in her dreams.

Annie searched the house for Alastair and found him in the garden as the sun rose. The light clouds had a soft pink hue. He was sitting on one of the garden benches, staring off at nothing, motionless. As she sat beside him, he turned and smiled at her.

Alastair placed his hand on her knee. "Morning. It initially took me quite a while to sleep at night, but you seem to be taking to it."

Annie could see that something was bothering him. She hadn't been with him long enough to know all his idiosyncrasies, but she could read most of his expressions and how he tried to hide his moods. She hoped he wasn't hiding too much. "What are you doing up so early?"

A long pause before he answered. "Well, I got a call from a friend around four, and he had some interesting information for me?"

"Oh, great news or not so great?"

"Could be both, I suppose."

"What do you mean?" Annie stared at the dark pink petunias with white stripes. When she was a young child, she remembered thinking that the flowers could talk to one another and how she would try to listen in on the conversation. She had only been about five. It was one of her earliest memories.

He cleared his throat. "Well, I found your rose."

That information gave Annie a boost. "Oh, my goodness! Do you have it? Where is it?"

Alastair turned and faced her, taking her hand in his. She didn't like the way he hesitated. "The fellow that sold it to me had the boy steal it back. Who knows how many times he's sold that same flower?"

"What a weasel. Can we get it back? How did you track it down?"

He kissed her hand. "Well, I told Oliver how pleased you were with the gift. I told him what had happened. He went into the shop where I purchased it, looking for a gift for his wife Miranda, and he spotted the rose. A butterfly passed through its empty container and touched down on the rose."

"How do you know that it's my rose?"

"Remember, there were only three, and two were sold long ago. It's your rose, Annie."

Annie was angry at the dishonest fellow but looking forward to getting her rose back. She was a little fearful of what Alastair would do to him. He was a crook, but she didn't want him killed over a flower. "What are we gonna do?"

"The solution is not as simple as you would think. The shop owner is a wizard called Freder, a minor wizard but a wizard, nonetheless. Can't be too careful dealing with an unknown sorcerer, definitely not to be underestimated. He could have purchased several powerful spells to defend himself. His shop, made of magic, resembles an igloo made from glass and constantly changes its location. Visiting his shop is usually by invitation only, and a vampire must receive permission directly from him. Sometimes patrons show up by word of mouth without a problem, but it is risky."

"So, the flower is lost?"

"Not necessarily. Oliver told me that his wife had heard of a fellow that's a detective of sorts. He magically tracks down people. He is expensive, but that is not a problem."

"So, what is the problem?"

"Well, for one thing, he might not find him, so I don't want you to get your hopes up. Remember that he moves his shop around magically. What should we do to Freder if we find him? I know what I'd like to do to him."

She considered his words. "I don't want you to kill him if that's what you're implying, even though he's a thief and a lowlife."

"Okay. It's your rose, and I'll let you decide what to do with him."

"Maybe we should break everything in his shop over his head?"

"Remember, he's a wizard."

Annie was getting a little frustrated. "So, what exactly are you saying? He will turn us into a glass and smash us with a hammer?"

"I'm saying he's dangerous. But I have a couple of spells, too. I have one that might do the job if I can find it. I used to carry it, but I put it away somewhere. If we locate him, you'll have to go in first because he'll recognize me. We'll need the element of surprise."

"I can't wait to get my rose."

Alastair was trying to remember where he had put the spell. "Patience, my dear, I need some breakfast first. Oliver is searching for him as we speak. He has many contacts, and one should be able to help us. Hopefully, he hasn't moved out of the country because that would make him much harder to track down."

"Alastair, tell me how much you paid for the rose."

"Annie, I'd rather you didn't know."

"I'll ask the felon who sold it to you."

"That would probably bring unwanted consequences. You're not supposed to notice the rose, and you will ask him about it?"

"Why won't you tell me?"

"A lady doesn't kiss and tell. And a gentleman doesn't tell what he's paid for a gift to his girl."

CHAPTER NINE

ALEXANDER'S SOUL STOOD and looked down at his charred body; his presence was now ethereal. He couldn't describe how he felt, otherworldly perhaps? It had felt peculiar when his soul slid out, cold and slippery like slipping on ice, but pleasant enough once he stood up. Warmth had replaced the cold. Everything looked brighter with a glow, and he hated seeing Tessy in such distress. A demoralized dog was a terrible sight to see. It tugged at his soul, and to Alexander, it was almost worse than a downhearted person.

Alexander took stock of his surroundings and saw several ghost people walking around. A mother and her daughter walked hand-in-hand, were dressed in pink. A young man resembled an infantry private from the civil war and looked to be on the side of the North. The young man received a brief salute from him, and he returned it. Why would he still be hanging around after all those years? Perhaps when one was dead, time for a ghost was different. Maybe one couldn't differentiate an hour from a year. He turned to his left and could see the so-called light at the end of the tunnel with relatives gathered near it, but it appeared to be quite far away. A man entered it and disappeared into the mist.

What would it be like if he entered that light? He imagined he would have to, eventually; he couldn't just hang around here forever. The sheriff thought about Abbey. She had lost her husband, and now she had to deal with his passing. It would have been better had they never met. Alexander had warned her of the life of a sheriff, but she had been willing to take that risk. He hoped he wouldn't have to see her face at the news of his demise. Fate was a fickle witch that would only give you your heart's desire to take it away.

Alexander had spent much of his life helping people, but now he couldn't help anyone, including himself. How would Arym take the news? Would it ultimately lead her to the dark side? He hoped not, but traumatic events had a way of changing people, especially the death of a loved one, not that he had attained that status with her. But she had lost her father. Would this be a weight too heavy to bear? When the scale tilted too far, it was never a positive outcome.

Alexander wondered if he could attend his funeral and how utterly strange would that be?

Would he meet GOD if he went into the light?

He could feel the pull, but what should he do?

He knew no one got out alive, but felt it wasn't his time. Alexander felt cheated.

Tessy saw Alexander's ghost standing there. She tried to jump up and lick his face but couldn't. The German shepherd attempted to offer her paw, but it proved futile. Alexander tried but couldn't take it. He even tried to pet her but, of course, couldn't. She cocked her head at him and wondered what was going on. If the dog could have shed tears, she would have. Tessy didn't know what to do. The contact she desired was unattainable, and she so wanted his comforting hands. What would she do without him? It felt as if two magnets had been separated, unable to reunite even though the pull remained.

Alexander circled around his body with the dog following him and wagging her tail. Looking down at the pain on his face on his burnt remains was upsetting, even as a ghost. His mouth hung open. A fly was on him, but it was impossible to chase it away.

Distracted and annoyed as he remembered the agony he had suffered because of the skeleton. He would love to kill the wizard that had created it, but that was impossible. How much chaos was the thing going to continue to cause? His world was gone now. He did not know what the new one would bring. Alexander looked at his hand and through it, disconcerting. A crow cawed three times, and he knew it was like him as it flew over. It was translucent and headed for the light. It appeared to carry something in its claw, but he couldn't tell what it was.

"I know you can see me, Tessy. I wish I could touch you, but I can't." Again, she tried to give him her paw, but he couldn't take it. The shepherd had never been so confused, desperate to touch him.

A middle-aged man wearing a black suit torn from the impact with the bus that had killed him was carrying a black umbrella. He bumped into the sheriff, and Alexander felt it. He looked distressed as he excused himself. "That was stupid. I shouldn't have been jaywalking. Stupid, stupid, stupid." He headed straight for the bright light as if late for an important meeting.

It might take a long time to get used to being dead.

Everything would be new again.

The end was a new beginning.

Alexander felt like he was hurtling downwards with nothing to grab onto. Why was he frightened if he was dead? Felt it in his stomach. It resembled a gradual, accelerating fall off a cliff. What the hell was going on?

Tessy got down beside his burnt body, staring up at his ghost that now appeared to be fading. She barked at it, trying hard to make sense of it all. But she couldn't understand if he had passed, why he was still there? Several times she looked at him and then at his ghost. And again, the dog nudged his body.

It felt like the sheriff had fallen from a great height back into his body. He jerked back to life with his heart pumping a single beat for the first time in almost two months. Alexander shivered and shook. His blood rushed through his circulatory system, distributing its healing elements to every cell. Scorched skin begun healing, and the pain returned, which was something he could have done without. The sheriff realized he was alive the moment that he was in excruciating agony. It was hard to be happy while dealing with such pain. The dog licked his face, causing him even more discomfort. "Wait, Tessy, wait. Wait until I heal."

The German shepherd had never been so overjoyed. Every muscle in her body writhed with happiness. She squealed with delight as Alexander sat up, healed except for a small burn mark on his chin. "All right, girl, come on!" He smelled her scent as she licked him, petting and rubbing almost every inch of her body. She gave him her paw and was so enthused that he could take it. She gave him a hip check and knocked the sheriff over. "Oh, you want to play rough?" They wrestled for almost five minutes.

Alexander and Tessy entered the kitchen and sat at the table as Abbey made dinner. She never knew if he would make it home, but she always set his place at the table. The dog barked several times at her, trying to tell her what had happened to her master, but she couldn't understand. The dog attempted to show her mind-to-mind but couldn't manage it with a human, only accustomed to vampire-to-vampire communication.

Abbey gave him a hug and a passionate kiss. "What's wrong with Tessy? She seems overly excited."

"I guess she's happy to see you."

Abbey stared at him, and she could see something was going on by the look on his face. "So, how was your day? You look tired or something."

"Don't ask."

"Well, I am asking, so tell me."

He wasn't about to reveal that he had died and come back to life. He hoped he could soon forget that searing fire on his skin. "Let's just say it was a terrible day and leave it at that. Ok?"

Tessy lay on the floor like a big old bear and refused to move. Her mind and body were tired, and she went to sleep. Abbey went around her. "Even the dog looks beat. I don't know what happened, but I can tell it was no ordinary day at the office. I can only guess that you saw something horrible. Wish you could come home on time. Anyway, I made your favorite." She gave him two browned-to-perfection turkey legs, and after he had sprinkled them with blood, he devoured it, bones and all.

"Where's Arym?"

"Oh, she's out with a friend. She seems to be in a better mood lately."

"Glad to hear it." She might just have an easier time of it than I initially thought. For some, it's just realizing that you can't go back, so you must move forward. It's easier to say than to do when your life is forever changed. He adjusted himself in the chair to get a little more comfortable, but looked tired. "I know a young woman that was turned against her will, and she took to the forest. She found a deserted log cabin, fixed it up, and, as far as I know, she's been there for over a century. The last time I saw her was about five years ago. She seemed happy enough, but she's all alone out there."

"It's a hard thing to deal with, I'm sure."

"You know, I actually think I need a nap."

"If you need one, take one."

Alexander went into the bedroom for a nap, and Tessy followed. Within minutes, both were snoring and reliving the terror they had gone through.

CHAPTER TEN

WEI WAS COMFORTABLE ON HIS BROWN LA-Z-BOY RECLINER, his long queue of hair still damp from the shower. It was noon, and he was looking forward to the day progressing. Wei had a date with Margat, an old but beautiful vampire from Detroit who had just moved to New York City. He had encountered her once before. However, they were going in opposite directions, so their encounter didn't lead to anything. However, Wei had felt their mutual attraction. He had had recurring dreams of her of the erotic kind.

They had rescheduled the date three times already. A red sheriff's life is not his own, with promises to the Master to defend the defenseless. Lives were on the line, and so many people dying. He couldn't allow people to be killed while he was on a date.

Bao exited the kitchen with one of the biggest ham sandwiches Wei had ever seen. Four slices of ham, four pickle slices, two slices of cheese, tomatoes, and lettuce, all covered in mayonnaise on homemade bread, had just come out of the oven. Eating for a vampire wasn't required, but it was a comfort. He showed the sandwich to Wei as if to say *mine.* And when his attention lapsed for a second, he discovered Wei had taken the first bite of it.

"Hey!"

"That is good. You should make me one." Wei wiped the mayonnaise from his face.

They were watching the Price is Right as Bao sat in the matching recliner and chowed down on the sandwich. He ate it so fast that it must have been a world record, with an enormous belch following. Afterward, he ate some crumbs off his lap. "Pardon me. I need another one."

"Think I'll actually make it to dinner with Margat?" Wei ran his hand over his Cute Boy hairstyle and then stretched. He knew she knew the importance of his job, but it didn't make it any easier. Wei didn't know how many times he could delay the date before she would tell him to forget it. He was eager to see if they could start a relationship, and he looked forward to getting to know her better.

"I'll bet you a hundred bucks that you don't." Bao drank his glass of blood and placed the empty glass on the square coffee table.

"That's one bet I'm not taking. She's gorgeous, though, isn't she? That black hair and those beautiful brown eyes."

"I think what you're interested in is a little lower than her eyes. She's a classic beauty and reminds me of old Hollywood. I might steal her from you if things don't work out." Bao smiled because he knew they had a lifetime of friendship and honor, and neither would trample on that bond.

"If it doesn't work out, it wouldn't be stealing. Though seeing you with her might make me chop you in two." Wei watched the credits roll and then took his sword and sharpened it. "Look at this. As soon as I sharpen my sword, the edge immediately changes. Look, you can see it."

"Your sharpening skills are not as good as the magic that keeps the blade perfectly honed. Why do you continue to try to alter perfection? Wasting your time."

"My sharpening skills are second to none."

"Second to the magic in that blade." Bao smiled and raised his eyebrows, showing more of his brown eyes.

"Remember when you cut the cement block in two?"

"Oh yeah, I didn't think it would work. Didn't even take the edge off it. That was stupid, though, risking my blade like that. I know it's supposed to be indestructible, but still. For all I know, the magic weakens."

"That was a long time ago. I'll trade swords." Even though he knew its magic wouldn't work for him, Bao had always wanted to wield that sword.

"I'm the wizard. It won't work for you." Wei had been told he was a high-level wizard but had never practiced. His father taught him that all magic was evil, and although he knew that wasn't true, it was hard to escape his father's influence. He wondered if he was looking down on him from the other side, continuing to judge; he was such a strong-headed person he wouldn't doubt it. Wei was aware it was a waste of talent. Perhaps he could have taken care of that damn skeleton if he had been skilled in the art. But his father's beliefs still pressed on him.

"A wizard that doesn't use magic may as well be a coatrack."

"I use magic. The sword is magic."

"That's not what I mean, and you know it."

The laptop lit up with multiple locations flashing red and there looked to be at least six. They grabbed their swords and studied the information that was coming in. It looked like diversionary tactics, which weren't bad because of insufficient red sheriffs. They thought Dracula needed to get those new sheriffs in play, but nobody could demand anything from the Master. The red flashing locations circled in green showed that sheriffs were on the scene, but three areas were devoid of the reds.

Bao shook his head. "Where do you want to go? Want to split up?"

"Hell no, we've survived this long by sticking together. One attack looks to be in the stadium parking lot. Let's start there."

They blurred out the door and down the street.

Almost a dozen zombie-like vampires with strange faraway looks in their eyes were killing people. They all emitted a slight red glow, and their fighting abilities were enhanced. Most of the vampires had swords, but two used their superior strength to rip people to pieces. One was beating a young man with his own leg.

"Watch it!" A vampire attacked Bao, but Wei cut his head off.

They were too late to save an old man with his grandson. As the 10-year-old boy ran away screaming, someone tore off the man's head. Wei split the one responsible in two. As the pieces attempted to reform and heal, he severed his head while the skin turned to dust and the bones remained split in two.

Bao's reverse turning kick knocked the head off one dressed in a black Armani suit with a green tie, sending people screaming, while two others fainted. He was as furious as Bruce Lee at the horror they were causing. He cut into the evil bastards with no mercy, killing five of them in two seconds.

Two vampires attacked Bao. One had a T-shirt with palm trees on the front, and the other had khakis and was bare-chested. He ducked to avoid decapitation, and the other vampire unintentionally sliced the bearded fellow with no shirt at the upper part of his chest just below his throat. A deep gash sent blood flying onto Bao's new Black Mandarin Collar Jacket. He side-kicked the one that was cut, sending him flying into several people. Then decapitated the blond in black, and reverse-crescent kicked the head into the air and across the parking lot. Wei grabbed the one in black and threw him into the parking lot where there were no people. He engaged him in an epic, brief battle as swords clashed fast and ferocious. When Wei broke the fellow's sword with his weapon, he quickly decapitated him.

Once the other vampires noticed the red sheriffs, they obediently shifted their focus towards them. The first one that approached Bao was snap kicked in the face so hard that it partially crushed his skull. The pain was enough of a distraction for Bao to swiftly remove his head. However, he sliced across the chest from right to left, with blood from the gash dripping down. Backing up allowed him time to heal as Wei removed the foe's head.

As they fought back-to-back, the sound of clashing swords echoed around them, each strike a reminder of the danger they faced. Two vampires grabbed Bao by both arms, pushing him so hard against Yankee Stadium, there was a resounding splat. As a third vampire rushed in for the kill, Wei intercepted him with a prone kick to his throat, incapacitating him and preventing him from striking Bao. And plenty of time for him to remove that ugly head.

The two continued holding Bao against the wall as another blurred in to take care of the sheriff. Bao moved just enough so that the evil biter tagged the one holding his left arm, inadvertently cutting his arm off, and with that. He was released as the two red sheriffs disposed of the others.

Bloodstained sections of the parking lot as the sheriffs observed the remains of the horrific scene. It was time to call an ambulance and help the wounded.

CHAPTER ELEVEN

VINCENT FED ON HIS GIRLFRIEND'S NECK, biting her and drinking blood. A little ran down Adeline's shoulder. She was a strawberry, and he twirled her hair as he bit her. Nourishing and oh-so-satisfying, like nectar to a hummingbird. The famous red sheriff wasn't being aggressive. Hoping he would turn her, she desired it intensely, but there was no chance he would accommodate her. They had met less than a month ago and seemed to mesh, but the sheriff never stayed in one spot for long, so he wasn't sure how this would work. It was likely that eventually, he would leave her behind. But he had been upfront with her from the beginning, and it had been her choice to hang around.

The apartment on the Upper East Side was large and stylish, and fully furnished. Mostly modern and expensive-looking furniture filled the room, except for a commode in the bedroom that seemed oddly out of place. A chest of drawers from the 1700s puzzled Vincent as it sat among modern items. He had contacted the landlord to have someone retrieve it, but they had yet to arrive. Vincent wasn't sure how long he would be there, even though he had signed a year-long lease. He knew Dracula was about to ordain more red sheriffs and wasn't about to miss that. Word was it would be at St. Patrick's Cathedral on Saturday night at midnight. He had talked to the Master and received his personal invitation.

"That's enough." Vincent saw the disappointment in her eyes, but she would get over it.

Adeline Reed flicked her hair out of her gorgeous green eyes; she was twenty-seven and pretty. "Oh, come on, just a little more."

"Listen, enjoy being human."

Despite her disappointment in his attitude, she couldn't compel him to take any action. Adeline would continue to try to get him to turn her. "Easy for you to say, but I'm at risk from every vampire out there." She was frightened because of all the killing that was going on.

You couldn't look at any news source without hearing about more vampire murders. It seemed they were all over the damn place.

Adeline felt like a frightened rabbit in a forest of wolves, and she believed she had little chance unless she transformed into a wolf. She had been so happy when she met Vincent, recognizing him as a red sheriff, practically throwing herself at him. He considered turning her but thought her fragile nature might make her miserable as a vampire for years to come. He was uncertain. Some timid people had difficulty adjusting to being a vampire because it was like being born into a nightmare.

She kissed him intensely, wanting to take things further, hoping he would lose control. It hadn't worked in the past month, but it might work now. She wouldn't stop asking because she couldn't even get a night's sleep anymore. She had moved out of New York but then moved back when a sheriff had saved her in Lewiston, Maine, from not one but two vampires. As soon as the sun went down, the little courage she had had during the day sunk with it.

Alexander's enhanced hearing heard a single scream, and he sat straight up on the black leather sofa. No matter how often he heard it, his heart was always tugging at the sound of a woman screaming.

"What is it?"

"I'm not sure." He blurred to the window and looked down. The flaming skeleton was in the middle of the street, halting traffic. Two police officers were off to the side, away from it, discussing what to do next. They had heard that bullets wouldn't hurt it. The officers were deliberating whether to run away. They would have already run off, except a New York Times photographer was on the scene; they didn't want to be on the front-page fleeing.

"Stay here. I must go down there and see what that thing is doing."

"Be careful. Escape if necessary."

He shook his head at the thought. "Adeline, that's not how it works. Red sheriffs don't run. At least I don't."

"Even if you knew it would kill you, you wouldn't run?"

"No, I wouldn't."

"That's crazy."

At street level, Vincent saw the skeleton appeared to be confused. It looked left and right as the blazing sword rested on its shoulder. It lost track of a wizard it had been locked onto. The wizard Abraham had conjured up a black cloak when he saw the skeleton; he thought the thing was killing wizards. He had just gotten out of sight, put on the cover, and ran for a red Dodge minivan. The family of four agreed to let him in when he told them he was in danger. Now the skeleton searched diligently for the wizard but couldn't locate him. It rotated leisurely in the middle of the street as it attempted to reconnect.

"Hey, you need to move! You're impeding traffic." Vincent shouted at it. It unhurriedly turned its attention to Vincent, and it was a disturbing look.

The skeleton blurred to within several feet of Vincent, knowing he was a sheriff. It could see his swirling aura. His energy wasn't as high as a wizard's, but still quite impressive. It looked at the sheriff as if he was beneath him. Without hesitation, it pulled a fist-sized skull out of its chest cavity, hurling it at the sheriff. The skull bit into his trench coat at the shoulder and held fast, setting him on fire. The beast was evolving. Vincent slid out of his trench coat and it disintegrated on the sidewalk. The skull wobbled, smoke rising as its fire faded away. Vincent pulled his Colt faster than Billy the Kid could and fired twice; both rounds deflected off in strange directions.

The skeleton looked at the sheriff and cocked its head; it couldn't decide whether Vincent would be a challenge.

Vincent unsheathed his sword and smiled, hoping to surprise it with a sudden attack. He tried to take its head off, but an unfortunate deflection. Their blades clashed, creating a shower of sparks and a symphony of metal on metal. Their swords came together, and they were seemingly at an impasse. The sheriff adeptly somersaulted away, skillfully evading the line of fire launched by the thing's mighty swing. Again, their blades met in rapid succession, and he could feel the heat from its fire and again an impasse as it stepped away from Vincent.

Adeline showed up as the last thing she had observed from the window was Vincent on fire. The creature hit her with a skull from inside its chest, catching her left arm; she burst into flames and was almost instantly turned to ash, more efficient than any crematorium. So beautiful and full of life one second, dead and gone the next.

Vincent was furious and attacked with a barrage of chops and slices deflected by its sword; he kicked it and sent it tumbling down the sidewalk while blazing embers bounced around. As the skeleton laughed, the fire was spreading up his leg, but when he saw the sheriff concentrate and extinguish the fire with his mind, it left the area. Vincent tried his best to catch the thing, but within a few minutes, he lost it. Unfortunately, it had been just fast enough to escape.

CHAPTER TWELVE

JENNY TOPPLED TO THE GROUND like an inanimate object being pushed over; she was turning into another shadow thing, and she didn't know how to stop it. She now saw the forest and the shadow beast through a darkish lens, the colors of the forest muted. Everything had a darkish sheen to it. It felt like she was tied up. She struggled to escape, but to no avail. A puff of smoke came out where its mouth should have been, making her wonder if it was laughing at her. Then several more puffs of smoke. Was it talking to her? Magical things were the most difficult to fight. She did not know what had gone into that enchantment.

The shadow had drawn back the string on its bow, and Jenny figured it was preparing to finish her or complete the transformation. She thought one of the worst sensations a person could feel was feeling helpless; she knew she couldn't save herself. It shredded an individual's will to struggle, leaving pieces of what a person could be and should be. She imagined her mother's face when she returned home. *Hello, Mother; I'm a shadow now.* They would be one big happy family, Dracula, the lion, Zacharia's ghost, Jenny the shadow, and a bratty brother on the horizon.

The girl tried hard to sit up. She struggled to unleash some form of magic, but nothing was happening. She concentrated, going deep into her own mind. Down, down, down she went. There had to be something in there that could aid in her escape. Jenny felt her left hand getting warm and then hot. A lightning bolt shot out, missing the shadow by inches but hitting the lion. The energy revived Sarah, and she stood up fiercely, immediately charging. The lion jumped and grabbed the shadow by its neck, tearing through it. After a battle, it fell, and the feline jumped on it. The arrow had been unleashed almost simultaneously, grazing her ear. Blood gushed from the shadow as the lioness tore into its neck, getting blood all over Sarah's face and chest. But she was determined not to let it escape from her death grip. It was facing down, and she tightened and chewed until, finally, the head was severed. Batting the shadow's head, it rolled as she played with it, but it just disappeared. No sign of it remained except for its blood.

Dracula's daughter stood up. Dracula's daughter stood up and watched as the shadow that had taken over her retreated, with all its elements of magic dissipating. Felt like a mighty hand forced to let go. Jenny wiggled her fingers and realized she had fully recovered.

The lion continued to search for the head, but it had disappeared. The bow and a leather quiver with three arrows were on the forest floor. She stared at the weapon, wondering if she should dare touch it. What if it started turning her into a shadow again? If Sarah hadn't killed that thing, it would have finished her. How long was her luck going to hold out? The lion stepped on the bow as she ran to Jenny for affection, and nothing happened to the cat. She examined the bow when she fished playing with Sarah.

"What a good girl you are!" She kissed the cat's big head and received a rough, wet tongue.

They played and wrestled for several minutes, and the lioness rubbed her face against the girl, delighting in the interaction. She grabbed Sarah by the tail, who turned and playfully swatted at her. They shared a hug and a laugh when it bumped her over.

A branch cracked in the distance somewhere. Was there something else out there coming for her? The lion turned, listening and watching the forest in the direction where the sound had originated. Jenny stooped and picked up the bow. It was strange and slippery, and she had to grip it tightly. Her fingers went into it, yet some form of energy pushed back, maintaining its shape. It was a puzzle to one's senses because smoke should have been impossible to pick up. However, there it was with weight and substance. Jenny placed the quiver over her left shoulder, followed by the bow. She had taken some archery lessons several years ago. It might be foolish to attempt to tag an assailant with it, but she would bring it along just in case.

Again, another branch was not cracking this time, sounding like someone or something was shaking it, rattling leaves. An invitation to come and get eaten, she imagined. The lion took off toward the noise as Jenny screamed at her. "Sarah, no!" She didn't know what to do, pursue her into what might be some sort of trap, or just wait for her to return. Either action could have been in error. The lion was out of sight within a few seconds, so she waited.

"Please don't get killed." Jenny took an energy bar from her small backpack, sat, and waited. It only took about a minute for her to spot Sarah chasing a black bear, making her laugh at the sight of it. The lion broke off the chase and returned to the wizard for more affection. She would have thought the bear would have fought more, but of course, it had never seen a lion before.

"You silly lion, chasing a bear." Had it been a real bear or a magical distraction? She was questioning everything, but wizards were notoriously sneaky. She scanned the forest, expecting something like the lion lying beside her, but then jumped up.

Jenny looked up and saw Achak in the distance. He stood as still as the surrounding trees, dressed in furs and holding some sort of white staff. He was far away, and she could only see him partially through the trees. However, it impressed her with such a foreboding feeling that frightened her. Achak tried his best to penetrate her mind but couldn't; it was as if he was attempting to kick down a solid steel door. No way he was getting in there.

As Jenny stood up, he transformed into the blackest smoke she had ever seen, which approached and went around her. Then right through her, and she couldn't breathe for a few seconds. When Jenny finally shook off its effects, she knew it was a threat and a powerful warning. He was telling her to flee or else.

CHAPTER THIRTEEN

MOON DIAMOND LAY LIFELESS, curled up in a ball, pushed under the stand of the big-screen television in the living room. Allison felt like vacuuming the cat when she did the floors. The Siamese appeared dead to her; there was more life in the vacuum cleaner. At least once a day, she listened to its chest, hearing nothing. She didn't know what to think, but it wasn't emitting any foul odors.

Zacharia's ghost sat on the sofa as best he could and tried to pay attention to CNN as Dracula and Allison were in the kitchen having coffee. The occasional booming laugh filled the room from the Master. An incident involving gunfire had taken place near the Empire State Building. The scent of bread was throughout the house, and the loaf was just about ready to exit from the oven. The smell made the ghost hungry, even though he couldn't eat. Another part of death that annoyed him.

The funny thing was that earlier, he had observed another ghost walking right through the walls, which scared the shit out of him. It had been a tall fellow dressed in blue overalls with a double-edged ax. Whoever it was did not notice him.

"I'm so tired of this." His words went nowhere and had no sound or vibration. He thought about a silent film with no piano to accompany him and no words written. Zacharia felt displaced and discouraged. He hoped that heaven was better than being a ghost on earth. Perhaps this was hell? What would be the point of being bored for all eternity? At least he could sleep if he put his mind to it. Had he noticed the cat twitch? He now stared at it, fixated, but saw nothing. Was it wishful thinking? He floated over Moon Diamond and stared down at him. Did the cat now have a perceptible glow to it?

Zacharia called to the cat. "Moon Diamond, are you in there?" He started feeling a pull, like two people having a tug-of-war with one side winning. Would it recover? And if so, what would happen to his soul? Would he go back in there? Or remain a ghost? One thing was for sure; with his body destroyed, he would never be the old Zacharia. At least the situation had him curious, which was something. The cat started kicking its back leg as if running in its sleep. He guessed it was chasing a mouse. Then Moon Diamond stood and shook vigorously, as if wet.

"It's alive!" said Zacharia, talking like a mad scientist. He was instantly sucked back into Moon Diamond, never expecting to be happy to be back inside that cat, but he was. He had control of the cat but couldn't even pick up a matchstick when he was a ghost. Zacharia lifted his right front paw and stared at it. "Oh yeah, I'm back." The feline showed him an image of a dead mouse, which made him smile. Situation normal for the feline.

"Meow," the Siamese cat stated. The feline walked toward the kitchen but was so weak it fell over. It rose and continued toward the kitchen, bumping into the wall and staggering around as if inebriated. It sat and looked up at Dracula.

Dracula was happy to see the cat on the kitchen floor. "Zacharia?"

The cat nodded as Dracula got up, opened the fridge door, poured some blood into a saucer from a large beaker, and felt satisfied as the cat licked it up. The Master went into Zacharia's mind to re-establish contact. They gave one another a virtual hug. Zacharia was talking so fast that he had to be told to slow down.

Allison was happy to see the cat back amongst the living. "I thought you were going to stay in that coma forever. I was soon going to use you for a dust mop. Poor thing."

Dracula petted the cat and made it stick its butt in the air. "Zacharia, what was it like?"

"It was the strangest thing, floating around and having no one to talk to. It was quite maddening. By the way, I saw the bright light that would have taken me to heaven or hell, but I refused to go. I can tell you that the bright light is a genuine entity."

"Interesting."

Allison's curiosity grew as she was excluded from the conversation. "What is he saying?"

"He said he could see the bright light but refused to enter."

"Yes indeed, and I saw another ghost." The cat brought up its hind leg and scratched behind its ear. "But I don't want to talk about it. I'm happy to be back in here."

"How do you feel?"

"A lot better after having that blood. Moon Diamond appears a bit confused. I guess he's just missing time. Never in a million years would I have thought I'd be pleased to be back inside this fur ball."

Dracula tossed the cat a piece of ham, and it growled as it ate. "Still aspire to be a sheriff?"

"Hell, yes! When is the ceremony?"

"Soon. The last count should be over five hundred. I'll have the service in New York and keep them there. My Blood Book tells me I will be the center of the battle. We're waiting for Jenny to come, but we'll have to proceed if she doesn't return soon. It's difficult to say how long she'll be tied up with that wizard. I hope she's okay."

"That bread smells delicious. Even as a ghost, I could smell it. And there's something else in the air, something unpleasant."

"That's the stench of black magic.

"Some wizards can't resist turning to the dark side as it appears to be a challenge to see how much damage they can accomplish." Moon Diamond began washing his face.

"Zacharia, it's all about power."

The cat finished the ham and clawed at the fridge for another piece.

CHAPTER FOURTEEN

KEITH WENT DOWN WEST 18TH STREET in Manhattan, where Mannequin Hub was receiving a delivery of mannequins. The overcast and muggy morning caused people to perspire. His reality was now slip-sliding away. Earlier that morning, he had argued with himself in the mirror for over an hour, almost coming to blows. Insanity had grabbed him with formidable hands and would never let go. His mind tried hard to make the proper connections, but it just was not happening.

"*You* there!"

Keith's weathered face and small beady eyes took notice of the mannequins. He blurred to one and showed his fangs. The two workers dropped everything and ran for their lives. The two figures remained standing. Keith scrutinized them and was sure that one had given him the finger. Being a powerful vampire, he wouldn't endure such an insult without retaliating. He was trying to find out how old and powerful they were, but he couldn't read them.

"What the hell are you looking at?" Keith gazed directly into the mannequin's eyes, staring it down. His breath was almost sick enough to melt it. He waited for its response, and when none came, he took that as an insult. Keith gave the mannequin the finger, touching its face with the offending digit, trying to instigate the first move, impressed by how calm and collected he was.

Mike, the male mannequin, took the comment as a personal affront. "I'm looking at a fat piece of shit. That's what I'm looking at! You'd need one of those dock scales to properly weigh yourself."

Those were confrontational words that Keith would not forgive. The fellow desired a fight. A struggle ensued, with Keith getting Mike on the ground, tearing into his neck with his fangs, and when his head came off, he knew the mannequin was dead. He must have had low blood sugar or something because he didn't taste terrific. He shook the head, removing it from his fangs and watched it roll on the street.

Keith stood up, satisfied that he had done justice, defended his honor, and emerged victorious once more. Why he didn't turn to bones was a puzzle. It must be some sort of spell. The beautiful female stared at Keith, and he could tell she was frightened. But the vampire, outnumbered, believed they all jumped him as he tripped. Keith had to run or they would kill him.

On West 22nd Street, a vagabond with his hat in hand approached Keith. Many knew him as Bernie the Bum. Bernie was a short fellow with enough grime on him to make most people topple over from the stench. His gray hair was matted with blood, causing his blue eyes to appear as dull as a doll's. He wore a gray jacket that in the past had looked exceptional, but time and grime had not been kind. It appeared as if a person couldn't add more dirt to it, even if they wanted. It smelled like a dead rat, likely because he had slept on a decaying one for three nights.

Bernie was in a foul mood and as drunk as he could be without being unconscious. Liquor was his life. It was all he had to dull the vision of finding his wife, and two boys slaughtered some twenty years ago. He was not the man he used to be, nor would he ever be again. Some people could not get beyond tragedy; Bernie was one of them. The more life was a blur, the better he liked it.

"Can you spa, spa, spare a dollar or two? Or some change? I'm not gonna lie. It's not for food. It's for wine." The fellow tried hard to steady himself.

Keith looked at him up and down. Keith looked up and down at the vampire, whose vision was almost as distorted as the inebriated fellow. He blinked rapidly and tried to focus. "You want me to change you into a vampire?"

"What?" Bernie staggered around as if he was in an earthquake. "Listen here, you, you, you fat bitch." Bernie lost his train of thought and cried, the tears rolling down into his scruffy salt and pepper beard. "I, I, I forgot what I was saying. Probably had something to do with wine. You, you know what happened to me today?"

Keith felt sorry for the drunk and that surprised him. "I can smell O-positive blood in your hair. What happened to you?"

Bernie was surprised that someone took the time to have a conversation with him, because most people would have dismissed him by now, but considering the stench, it was understandable. "I don't know how positive it is. I was, ah, what do you call it? What was I saying? Oh. Someone mugged me. I came out of the liquor store with a brand-new bottle of wine. And I, I, I was kissing it, and then this big bastard came out of nowhere. He must have been twelve feet tall, took my wine and knocked me out with the bottle. He, he, he could a broke it! Look at this lump, but don't touch it. What is this city coming to when the winos are getting mugged? Who's next? What's worse than a wino? I know two winos."

The vampire nodded. "I'll kill him for you if you want me to? Just point him out, and I'll rip his head off and give it to you."

Bernie the Bum was most impressed as he imagined it. He visualized holding a severed head. "Would, would, would you do that for me? I, I, I don't know what I'd do with his head, though. Do you think I, I, I could trade it for a bottle? There are some sick people around here, and I might be one of 'em?"

"Just point out the bastard. I'll kill him. You say he was twelve feet tall?"

"At least, maybe bigger. You one of those vampires? Are you Drakata?"

"What?"

"You know drink! The king of all vampires. He lives in a castle in transkelmania."

Keith became puzzled. "No, my name is Keith."

Bernie studied Keith as best he could. "I, I, I have such a headache. If I had some wine, it would go away."

Keith put his hand on Bernie's shoulder. "I can get you a bottle of wine."

That took Bernie's attention. "Thank you, God. You're not as fat as when you first walked up here."

"Come on. Show me where the liquor store is, and I'll buy you some wine."

Bernie smiled for the first time in months, but he had lost most of his teeth long ago. His eyes were full of wine bottles. "Will you be my friend?"

Keith was going to hug Bernie, but decided not to. He would have crushed him for sure. "I was going to ask you the same thing. It's important to have friends. You could be my best friend."

"Really? We think the same stupid things." Bernie laughed until he coughed and spit up blood. "Okay, let's go get that wine. Watch out for that fire hydrant, jumped out in front of me last week. I tried to get them to take it away, but they wouldn't."

"Bastards."

"That's what I said. I, I, I tried to pull it out, but I couldn't. It's hard to fight one of those things. Oh, hey, see that post over there?"

"Yeah."

"Don't go over there; I farted there last month. And then the next day I, I, I found a dead crow in the same spot."

Keith ripped the hydrant out of the ground, the water surged, and then they headed for the liquor store.

CHAPTER FIFTEEN

ANNIE AND ALASTAIR WERE ABOUT A MILE INTO THE MASSACHUSETTS FOREST, waiting, watching, and planning. The fragrant scent of pine was in the air as a Red-bellied woodpecker nosily pecked on a pine tree, sounding a little like a machine gun. Annie observed the woodpecker and cherished its beauty because, to her, nature was meant to be enjoyed. It existed to be appreciated, and those who didn't were fools. They had followed a winding forest trail that looked like it had been there for years. However, it had been there for only days, all part of the spell that led to the shop.

They studied the domed structure in front of them. Fabricated of opaque glass, with a single large section of the roof showing an image of a large hand casting a spell. A circle of petrified salt surrounded the place, as thick and wide as any speed bump.

Alastair was taller than Annie, so he bent to talk to her. "He'll know what's coming when we step beyond that barrier. He'll sight you and watch as you enter. Don't look back at me. Annie, once you're inside, you can look around, but if you spot the flower, don't pay any attention to it because he'll be on guard. Don't ask him how much the flower costs because you'll jeopardize both of us. Always remain calm, no matter what he says. He wins if you get angry."

The idea of an entire building being transported from one location to another impressed her, but such was magic. "I know, I know," said Annie. "And wait until he takes his eyes off me before throwing the spell at him. We wouldn't want him to dodge it and turn me into a spider." Annie was both eager and nervous. She had no experience with wizards and had heard awful things about some of them. They would both be in big trouble if she didn't hit him with the spell, but she wanted her rose and was determined not to miss.

Alastair kissed her and went further into the forest to hide. When Annie couldn't see him anymore, she headed for the barrier and then over it. Suddenly there was a Great Horned Owl on a tree by the door. It hadn't been there until she crossed the barrier, and neither had the tree. Or if it had, then some enchantment blocked her from seeing it. The bird turned its head and looked straight at her. It was lovely, but the thought of Freder seeing through its eyes made her uncomfortable. Annie hoped she hadn't been ogling the bird too long. It was best not to overthink things.

"Who?" said the owl.

"Oh, shut up."

Alastair watched from a distance and was worried. If something happened to her, he would never forgive himself. Annie needed to keep calm, but would she? She was opinionated and wasn't one to hold her tongue. If Freder annoyed her, she just might let him have it. She loved that rose, but he knew it was all the butterflies it brought forth. He might not be able to save her from an outburst should it come to that? She could also flatten him like a bug, which wouldn't be so bad. When a loved one was at risk, time appeared longer than it was. Seconds dragged on as he waited.

Annie stared at the owl about a dozen feet from the entrance. She had been told to flee if the front door didn't open within a few seconds. The translucent door only took about four seconds to open, but it seemed longer. Just before it swung open, she was ready to run.

Annie stepped in wearing her black dress and red purse; she was calm and unruffled. Freder was standing behind a semi-circular mahogany countertop, and it was a mess. Small books and uniquely shaped beakers containing liquids and powders were everywhere. In front of him was a small space where he created some concoctions. She attempted to search for the rose without being obvious, but she couldn't see it. The shop was white. The floor, walls, and ceiling. From the floor to the ceiling, the spells floated against the walls, with some near the sectioned roof. The expensive-looking chandelier that was floating up there impressed her.

"This place is so beautiful."

Freder loved a compliment. He was a tall fellow with a Mutton Chops beard and a crooked nose. He had suspicious green eyes and grew wary of Annie because ninety percent of his clientele were repeat customers. She thought his face would fit nicely behind the bar of an old western saloon. He was a distinctive-looking character, wearing a white apron with a red dragon image; the dragon was chasing another dragon, trying hard to hit it with fire, and then the scene would repeat itself. It was like watching a high-definition television on his apron. She didn't know if she would ever get used to paranormal stuff, but she loved her magical rose.

He placed the small teal booklet he had been perusing onto the counter and glared at her. Unfamiliar symbols covered it. "It's taken me a while to get the place just how I like it. My name is Freder, the proprietor, and you are?"

"I'm Annie. I'm looking for something special for a good friend."

"Who told you about this place?"

"It was an old friend who doesn't want to be identified. I paid him a shitload of money to get it out of him. I hope you don't mind? He said you weren't one to take to strangers."

Freder smiled a crooked smile. He liked the shitload of money part. "Indeed. What are you looking for, Annie?"

"That's the problem. I don't really know what I'm looking for. Molly has always been fussy and more than a little judgemental, for that matter. She's a tough bird to pluck."

"I see. What does Molly like to do?"

She was enjoying the ruse more than she had expected. "Well, she used to like to paint, but now she's too shaky. She's human. I asked if she wanted me to transform her, but she refused. It's her loss." It was fun telling tall tales. Felt like acting. She continued to look at all the spells and knickknacks, searching for her flower.

"I see. Humans are easier to impress. I might have something here that's primarily designed for an artist. Now, where the hell is it?" He stood motionless as he tried to remember.

"Take your time."

Freder ducked down behind the counter, and it was the perfect opportunity for Annie to hit him with the blue balloon in her pocket, which was the size of a quarter, but then she saw the rose hiding directly behind him. It took her attention more than it should have, and the opportunity was lost when he stood up.

"Does it take a lot of magical energy to keep everything floating like that? That chandelier won't fall on me, will it?"

"I can guarantee that it won't. It's a basic spell that gets its energy from the sun. This is it. One of these days, I will have to organize this place a little better. I hate it when I can't find what I want." He pointed to a small rectangular yellow box in his hand's palm. He noticed that her expression had changed. Was she apprehensive now? He widened the box, putting his hand down into it. Then pulled out a white canvas way more significant than the box, surprising Annie as he struggled to get it out. Such a distraction helped her to feel a little more at ease.

"This is no ordinary canvas, Annie; it's painted with the mind. Watch this." Freder stared at Annie; in less than a minute, he had a likeness of her standing in the shop. Although he was no artist, she recognized herself. "I have little talent as a painter. Your friend will probably do better."

"That's amazing. How much?"

He nodded as he tried to determine a price, strumming his fingers on the counter, cocking his head as he attempted to decide. "Things are not cheap here. I'll let you have it for seventeen thousand. Think of how much fun your friend will have if he can paint again. If she doesn't love it, I will discard her as a friend."

Annie raised her eyebrows. "I'll give you ten."

He despised people who thought they could haggle down his price. "No, no, no. There's no haggling in my shop. I set the price, and that's it. We'll move on to something else if you don't want it."

She couldn't let him see her thoughts were fixated on her flower. "All right, don't get your panties in a bunch. I'll tell you what. If you throw in the box, I'll give you the seventeen thousand."

His face showed consideration as he thought of it. Freder nodded the slightest nod. He looked undecided for a moment, but then agreed. "It's a deal. MasterCard or Visa?" In that moment, he carelessly knocked down the cover of the box, and when he stooped to retrieve it, Annie pulled her spell and struck him with it as he stood up. He had started a counterspell but couldn't cast it fast enough. Freder found himself frozen in place and would remain so for quite some time.

"How do you like that, you weasel?" Annie went to the door and beckoned for Alastair; he blurred into the shop and watched as Annie went behind the counter to get her flower. He went over and stared at the frozen Freder. Just then, a butterfly flew into the case, making her smile; it lit on her left shoulder before it flew off, but when she tried to get the rose out of the case, she couldn't. "Alastair, can you open this? Don't tell me it's spelled!"

He tried to open it but couldn't. He turned the case round and round. "I don't sense a spell attached to it, yet I can't get it open."

Annie took the flower and case and broke it over Freder's head. "No spell. I guess it was just hard plastic. How long will he be stuck like that?"

"Exactly fifty years from today, he'll awaken, and the first thing he'll think of is you."

"I'm taking this canvas. It serves him right for taking my flower. That is a long time to be stuck in that position, and I hope he gets a crick in his back."

Annie took the large canvas and pushed it back into the small box. Even seeing it was hard to believe. "Isn't that amazing? It defies the laws of physics; it should be impossible for that thing to fit in."

"Magic can be both a blessing and a curse, dependent upon who's wielding it."

Annie gave Alastair a big hug and kiss. "The important thing is that I got mine, and he got his. Tonight, you are going to get yours."

CHAPTER SIXTEEN

DORIAN SAT OUTSIDE ON THE CROOKED PORCH with his brother sleeping in the coffin at his feet. He was going through the Blood Book, page after page, with sounds of Lemuel snoring and disturbing his concentration. It was a daunting task to go through every page of the tome. And it was as if the book refused to give up the proper spell, and for all he knew, the task was futile. But he wasn't about to give up yet.

The early morning air was cooler than it had been in a while, and the sky was blue with some haze off in the distance. The summer's heat would take over before noon. A bee accidentally buzzed him, and he glared at it, zapping it out of the air with a small amount of electricity shooting from his index finger. He could hear his brother talking in his sleep but couldn't make out what he was saying.

Dorian got up and walked into the nearby forest, looking through the book. The book showed everything except the spell he wanted. It was maddening to think that the enchantment put on the coffin so long ago now affected the book. And as his effort increased, so did the frustration. He knew Lemuel would be frantic if he didn't get his brother out of that coffin soon. His wailing and complaining were already bothering him. Would he have to abandon him and search the world for a spell to get him out of there? He couldn't carry around a dirt-covered coffin.

Dorian walked face-first into a spider web, then tripped on a dead branch and fell over; he sat there for a while going through the book. Minutes turned into an hour and then another. The book always gave up the spell needed, so what was different? Could they have made that spell so complicated that it could disturb a Blood Book?

Lemuel awoke inside the coffin and immediately called to his brother, but there was no answer. After several more shouts, he panicked. The vampire talked to the spider, but it gave him no comfort. As a matter of fact, the arachnid ignored him. He screamed as loud as he was able, but still no response. Where had his brother gone? Had it all been a dream? Did he remain buried? No, he wasn't still in the ground because the light was different. Perhaps his brother had gone to the store for supplies or something. But what if he didn't come back? What if he couldn't get him out of there and he had run away? A life trapped inside that box was worse than death. Dorian had run off; he was sure of it.

A tear ran down his left cheek. "Dorian?"

Dorian walked deeper into the forest when he got an idea. If the coffin influenced the book, what if he got further away from it? Would the interference stop and show him the proper spell? He blurred off deeper into the woods, and when he passed the three-mile point, the book lit up and showed him the correct incantation. At least he hoped it was the right one. *How to deactivate a level four containment spell*, and the letters were bright red on top of the page. "Yes!" The enchantment appeared to be simple enough. His smile was as big as he could manage.

"Dorian?" Lemuel repeated.

The vampire blurred to the coffin and tapped on it. "Lemuel, I think I have it. Believe it or not, the defensive spell attached to the coffin reaches for miles. But the book showed me the spell when I was far enough away from it. I'm pretty sure I know how to break the enchantment. At least, I think so. I need to get a pen and paper, head back into the woods, and work on it."

"You can get me out of here?"

"I can't promise it'll work, but I think it will."

"Hurry."

It didn't take long to get the spell written, but Dorian soon discovered he was missing one ingredient, a jumping spider. Back out at the coffin, he called down to his brother. "Lemuel, what kind of spider do you have in there?"

"How the hell am I supposed to know that? Why?"

"Well, I need a jumping spider to complete the spell. Does he jump?"

"Yeah, he jumps." Lemuel was becoming more annoyed by the second.

"Of course."

"What kind of jumping spider?"

"It doesn't say."

"That means any jumping spider will do. Find one."

"This could take a while. What if I collect twenty different spiders and mash them all up, hoping that one is a jumping spider? Will that work?"

"You know it won't. All the other spiders would contaminate the spell."

Jumping spiders were common, but he figured catching one was likely simpler than it sounded. However, there was nothing else to do but search out a stupid jumping spider. He searched the forest and found a lot of spider webs, some quite large, but he couldn't make any of the arachnids jump. He thought jumping spiders were small, which would probably make them that much harder to locate. For all he knew, some had been jumping spiders that refused to jump.

Dorian discovered a striped arachnid on the underside of a leaf. He guided it to the palm of his hand and stared at it. "Jump, you little bastard!" It did jump, but unfortunately, it landed on the forest floor. He got down on his hands and knees and searched for it, but it was gone or camouflaged? Dorian hunted frantically. However, it remained elusive. It was crawling on the side of his pants. Finally, he spotted it, gave it a whack, and squashed it. It didn't matter, because it needed to be crushed for the spell. He scraped it off, rushed back into the cabin to create the enchantment.

Dorian exited the cabin within the hour with his two hands closed. The wizard rubbed his hands, fusing the ingredients as he sprinkled the coffin, with red dust turning to blue turning to black. A mist enveloped the entire casket. There was a loud sizzling noise and a bang, but nothing after that. The box didn't open. He turned away from the coffin and shook his head. Dorian couldn't believe it didn't work; he rubbed his forehead at the thought of it.

"Hello brother, long time no see." Lemuel was out of the coffin and finally breathing some fresh air. "You did it!"

They hugged as Dorian patted his brother on the back. "You scared the shit out of me!"

"We need to make some zombies and take over this place. Let's get busy."

CHAPTER SEVENTEEN

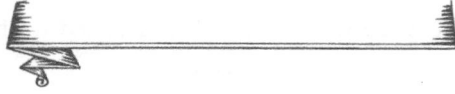

DRACULA, PIERS ANTHONY, AND MOON DIAMOND arrived at Dracula's loft on Hudson Street with the Tribeca skyline and panoramic views. An ample space that was both elegant and modern. He had paid just under fifteen million for it in 2008. Allison had stayed behind in Moncton to await news from Jenny, and when she returned, they were to just on the next flight and head to New York as well. Dracula knew that the initial push from the evil ones would originate in the Big Apple. The evil vampires and nasty wizards would take a massive bite out of it, leaving the city covered in foul saliva. Part of it had already started, but he knew the most significant threat was yet to come. The Master's Blood Book showed disturbing things and dire scenarios that were possibilities for the city. None of the dozen scenes it showed were positive; they were all dark.

Zacharia went off to explore New York City, being quite happy to be back inside the feline. But more importantly, he was looking forward to becoming a red sheriff. He remained unaccustomed to everything appearing so big even a doorknob looked to be ten feet above him. The windows were as large as a movie screen at the drive-in. A cat's perspective was no fun for a vampire.

While the Master stared pensively out the window, reminiscing about the last time he had been in the loft in a foul mood, Piers had permission to take a tour. The author walked around the loft and was captivated by the views of the city and the expensive furniture. One room entirely white, another black. The dining room had floor-to-wall windows and plenty of them. There was a beautiful bar that could seat eight, with a large painting of Earnest Hemmingway standing at his typewriter. A statue of Alexander and Tessy was in the corner that he had commissioned a few years ago. The figure was created from a photo, and Alexander did not know it existed.

"Impressive." Piers stepped into Dracula's master bedroom.

The bedroom was bright white, and on closer inspection, swirls of light texture were also present within the paint and white bats that were almost imperceptible. In the room, there was a massive bed, bigger than any he had ever seen. Of course, the mattress had been made specifically made for the bed. Three walk-in closets and an antique armoire. On the wall, at the foot of his bed, was an old wooden shield that looked ancient enough to be genuine.

Above the bed were three swords, one Arab sword that Dracula had taken from Napoleon Bonaparte, and it had been one of two identical weapons. Another was a rare Katana he had taken from a Japanese vampire who attacked him in a bathhouse. The third was Joyeuse, Charlemagne's sword when Emperor of the Romans in 800, also known as Charles I, the first Holy Roman emperor. Others claimed to have the sword, but Dracula had the real deal on his wall.

In the living room, Dracula stared down at the street below and saw vampires walking on the sidewalk, attacking many humans. That was the thing about New York City; one could always find a sea of people walking somewhere. The Master grabbed his sword, dashed to street level, and began cutting necks. Sharpton had sent yet another bunch, and the author was surprised to see the battle below as he looked down.

Piers rushed down to street level and engaged in combat. Although he didn't enjoy fighting, he knew it was all part of hanging around with the Master. Besides, he couldn't let the innocent get slaughtered. The first thing he noticed was the deadness in their eyes, and he got his back slashed open for his efforts. It made him dance with the pain. It damaged his spine, but rapidly healed. Dracula beheaded the perpetrator, and the black man in the gray suit caught his own head in his lap. Both Piers and Dracula had noticed it as he had turned to bones.

The Master took three heads at once as they rushed him, their skin turning to dust and their skulls hitting the sidewalk and bouncing in different directions. As people ran across the street screaming, they were surprised to see Dracula in person. Piers Anthony cut one in two from his right shoulder through his left nipple, with the blood hitting him unpleasantly in the face.

"Watch out!" Piers warned Dracula, as the last one was attacking him from behind.

He turned and slapped the assailant so hard that he dropped his sword. The Master picked him up with one hand and shook him. "Who sent you?" But the fellow in coveralls either refused to answer or was incapable. The Master snapped him in two and then forced his head from his body with his right foot.

"I think that was the last one."

"Indeed."

An old man with a torn throat was bleeding out, got Dracula's attention with a wave of his right hand. He couldn't talk, so he went into his mind and discovered he didn't want to die and aspired to be turned. Shown how different his life would be. The man was okay with it. The responsibility of caring for his two grandkids fell on him after their parents tragically lost their lives in a car accident. Dracula disliked making those decisions, but the fellow had a pure heart. He stooped, and his fangs shot out.

"Dracula, what are you doing?"

"He wants to live, and he has serious responsibilities." The vampire turned him and watched as he bounced up. The poor fellow had had less than a dozen heartbeats remaining, and now he might have ten centuries or more to live.

"Wow, I feel strong. Thank you so much. Are you Dracula?"

"I am."

"I thought I recognized you."

Dracula gave him a white card with a New York address on it. "You'll need to attend these meetings. They'll help you through the initial, how shall I put it, the differentness of it all. Do you understand?"

"I do."

"Beware of your new strength. Be as gentle as a butterfly."

"I will and thank you again."

Dracula had observed the fellow's well-dressed appearance. He had a white shirt and purple tie, although now the shirt was covered in blood. He blurred off but not before smashing into the side of the building, unaccustomed to his newfound speed, then decided that it was probably safer to walk.

CHAPTER EIGHTEEN

N ight had fallen in the forest, and it remained unnaturally
quiet. A slight breeze flowed around the trees. The stars were
bright and quite spectacular, with no city lights to obscure them,
with a shooting star streaking high overhead seeking attention. It
would have been enjoyable if there hadn't been so much at stake. The
showdown with Achak was approaching, and she wasn't looking
forward to the confrontation.

Jenny was lying on the ground, using the lion as a pillow. Her
mind was silent. Sarah was prone but wasn't sleeping. The cat's
glowing eyes were alert to something nasty that might approach. She
could detect the scent of an acrid bonfire somewhere in the distance
and also the smell of marshmallows toasting, deliciously sweet.

Jenny stayed at her current location until dawn, giving Achak
time to think about whether she was coming. A place where the
wizard had spent years was unlikely to be vacated soon. When a
wizard remained in one location long enough, surrounding magic
from previous spells augmented one's abilities.

The girl's thoughts went back to her parents, and she wondered
what they were up to; she knew her mother would be worried, but
she wasn't sure what her father would be feeling. Having lived so
long, centuries instead of decades chiseled his personality. What
transformations he must have gone through over the years as
everyone changed. Perhaps living for so long muted his feelings. She
couldn't imagine it. But lately, he appeared to be loosening his gruff
exterior, and she could see it day by day. Family life seemed to agree
with him.

Jenny sat up, took several Hot Rods out of her backpack, and
chewed on the dry sausage snack. She gave one to the lion, but Sarah
didn't seem fond of it, and Jenny laughed at the faces she was making.
It was spicy. The cat took the wrapper and tore it open with her teeth
and then sneezed.

"I love these things, but I guess it's not for lions, huh?"

Dawn remained several hours away, and the wizard didn't dare sleep as she didn't want to wake up dead; she smiled at that thought. Quiet time was sometimes strange, being alone with one's thoughts and fears, especially now. One could get lost in there. The inevitable could be scarier than the unknown, especially regarding a life-and-death battle. A showdown with another wizard was more than a little frightening because of her lack of experience. She was at a definite disadvantage. When the lion stood up, she did as well; something was coming, but what? She couldn't hear or see anything, but she could sense it. Jenny used a simple spell to light up the area and saw a cluster of spiders approaching.

"What the hell?" She wasn't terrified of spiders, but so many couldn't be good, and they weren't approaching to engage in pleasant conversation. The girl turned to run, but they were behind her as well. They crawled on the ground and through the trees, falling from leaves and branches, and what a horrible sight it was. They were crawling over one another to get to her.

The sight of what was perhaps a million spiders puzzled the lion and wasn't sure of her next move. Should she bite them? They swarmed around Sarah, and she shook them off as best she could. Jenny formed an energy ball, but before launching it, they were all over her, biting and crawling. Each bite was poisonous, and although a single bite wouldn't do much, thousands just might do her in. A wave of arachnids covered her after she fell.

"Get off me!" She accidentally dropped her ball of white energy, and it burst. A circle of power went through the forest, radiating out from where it had fallen, killing every spider. However, the proximity to the explosion knocked both her and the lion unconscious. The wizard was awakened by Sarah licking her face. The energy sphere had singed areas of fur off the big cat. Most wizards had protective spells against their own magic, but she wasn't yet aware of how to accomplish it. She had researched some information on the Internet, but she couldn't be sure what was accurate and what wasn't.

"Sarah, that's quite the punk haircut." Jenny laughed at the lion's new hairstyle.

The lion shook vigorously, and fur went flying everywhere. More than half of her hair fell out but instantly returned, just a little thicker than before. Jenny was now angry at the assault. If that son-of-a-bitch could attack from a distance, she could most likely do it as well. She concentrated hard while forming another energy ball, pressing hard on it with the palm of both hands while talking to it, telling it to get the wizard. She threw it hard, watching as it dodged through the trees as if it had a mind of its own and was then out of sight. Then it exploded somewhere in the distance. Jenny observed its glow through the trees, wondering if it hit its target.

Achak was enjoying the magical properties of the bonfire, its warmth, and its color, although his thoughts were on Jenny. Sparks drifted into the night sky, the contrasting beauty of light against dark. He had a broad smile at the thought of all those spiders attacking her, even though they weren't likely to kill such a powerful wizard. Being a girl, there was a chance it would scare her off. He knew how powerful she was because even though she was miles away, he felt her energy, which appeared to be equal to or surpassing his. He had summoned the flaming skeleton to his defense, but so far, it either fought in battle or simply ignored his call, as there was no sign of it. It was exasperating.

The raven jumped off his left shoulder and up into a pine tree. Achak found it a little peculiar at how fast it had departed. Just as he was going to ask if it sensed danger, an energy ball hit him in the shoulder, causing significant bleeding. "Aaaahh!" Fifty percent of his shoulder was missing, with part of the mangled bone sticking out. Achak screamed out in pain as it began to heal. Because of the high energy level of the impact, it took longer than expected for it to heal.

Another sphere struck him in the hip and knocked him down; he tried to get up but couldn't. The gaping wound took even longer to heal than the first. When he finally stood, he formed a translucent red shield, and as another ball exploded, it stunned him, making his ears ring from the explosion. That little vixen!

Although he wanted to retaliate for the retaliation, he had never seen such destructive energy in a ball of power. Because of his weakened condition, he decided not to bother her for the rest of the night, as he would get busy preparing something nasty for Jenny's imminent arrival.

CHAPTER NINETEEN

LAUREN AND MICHAEL WERE WALKING PAST THE BRILL BUILDING on Broadway and enjoying the afternoon. Hand in hand, their souls touched. Michael was wearing a smart-looking gray suit with a purple striped tie. And Lauren was beautiful in her black skort and blacktop with a spectacular-looking bat with red eyes on her left breast. A blond young fellow in a tuxedo walked by carrying a pizza and a six-pack of beer, and it was such a delicious aroma that it made them both hungry. Lauren's attractiveness caught his attention, and as she walked by, he flashed a big smile, almost walking into an older gentleman.

Michael recognized that look and didn't like it. "Lauren, did you see the way his eyes devoured you? I should punch him."

Lauren shook her head. "Michael, he's human. I get those looks all the time. You get some too."

"I know, but did you see how he looked at you? He was undressing you with his eyes."

"Really?"

"He would have walked off a cliff and smiled all the way down. Shouldn't you be wearing your trench coat? You look too sexy."

"A woman can never be too sexy."

"They can because you are."

Lauren stopped. "Michael, we're together, we're having a baby, and we're getting married. You don't need to be jealous because it's very unattractive. I don't think you ever will if you don't feel secure now." Her cell vibrated. She read the text and then showed it to Michael. *I'm in the city. Congratulations on the baby. We're having one as well. Talk soon. Dracula.*

"Was that the real Dracula?"

"No, the fake one."

"Dracula's here? In New York? Could we run into him? He's having a baby?"

"Men don't have babies."

"You know what I mean."

"Apparently."

"Wouldn't it be cool if our kids played together? And our baby beat up his baby."

She gave him a look that made him stop. They started walking, and he wanted to admit something to Lauren, but then again, he didn't. The way she read his mind, there was a chance she already knew. He always tried to show confidence, but he wasn't all that self-assured. How was he to put it? "Honey, I hate to admit this, but I'm scared."

"Scared of what?"

He hesitated, unsure of his next words. He didn't want her to think less of him. What would be the best way to spit it out? "Of meeting Dracula? Scared of the ceremony? There will be ancient vampires there that have seen and done so much. What if I faint?"

It was Lauren's turn to hesitate as she imagined Michael falling flat on his face. "You will not faint? If you do, it'll be a story that you can tell our daughter, that you met Dracula and fainted. Not everyone gets to meet the Master."

"Oh yeah, that's some story to tell my son. Daddy pooped his pants when he met Dracula."

Lauren laughed and then brushed her blue-black hair out of her eyes. "You know, you don't have to become a red sheriff. I would think that one in the family is enough, but it is your decision. It really doesn't matter to me if you do or don't. Do it for you, not for me."

"So, you're saying I should be home changing diapers?"

She thought he was in a strange mood. "Michael, that is not what I'm saying, and you know it. Do whatever makes you happy."

"You make me happy."

"Well, then, do me."

"Ha, I can't; we're in public."

Lauren took him to the side and gave him a hug and a kiss. "I'm going to say one last thing on the subject. If you don't become a red sheriff now, it might be quite a while before you get another opportunity. It's a simple fact."

"I thought about that. I'm still not sure what to do."

She initiated another kiss. "Come to the ceremony, and you can decide there. What the hell is that?"

Across the street, the burning skeleton attacked a tall fellow and made him scream; Lauren pulled her swords and rushed over. The thing dropped the wizard Karis and blocked several swings from her blades. When she punched through her sword, she went right through it touching nothing, which threw her off balance. Michael was there to deflect the blow from the blazing sword that would have taken her head.

The wizard lay on the ground near death as the flaming skeleton had consumed ninety percent of his energy; he tried to crawl away but didn't have the strength. His eyes fluttered as he went unconscious. It aimed the palm of its hand toward the wizard and sucked out the last of his energy, killing him. Michael was ready with his sword when it turned its attention toward them.

"Michael, wait, my sword goes right through it."

"What should we do?"

Lauren saw the skeleton was looking at her stomach. Did it somehow know that she was pregnant? She attempted to read the thing's mind but couldn't. "How do you destroy something that you can't touch?"

The monster swung its fire blade in Lauren's direction, and fire flew off it like paint on a brush and tagged her. She was suddenly on fire. She patted herself with impressive speed to extinguish the flames, but it didn't work. Lauren fell as the fire consumed her.

"Noooo!"

CHAPTER TWENTY

S HARPTON AND OBLIVION HAD ALMOST A THOUSAND spelled vampires at attention in front of the military-style buildings. Like proper soldiers, they were prepared to follow orders no matter what, because the enchantment had robbed them of their own free will. They would all stand on their heads if told to do so. The pile of dead animals continued to burn with black and orange flames, radiating heat and magical energy. The tiniest bugs now crawled around in their brains, telling them whatever Sharpton said to the microbes. He smiled as he gazed upon his army. It was a good beginning.

Oblivion smiled. "Aren't you glad that you didn't kill me?"

"I am." He was unsure of his next move, but time was on his side. Every day that went by made him feel more in control of his destiny and of the world as well. Power was as satisfying as sex, and he figured the outcome was likely.

"Frankly, I wasn't sure I could get the spell to work properly."

Sharpton wondered if he should unleash them all at once, creating a living hell for every New Yorker, with those not being attacked hiding in fear under their beds? Or should he release them a hundred at a time, day after day, until the government called a truce and conceded the city? Both options were promising, and he dreamed of New York City as dark and nefarious, utterly devoid of humans, unless invited to dinner.

"I have never seen such a precious sight. You know, they've called out the military in some parts of New York, but a thousand of them remain vulnerable to a single one of us." The military has been called out in areas of New York. Sharpton's proud expression diminished as he examined the vampires, because of his initial doubt about the possibility of gathering so many in one spot.

Talks were ongoing with the government in surrendering New York City to him and the vampires. He hadn't believed such a prospect was workable, but tens of thousands were moving out of the city because of the recent attacks. It was the topic of every conversation, every newscast, and every nightmare.

Oblivion cocked his head to the right. "Do you feel that?"

"Feel what?"

"Someone dominant approaches."

Then Sharpton spotted it from the forest, past a hundred trees too far away to tell what it was, but it appeared to be a walking fireball. Some trees were catching fire as it passed, but it was self-extinguishing on the trees because the skeleton had wished it so. As it approached the edge of the forest, it stopped. Then it saw it was a walking skeleton. Oblivion was alarmed. The entire country was talking about the flaming skeleton destroying wizards, and since Oblivion was the only wizard there, it wasn't difficult to figure out that it had come for him. What was the proper course of action? It might be faster than him, as he was far from the most rapid.

"That thing is coming for me."

Sharpton didn't need such a complication. "You said that this place would be invisible to all that would do us harm."

"Well, powerful magic has apparently created the skeleton; as a matter of fact, I've never felt such destructive power. I can only imagine how powerful it could be if it's destroying wizards. Perhaps I should flee?"

"What happens to the vampires under my control if you die?"

Oblivion had formed a destructive ball of energy. "Your concern is touching. The ingredients in the fire feed them, so nothing unless it destroys the fire. Why don't you send some vampires after it and see what happens?"

"I think I will. You twelve in front, pull your swords and kill that thing!"

A dozen vampires with dead eyes rushed toward the skeleton, but the blazing monster set them aflame before they could reach within twenty feet. They all died in a gruesome manner, transforming into burning bones. The skeleton's strength and intelligence were both on the rise, which was not good for the world. If it continued its current path, it could become unstoppable. As if the world didn't have enough problems.

Sharpton was both surprised and shocked. "That thing might kill all my vampires! Can you kill it? What the hell is it doing?"

Oblivion watched as it paced just feet from his line of protection. "It looks like it's trying to judge whether it will survive my security."

The skeleton stood at the edge of the spell that protected the camp. It felt a considerable energy that encircled the place, attempting to evaluate what would happen if it took another step forward. It shot a stream of fire over the line and studied it. Then it just walked through the barrier, not affecting it whatsoever. Sharpton pulled his sword, uncertain what to do because unleashing his vampires could cause their destruction. He would be right back at the beginning. Oblivion blurred to within a car's length of it; he was sure that if the sphere didn't kill it outright, it would hurt it and give him time to flee.

Sharpton called out to Oblivion. "It's best that you don't wait until it attacks."

Oblivion's attack caused an explosion in the sky, creating a black hole-like outline. They all stared at the heavens, watching as it healed and again turned blue. The sword's magic had combined with the energy ball and had altered it somewhat. "Un oh."

The fiery beast rushed Oblivion as he tried to run away, bumping into him and sticking to him like glue to paper. His skin turned to ash after a single scream, and then he was bones, with the skeleton taking all the wizard's power and talent. The beast glowed even brighter than it had before. It rested its sword on its right shoulder and scanned the area, staring directly at Sharpton.

Sharpton looked at it, thinking that he was most likely facing death as well, positive that he was no match for it, so there was no need to initiate an attack. They stared at one another for over ten seconds, with the skeleton finally turning and heading back into the woods. Those moments had seemed interminable as Sharpton was happy to see it go. But losing his wizard was a blow.

CHAPTER TWENTY-ONE

ZACHARIA TOURED NEW YORK LOOKING FOR TROUBLE. Being restless, he hoped to run into an evil vampire so he could kill him or be killed. Either way, he was okay as long as he didn't end up in a coma with his ghost floating nearby. Any fight was risky but being inside a cat complicated it. He had different weapons as a feline, his strength and cunning being his best weapons. His thinking had to be altered. It was like fighting giant vampires, but being ancient, he was faster and stronger than most.

Passersby gave the cat plenty of looks, and he almost tripped over a few times. He was a handsome Siamese, and some people wanted to take him home, and he even had to show one guy his fangs to dissuade him; the look on his face made him laugh. He would never, ever get used to being cute.

Zacharia toured the Statue of Liberty; he had visited it once before, but of course, being cat-sized, the 305-foot statue, including the pedestal, looked massive. Everything was new again from that perspective. He crossed the Brooklyn Bridge into Brooklyn and enjoyed watching the traffic as he traveled, seeing people's faces that noticed him, almost causing not one but two accidents. Still, one guy had been using an electric shaver and not paying attention.

Moon Diamond toured the South Street Seaport Museum, walking on cobblestone streets. He chased a mouse that got into a crack in the side of a building that was too small for him to dig out. Moon Diamond checked out the 19th-century print shop, remembering he had a close friend working in such an establishment. He had been killed, and Zacharia had tracked down and killed the killer. Zacharia continued to think of his old chum, how he had been a person who lit up his day. Remarkable people with such pure hearts were challenging to find. He had almost always been in a good mood and had lifted Zacharia's spirit many times. Old memories were sometimes like old ghosts that came back to haunt.

Zacharia visited Grand Central Station. The place was 407 feet long, 160 feet wide, and 150 feet high. He knew that a French artist had painted the ceiling's zodiac constellations named Paul Helleu. Light entered through six arched windows, with a double staircase in Botticino marble, a unique place. Beauty came in many forms, and this certainly was one of them. People went about their business, and he enjoyed observing. A police officer tried to catch him, but as soon as he blurred, he gave up the pursuit, realizing that Moon Diamond was no ordinary Siamese.

Zacharia saw a suspicious-looking character following an old married couple in Madison Square Park. Many vampires were good at concealing their intentions, but this guy wasn't, at least not to the cat. The couple in gray shorts and black tops were unaware, each carrying an umbrella even though there was no rain, and none predicted as they were replacing their old ones. From any position in the park, one had a view of the nearby architectural landmarks, and it was a nice place to gather one's thoughts. Zacharia followed him and the seniors to the park's southeast corner, where they stopped to look at a 19th-century statue of the bearded Senator Roscoe Conkling. He had perished from the great blizzard of 1888. There, vampire Remington made his move, attacking Harold while his wife fainted. Moon Diamond attached himself to his neck and tore chunks of skin out.

"Aaahhh! What the hell? Get off me!" Blood went flying as Zacharia tore out more chunks of skin. The miscreant had to fight for his life, so he disengaged the attack on the senior. The idea was to rip through his neck until his head fell off. With the cat's strength, he could accomplish it. The seniors exited the area as fast as they could, the man helping his wife along. Remington tore the cat from his neck and attempted to smash the life out of it on the ground. But on the way down, it grabbed his arm near his elbow, and the pain of it made the vampire dance, Zacharia's claws sinking deep into his skin.

"How do you like me now?" Zacharia said in his head.

Wei and Bao blurred into the battle. Wei took Remington's head with a single slice that pissed off Zacharia. A good fight was the only thing that made Zacharia feel alive these days, and he had been robbed of the kill. He slammed his front paws onto the ground with great speed, so fast that they were a blur; he was furious.

"I wanted to kill him!"

Wei shrugged. "Sorry, Zacharia, we thought you needed help. I apologize."

"You don't know how bad I'd like to scratch all your damn skin off! He's the one that needed help. Damn it!"

"He'd take it back if he could, Zacharia." Bao gave the cat a slight nod of respect.

Two young blond women stopped to stare at Wei and Bao. At a distance, the two young women stared in the direction of Wei and Bao, showing their attraction to the Chinese sheriffs. Their handsomeness almost always invited the ladies and wearing black Kung Fu uniforms added to it. They both had boyfriends who had gone for drinks, but they couldn't help being impressed by the sheriffs. Both so wanted to flirt. They had observed the beheading, and it had not frightened them because there was a lot of that going around. This was the second beheading they had seen this week. New Yorkers could get used to just about anything.

Bao looked down at the cat. "I hear Dracula's in the city."

Moon Diamond had licked his right paw and cleaned his face, although Zacharia wasn't aware he was doing it. "Yes, he's here for the ceremony. I'm going to be a sheriff."

"Yes, congratulations are in order." Wei felt weird talking to the feline as more and more people were stopping to watch. He was reading his mind but engaging in ordinary one-sided conversation. "I guess we should get going."

"Sure, now that you've ruined my fun, you can just saunter off. What do you say to a little sparring?"

Wei shook his head. "Oh no, I don't want those sharp nails in my ass."

Bao showed his charismatic smile. "Shall we saunter?"

The two attractive girls had just gotten the courage to approach the sheriffs when they blurred off, but it was just as well as their boyfriends were back. Then Wei and Bao rushed back and looked down at the cat.

Moon Diamond continued to clean himself when Zacharia realized what he was doing. "Stop that. Yes, I know, there's a mouse over there a car has run over."

Wei waved at the cat to get his attention. "Zacharia, we have a possible terrorist thing going on. We can use you if you want in?"

The request picked up the old vampire's spirits. "Let's go."

$$\times$$

THE POLICE HAD AN APARTMENT surrounded on the east side. They had been watching the two Iraqis for months when they noticed that their level of excitement had increased. The police snaked a small camera under their door and observed them in the process of creating a powerful bomb with C-4. Unfortunately, one had noticed the camera. Abbas had grabbed it, sounding the alarm, and now they were threatening to blow themselves up. Falih wanted to detonate the explosive as soon as they got it together, but Abbas had not wanted it to be a suicide mission.

The Iraqis were both human, but the police feigned one was a vampire so that they could get the sheriffs in. Two FBI agents had taken control of the scene but were waiting for further help. When Wei and Bao showed up with the Siamese, they received puzzled looks, but were happy for the aid. After being informed of the situation, Zacharia noticed Falih was at the window near the fire escape with a grave look on his face. He stood in plain sight, making himself an easy target for the sniper. Of course, the other one would have set off the bomb if the sniper killed his friend.

Without hesitation, Moon Diamond took off up the fire escape and jumped into the apartment past Falih. The appearance of the cat made them smile, but as soon as Abbas took his finger off the detonator, the cat ripped his throat out. Falih went for his pistol but it was too late. Zacharia also grabbed him by the throat and tore through the carotid artery, and he bled out all over the cat.

Moon Diamond blurred down to Wei. "That's it. They're both dead."

Wei reached down with his hand to the cat. "Low five!"

Zacharia hit Wei's hand with his paw.

The tall and muscular FBI agent ran over. "What happened?"

"They're both dead."

"What? We wanted to question them!"

"So, who's stopping you?" Bao shrugged.

Moon Diamond, covered in blood, looked funny as he smiled. He blurred off in a better mood.

"What the hell was that?"

Wei shook his head at the agent. "It's complicated."

CHAPTER TWENTY-TWO

Annie rose as the sun was rising while Alastair continued to snore, grumbling as he stumbled out of bed. She got dressed and took her rose with her into the kitchen, placing it on the island. The 90-year-old poured herself a glass of blood, savoring it. Not long ago, it would have disgusted her, but as a vampire, she now cherished it. Annie could detect blood from across the street. She had assumed that her only escape from the agony she had been in would have found her in heaven. She continued to send Dracula thank-you notes for turning her, for not having to struggle for her breath.

A Blue Morpho butterfly appeared and landed on the island, then lit on the rose. It had a wingspan of almost eight inches. The insect's blue color had a metallic style to it, and it fascinated Annie. They usually spent about a minute on the flower, but this one was there for at least five. She hoped she would never get accustomed to the butterflies to where she no longer appreciated them, but she couldn't see that happening. With each and everyone, she was a little girl again, pursuing them in her grandmother's garden.

"Do you know how beautiful you are?" Annie smiled at it and was surprised when a second butterfly, a beautiful Leopard Lacewing that belonged in India or China, appeared. The colors included orange, yellow, black, and white. The day-flying insects took turns touching down on the rose, then simultaneously flew off, disappearing through the window facing the garden, right through the glass.

The sun was just peeking over the horizon, yet her day was made. Annie momentarily went through The New York Times, but there was too much negative vampire stuff, so she put it aside. Annie washed the two glasses left in the sink, put them away, and then looked down at the rectangular yellow box, pulling it closer. She pulled the top off and stared down at it. She saw shapes and shadows. It was undoubtedly a strange magical thing. Annie reached her hand down into it to her wrist; she could feel the corner of the canvas down there. Grabbing it, she pulled it out, and it must have been over twenty times the size of the box. The life of a wizard must be a fascinating one. How would one even think of creating such a thing?

Annie concentrated hard on painting a likeness of the Leopard Lacewing with her mind, but at first, it wouldn't work. Once she relaxed, the creation fascinated unfolding in front of her, and it was a pretty good likeness, if she said so herself. Some might call it amateurish, but thought it had a Picasso quality. Then she added the blue butterfly to it and then the rose. It was finished. Annie lay the painting on the island and again examined the rectangular box. She picked it up and thought it was much too cumbersome for its size.

"I wonder?" Could there be something else inside? She got the small flashlight from the cupboard drawer and tried looking down into it, but the beam couldn't penetrate. The light deflected in strange directions. How odd. She considered what to do next. Sticking her hand in there wasn't likely to be dangerous since she had already done it. What magical thing would she find in there?

"What have you got for me?"

Her hand went into the box, almost up to her elbow, and she felt around. She touched a corner and then felt something peculiar. Was it a tiny brush? It felt prickly. Annie grabbed it, pulled it out, and dropped it on the marble island top. She screamed and swiped it onto the floor; it was a substantial hairy Red Knee tarantula spider like the ones found in Mexico. Annie grabbed the Steven King novel, blurred and squashed it. Green goo emerged from it, and she wondered if she had overreacted. She supposed it had been pretty enough for a spider, pretty ugly.

Annie watched the spider regenerate as it returned to life. The legs grew out of its body, as if it had never experienced death. "Oh, my goodness, you have more lives than a cat? Well, you can't stay here."

The spider looked up at her with eight eyes, understanding every word she was saying. As she went for the broom, it approached the door, waiting to be let out. She looked down at the arachnid with puzzled eyes. "Go out into the garden. I like to sit out there, so you better not crawl on me. And don't you hurt any butterflies because I'll kick your spider ass."

Annie thought the spider was making a strange movement, almost as if attempting to shake its head no. In fact, it was telling her it wouldn't jump on her in the garden. She opened the door and watched as it crawled out. Once it got outside, it turned and looked up at her with sad eyes, all eight of them. She gently closed the door so she wouldn't scare it. Opening the door again, she looked down at it; the tarantula waved up at her with one of its legs.

Annie returned and drank another glass of blood as she stared at the box; she had had enough of it for the day and placed the cover back on it. She didn't know if she would ever have the courage to stick her hand in there again. Perhaps she would make Alastair do it. Yes, that was a much better idea. She thought her scream would have disturbed him, but he was a heavy sleeper.

"Oh, balderdash. Spider or no spider, I'm going out there."

Annie grabbed her Steven King book and checked it for spider goo; seeing nothing, she entered the garden. She sat on the nearest bench, and not seeing the spider, she opened the book, enjoying the scents of the flowers, but then she caught movement. Annie lowered the book, and sure enough, it was staring up at her. It brought its front legs together, repeatedly touching one to the other, and to Annie, it appeared as if it was thinking, or signaling? Clearly not an ordinary spider. Perhaps it wasn't really an arachnid, but a magical thing.

"What? You need something? Why don't you catch some flies?"

It jumped, and that made Annie laugh. "What in GOD'S NAME are you doing? What do you want, Hairy? I didn't think tarantulas could jump. But who knows what the heck you can do? I better not find you in my bed."

Hairy started toward the leg of the bench. "No, you stop right there. You turn around. Don't come any closer. You're too ugly. I'm sorry, but you are. You might look like Brad Pitt to another tarantula, but not to me." Annie shook her head. "Of course, a spider will not know who Brad Pitt is. Silly me."

When it turned around, she marveled that it understood what she was saying. "Hairy, can you understand me?" The arachnid turned to face her. She placed her bookmark down about two feet from it. "If you can understand, go to my bookmark and return to where you are."

The spider followed her words exactly.

"Oh, my." Again, it headed for the leg of the bench. "Oh, sit beside me. Just don't touch me." The spider climbed up the leg and sat beside her, about a foot away. "Alastair will not believe this." Annie tried to read but couldn't with the spider watching her. It attempted to get closer and closer when she wasn't paying attention. "Now, Hairy, what was the agreement? That you would stay on your own side." She could sense the spider's disappointment.

The spider began petting its own front legs. Every time Annie glanced at it, the spider would rub itself. "What are you doing? You want me to pet you? Is that it?"

Again, the Red Knee tarantula jumped as she had gotten it just right. She hesitated but finally agreed, but it took several attempts. The spider vibrated with glee, and the bond was complete. The spider was now attached to her by the act of kindness.

"That feels so good," the spider thought. "A little to the left."

CHAPTER TWENTY-THREE

KEITH CARRIED BERNIE THE BUM past the intersection of Fifth Avenue and West 34th Street. He crossed in the middle of traffic, and a yellow cab had to slam on his breaks even though he didn't want to; he gave the vampire the finger. Lucky for him that Bernie was sleeping, and Keith didn't want to wake him. Otherwise, his finger would have been all that remained. The vampire was getting a few looks from passersby, but he didn't care. He tossed the bum over his left shoulder, picked up a stray pit bull terrier, drank from it, and then let it wander off. That gave him a boost as he took Bernie back into his arms.

Keith turned and looked up at the Empire State Building and thought it was so beautiful. He leaned against the building on 1 West 34th, trying to concentrate on the skyscraper. "Whoa, when did they build this thing? It wasn't here yesterday. They work fast around here."

Bernie awoke and looked down at the ground. "Where am I?"

Keith placed him down on the sidewalk in an upright position. "You were sleeping, so I carried you."

Bernie tried to adjust his bloodshot eyes. "Hey, it's my best friend, the vampire. You, you, you got some wine?"

"You drank it all."

Bernie continued to try to focus. "That happens a lot."

Keith tapped Bernie on the shoulder. "See that gigantic building? That wasn't there yesterday."

"Are you serious? Who put it there? I'll bet he could get me some wine."

Although Bernie had been asleep for a few hours, he remained inebriated. They found a bench where they sat and watched people go by. They saw a red double-decker New York Sightseeing bus. "See that big bus? They probably came to see the New Building."

Keith looked at Bernie and was so happy to have him as a friend. He was a little worried about him. "You should eat something. You don't eat enough."

"Oh yeah? What should I eat? I, I, I know one thing. I should probably wash it down with some wine."

A teen started past them with a chicken dinner, and they could both smell it. Keith grabbed it and gave it to his buddy. When the guy was ready to fight, he showed him his fangs, and he was quick to get away from them. The vagabond finished the meal, leaned over the bench, and immediately threw up most of it.

"Are you okay?"

"Aw yeah, just making room for more wine."

The vampire stared and stared at him. "Hey, I don't remember you having two heads?" His blurry vision passed.

"I, I, I have two heads? Now I'm gonna have to drink twice as much."

"Bernie, what do you want to do today?"

"Well, I'd like to find some wine. And, and, and then maybe find some more wine." As an NYPD officer walked by, he let go with a loud belch. The officer studied them and didn't like what he saw.

"I'll get you some wine."

Officer Taylor could smell Bernie from where he was standing. "You two are going to have to move along."

"Hey, officer, that building down there wasn't there yesterday. Who put it there?"

"I'm pretty sure it was there."

Bernie stood up aggressively. "Are you calling me a liar? See this guy right here? He's a vampire; he'll kill you, drink your blood, and then buy me a bottle of wine. What do you think of that?"

That, of course, changed everything. It was best not to anger a vampire. Keith showed him his fangs and then pulled them back in. "Well, I'm going to check on that building and see who put it there."

The officer wanted to survive his shift, go home to his pregnant Katie, and get the hell away from those two. So the smart thing to do was just move along. He would remember their faces and not confront them again.

Keith picked up Bernie and blurred all the way to 37th Avenue. He went through the doors under the yellow Wines and Liquors sign, and when he exited, he gave Bernie two bottles of wine. Bernie had been standing there with a watermelon that he pinched from the supermarket next door, but he dropped it as soon as he saw the wine. There was nothing prettier than an unopened bottle of wine, except for two.

They found shade on 74th Street near some parking meters and sat there on the sidewalk, feeding off one another's energy. Bernie opened a bottle and took a big drink; it tasted like heaven. His liver didn't like it too much because it worked overtime, but if Bernie could have managed it, he would have given it a stern lecture. He offered a drink to the vampire, and then he consumed the remainder of the bottle. Bernie looked down into the empty bottle with a sad eye.

"Okay, that was your bottle, and this one is mine." Bernie was making a statement and sticking up for his wine.

"Okay."

Bernie looked at the Ford Focus, and he stood after a struggle. He staggered over to it and was most impressed by the white car. "Look how beautifuk that car is! Did I say beautifuk? They they-they don't make them like that anymore. Wait, I guess they do because it's brand new. We should steal it."

"You want that car?"

"I, I, I do."

Keith got up and pried the door open. Actually, he ripped it off. Bernie looked in the car and then got in. "It's so nice in here. It's like being in heaven."

"Hold on." Keith grabbed the car and heaved it over his head; he then ran down the street carrying it as Bernie held onto the steering wheel with one hand and his bottle of wine in the other.

He enjoyed himself as he drank the wine; he couldn't believe how fast he was driving. "The engine is so quiet I, I, I can't even hear it. Faster, Keith, faster!"

CHAPTER TWENTY-FOUR

D AWN IN THE FOREST, and Jenny hadn't slept. Another shadow creature could have been on them anytime during the night. Perhaps a vivid dream or two could have aided her in the upcoming battle; unfortunately, sleep had been too risky, even though the lioness would most likely have woken her if something had approached. She remembered a conversation from school that if a person's soul left their body when they died, they could indeed wake up dead. A silly thought to ease the tension.

It would have been nice if her father could have been there by her side, but it would have done her no good if the book had fused to him. Why couldn't some of life's complications lean more to her side rather than a pain in the ass? Now she had to fight a wizard that would probably kill or bury her alive or even something that she couldn't imagine. This day could end up being the last one of her brief life. It was best to push those thoughts into a deep hole, bury them, and press on.

People acted as if it was up to her to save the world. How fair was that?

There was wispy fog in the trees and coolness in the air. The woods were gray in the early morning light, and the morning clouds were now affected by sunrise. The summer sun would soon heat things up. And apprehension of the unknown was heavy on both wizards' minds; neither had slept. What would the day bring forth? Would victory shine or misery rain down? Trepidation could make one's mind as shaky as a fearful hand.

The girl got up and stretched, combed her hair, and petted her lion. She now hoped that her father's resiliency had passed down to her. Putting on a brave face was unnecessary when no one was around to see it. Sarah wanted to play, but she wasn't in the mood. Would Achak wait for her to approach him, or would he initiate the attack? How many battles had he fought and won? Jenny's green eyes scrutinized the forest, but saw nothing.

When the sound returned to the woods, they both realized it, especially with a nearby woodpecker making such a racket. But now they could hear a branch creaking with the morning breeze. A blue jay screeched. A crow cawed somewhere. She wondered if he had fled the area, and that wouldn't be good because it might be impossible to find him.

Jenny could sense the Blood Book, and so she thought it was likely that he had gone nowhere. He was out there, waiting and preparing his nasty enchantments. She could perceive his evil soul even though she didn't know what he was up to; she wished he would leave the book and run.

Even this close, Jenny wasn't sure what she could accomplish in battle; she had the energy spheres, daggers, and lightning bolts, but that was about it. She considered that the little training she had received wasn't worth much; Jenny needed spells to wield, of which she had few. The wizard had some instinctive magic, but would it be enough to survive a battle with another wizard? She could now smell what she thought was wood-burning somewhere in front of her. If she didn't return home, would Dracula avenge her? Of course, he would.

Jenny led the way, with the lion following; she told Sarah to stay behind her, and she did. She came upon a dead deer with its throat torn out and told Sarah not to eat it. It was either a warning or perhaps poison meat. Even with the uncertainty, she enjoyed the beauty of the forest. She had always loved being in the woods and always would. There was uniqueness, an atmosphere like nowhere else, nature's home. A couple of miles in, she could see the wigwam in the distance, but no Achak. The lion approached and listened for movement, but heard nothing. Sarah was as apprehensive as the girl, and Jenny would give odds it was some sort of trap. Either that, or he was about to jump out at her.

"What do you think, Sarah? Is it a trap?"

She approached the dwelling, her heart beating faster, but no wizard appeared. She instinctively knew something was wrong but didn't know what. The book's pull remained persuasive despite there being no sign of it. When the lion saw Achak appear from behind a tree, she attacked him, only she smashed hard into the see-through spell that now had them contained. It wasn't his real camp they were in but a mirror of it, minus the fire he had burning.

Achak smiled, not saying a single word, then he turned and blurred to his actual site about a mile further in. Jenny threw a sphere of light, but it exploded against the invisible wall, almost deafening her and making her lion jump. The entrapment felt solid, and they appeared trapped inside a half-sphere, a bit like glass but different somehow. It felt more like cement than glass.

Jenny began digging down to tunnel under it, but soon discovered they were inside an entire sphere, half underground. She kicked it hard, but it was unbreakable. The girl looked at her right hand and concentrated. When it glowed the prettiest blue, she shot lightning bolts at the sphere, but they ricocheted, and she narrowly evaded it. The lion wasn't as lucky because it singed her tail. Sarah shook her head as if she was judging her.

"Let's see you get us out of this thing if you're so smart?"

The cat tried to bite the sphere, but she couldn't; scratching accomplished nothing. Sarah let her head lean sadly against the hard surface, with her face being distorted from the outside. She sat and looked at Jenny as if to say it was her turn.

How could she break such a spell? What was that? A strange word popped into her head. Dachatromto? No, that was close, but not it. Dachatromtola? Yes, that was it, but what the heck did it mean? Achak was in front of her with three black knives, black but with small white snakes that wiggled around inside them. He stared down at the snakes and smiled.

Jenny spoke the word that was in her head just as the first knife penetrated the sphere. "Dachatromtola?" She found herself inside her gray protective bubble with an ancient type of hieroglyphic circling inside it. The knife hit the bubble and bounced, broke, and released the two white snakes. No variety that she had ever seen, entirely white with glowing red eyes. Achak's mouth dropped open because he didn't expect that.

Although Jenny was safe inside the bubble, Sarah wasn't. The first one struck at the lion and missed, and she bit the head off it. But while she was busy doing that, the second one caught her on the hip. She fell and shook from the toxins, dead in less than ten seconds.

"Nooooooo!"

CHAPTER TWENTY-FIVE

MICHAEL WAS FURIOUS AT THE SIGHT OF LAUREN, burning and dying in front of him. His anger brought his talent to the forefront, and he attacked the skeleton with all his might; his strength and speed had increased. The skeleton blocked three of his mighty swings, but it was inevitable one got through; he cut the thing in two at the sternum and watched as it fell into two pieces. It wasn't dead but temporarily immobile, but for the first time, it struggled and was fearful of being destroyed.

Michael jumped on Lauren, trying his best to put the fire out, but no matter how hard he tried, the fire got worse. Even if he could extinguish it, would the baby survive? He was ready to pick her up and head to the nearest body of water when the flames extinguished.

He looked down at her smoldering body. "Lauren, can you hear me?"

"Michael?"

"Are you okay?"

She sat up. "I feel awful. I think I'm running a fever."

Michael touched her forehead and couldn't believe how hot it was. Vampires seldom got sick because their immune systems were too vigorous. He would be lucky to find a single doctor in New York who could help her. He picked her up and turned toward where the flaming skeleton had been, but it was gone. Whether it had perished or escaped, he couldn't say, but he hoped he'd never see it again.

Back at Lauren's loft, she was prone on the sofa and looked miserable; she felt as if she had the flu times two. She needed to vomit but couldn't. Her muscles ached, and her head felt like it would burst. Although the sheriff didn't know it, the baby had instinctively extinguished the flames to protect itself; if not for the child, she'd have been dead. She attempted to vomit, nothing but dry heaves.

Michael was busy making calls to anyone he could think of, trying to find a doctor who could treat a vampire, but so far, it was a fruitless endeavor. He could not reach Dracula. It was awful to watch one's loved one suffer and not be able to do anything about it; he felt as miserable as she looked. Michael put his head on her stomach and was happy when the baby kicked him. She was so hot that he placed her in cold water in the bathtub. The cold water worked; she felt a lot better.

"It worked, Michael. I feel okay." Lauren got out of the tub with nothing on but a beige towel, but as soon as she sat down, she had a relapse. She had Michael help her back into the tub and again felt better.

Michael watched the pain ease on her face. "I can see that you're better in the water, but you can't live there. As soon as you leave, it looks like you're at death's door and trying hard to break it down."

"Did you kill that damn thing?"

"I split it in two, but when I turned around, it was gone. I don't know if I killed it or not."

"My hero."

"What will we do if you're too sick to attend the ceremony?"

"You're a big boy; you can go by yourself."

"I'm not going without you."

Lauren screamed and grabbed her stomach. "Michael, the baby!"

Michael did the only thing he could do. He fainted.

CHAPTER TWENTY-SIX

DORIAN HUGGED HIS BROTHER LEMUEL, and as their power came together with a *whoosh,* it killed every single bird within a radius of three miles. One wizard enhanced the other, becoming much more powerful together. The energy fed off each other's magic, a rare thing in the world of wizards. They could feel the enhanced level of magic flowing through their bodies like fire and fuel coming together. It was a sensation that they had both missed over the centuries and dreamed of their reunion.

"What happened to you that night at the wharf?" It was so long ago, and yet Dorian remained curious.

"Five against one, that's what happened." He was so happy to be out of that coffin, yet still fixated on zombies. Lemuel took in a deep breath and enjoyed the breeze on his face. "How many people are in the world, brother?"

Dorian thought it a peculiar question. "There must be somewhere around seven billion, perhaps a little less. Why do you ask?"

Lemuel looked deep in thought. "There can't be that many people. Graveyards must be enormous. How can there be so many people? Think of all the zombies that we can rise!"

Dorian shook his head. Not again with the zombies. "That didn't go over so well last time."

"Did you kill the bastards that put me in that coffin?"

"I told you I killed one, but the others got away."

Lemuel walked around enjoying his first taste of freedom, and it was as delicious as a three-course meal for a starving man. One might not think that open space could be so appreciated and essential to one's mental health, but humans needed to roam free. Lemuel was short, although a bit taller than his brother, young-looking and somewhat handsome, but with gray hair just like his brother. He only had half of his right ear from a long ago battle with another wizard. He examined the shack that Dorian was standing next to and disapproved. "You live in that piece of junk? It is so small and wretched."

"No, Lemuel, I tracked you to this point, buried under that little house. But it wasn't there all those years ago. They would have dug you up if it had had a basement. I was about to give up on you."

Lemuel looked puzzled. "Why is my speech pattern so different? I don't sound the same?"

Dorian shrugged. "You sound different. Perhaps goings-on from the outside world have trickled into your coffin. I can't even guess."

"I feel strength and weak at the same time. How is such a thing possible? I need to feed on you, brother."

Dorian tilted his neck, and his brother was on him, ravenously sucking blood. The wizard had to push him away lest he became weak himself. But it wasn't easy, as a brief struggle ensued. "That's enough."

"Help me find my spider. I hope he hasn't been injured. He has an awful lot of legs that could be broken."

Dorian said many unkind words in his head but kept them to himself. Lemuel didn't sound sane, which could be a huge problem. He guessed it was inevitable for him to have mental problems after being confined for so long, but would he snap out of it or would he forever be minimized? Would he ever return to the person who was buried so long ago? Or was he forever altered into something crazy? Too soon to tell. "You don't need a stupid spider. You are free, brother!"

Lemuel became quite emotional. "Stupid spider? He was my only friend. Don't you understand he could be hurt?" Lemuel said, becoming quite emotional. "My friend, not some stupid spider."

Dorian had many thoughts running through his head. *He sounds crazy. Maybe I should have left him down there? What the hell will I do with him if he cannot function? What if he's a danger to me? Look at those crazy eyes. I don't know if I should humor him or not?* "When you were released from the coffin, you might have stepped on it."

Lemuel searched what remained of the coffin, but there was no sign of the arachnid. Even though he spoke to his brother, Dorian thought he remained distant, as if he was more inside his head than not. "Do you think the spider has gone home to his family? That's what I would have done."

Dorian released a half snort, half-laugh. "Yes, I imagine it went home to his wife and kids. Maybe you'll see him later, maybe not."

"So, where do you live, brother?"

"I'm heading for New York City. I've rented an apartment there, in a very tall building. Just wait till you see it. Life had changed much in three hundred years."

He continued to scan the ground for the spider. "What is that smell?"

"The world is afloat with elements of magic. It's in the air. I don't think humans can smell it. They've never mentioned it."

"What does it do?"

"No one seems to know."

"The Blood Book is now functioning properly?" The book was bound to Dorian, but they could both use it, which was unusual.

"Yes, it appears to be back to normal."

"Good, because without it, I couldn't assemble a horde of the undead." Lemuel had a mind like Caesar's. He so wanted to conquer and rule. His dream of controlling an army of zombies was alive and well.

"Lemuel, everyone knows about vampires now."

"The humans know?"

Dorian nodded. "Yes, they know. The problem is the vampires are going crazy and killing people everywhere."

"Do they know about wizards?"

"Some yes, some don't."

"Where does Dracula stand?"

"From what I have heard, he is protecting the humans."

Lemuel was silent for a time as he thought about it. "Alright then, let's go to your place, and we'll return later for the spider."

Dorian's eyebrows tightened.

After a brief tour of New York City, where Dorian had tried to explain the new world to his brother's old way of thinking, he decided it was enough for one day. Dorian's mind was tired, and he needed a nap. While ascending in the elevator to the apartment, he noticed Lemuel had pressed himself flat against the wall and looked scared. He began to attempt to scratch his way out.

"Lemuel, what's wrong?"

"The building is falling!"

"That's just the sensation of the elevator rising."

"Are you sure?"

"Yes."

Three other men in the elevator had the same idea that Lemuel was some mental patient, as the building had a psychiatric office. Inside the apartment, Lemuel stood and stared at the ceiling.

"You look puzzled, brother."

"It's so clean in here. How do they get these things up so high? Why doesn't it fall over?"

"I suppose you might call it another form of magic called technology. They use gigantic machines and such."

Lemuel opened the freezer door of the refrigerator door and stared in. "It's winter in this box; impressive magic."

In the kitchen, they ate, drank some blood, and reminisced about days gone by and other wizards they had killed. Lemuel complained he missed his spider as he went through the Blood Book. He persuaded Dorian to compile a list of magical ingredients he possessed and was impressed, specifically because including dust of the Orchid Mantis. And seven drops of wizard's blood that had the power to create compliant zombies. The book had taken him back to the same zombie spell he had been tinkering with just before being confined.

"Dorian, I need you to take me to the graveyard. I can't wait. Let's go."

"As soon as the sun sets, we'll go."

Dorian and Lemuel arrived at the Calvary Cemetery in Queens at three in the morning. They had lost track of time, but it was to be expected after having not seen one another for so long. The size of the graveyard overwhelmed Lemuel. He wouldn't have believed it if he hadn't seen it with his own eyes. He tried to section them off in his mind and count them, but of course, it was impossible. Lemuel's blue eyes widened. He was as happy as a bat finding a swarm of mosquitoes.

"How many graves?"

"There's over three million."

"Dorian, just think of all the zombies we can make! Three million! We can take over the world. With the ingredients you have, how many can you raise right now? And once we raise them, we can send them for more ingredients."

Dorian looked at his brother and had never seen him so happy. "Probably less than a hundred, but where will we keep them?"

"We can hide most of them in the forest. Bring one or two back to the apartment with us for now." Lemuel continued to be fascinated by the number of graves. "Give me the pouch and let me cast it."

"You know they're going to want to eat human brains."

"Why should we care if they want to eat brains? It's their nature. Dogs want to eat cats, it's the way of things."

Dorian had always followed his brother's desires even when he disagreed, and this was one of those times. They would probably have more wizards after them. He could envision both in a box in the ground, or worse. Their bones resting in the sun were also a sight that came to mind.

CHAPTER TWENTY-SEVEN

I T WAS A MUGGY AFTERNOON. Dracula and Piers Anthony were in front of the Chrysler Building entrance waiting for a wizard friend to appear. There was a lull in the conversation that they were both enjoying. Precisely one hundred vampires with strange-looking eyes began attacking people. Dracula pulled his sword and started killing as Piers did the same. Wei and Bao appeared as if they had been following the group. Vincent also showed up several seconds later. So many vampires fighting in proximity were quite something to see. A blur of swords collided, and the sounds echoed off the buildings. Heads popped off, and skeletons collapsed.

Vincent took out his gun and shot six vampires, and before each could recover from the pain, he removed their heads. Then he rushed and killed those on his right flank. Dracula had almost killed twenty of them when he discovered a sword sticking through his abdomen. He removed it and tossed it aside as if it had never happened. The Master was a killing machine, an artist at the top of his game; his style and gracefulness were impeccable. He could see multiple moves ahead.

Piers took two heads at once, surprised that it had happened as he only meant to take one; one had jumped at him while he swung his sword. He kicked one skeleton across the street. Wei and Bao fought back-to-back as they were also killing machines. Wei jumped up with a reverse-turning kick and launched a vampire's head down the sidewalk. The skull rolled amongst people as they ran screaming, going all the way to E 43rd Street. Five humans lay dead on the sidewalk, with one of them having been eviscerated.

Battle screams continued to punch through the air.

One of the evil ones was preparing to kill a 5-year-old boy, and his mother cloaked him in her arms when Bao threw himself in front of them. He meant to block the blow with his sword, but he tripped, and the assailant's blade with through his neck. He fell with his head hanging by an inch of skin. Such blows took longer to heal, and Piers killed the attacker before he could wield the fatal crash. Wei protected Bao until he fully healed, a process that took almost a minute, which was a long time considering the constant threat of sharp swords coming from every direction.

Margat joined the battle with her long black hair flowing behind her; she was as skilful with a sword as she was beautiful. "Hey Wei, not much of a date, but I'll take it." She wielded a scimitar she had bought from a Saudi Arabian prince. She was splitting them in two and then taking their heads.

Wei had to keep his head in more ways than one; he knew he mustn't lose concentration, or he could get himself killed, or Bao or one of the others. Despite emotions often hindering in battle, he experienced fear for her. He had heard that she was extraordinary with a sword, but had never seen her fight until now. Her leaping and slicing with such style impressed him. Margat made tiny *SHA* sounds with most of her swings, which her master had done while teaching her in the 12th century.

Dracula picked up one vampire wearing a jacket that said *I'm going to hell, and I'm taking you with me;* he picked him up, broke him in two, and decapitated him. The sounds of swords clashing were loud, the battle ferocious. Wei prone kicked a female biter with such force that he got his foot lodged in her ribs for a moment. As far as he could tell, the brunette had been the only female felon. Bao's flying sidekick sent a man in a trench coat with a rapier sword against the wall so hard it crushed half of him. And then he finished with his katana.

Vincent was a big fellow, chopping vampires like a lumberjack cutting wood. He held one down with his foot as he killed two others. It had been over a century since he fought alongside Dracula; he loved seeing him in action. The Master was assertive. He was at home in battle. It was an honor to fight with him. He would have loved to have just stood there and watched him in action. He ripped one guy's arm off and took his head with a 360 spin, splattering the building with blood.

The number of assailants had dropped to less than twenty-five when a photographer showed up and started shooting with his high-speed camera. A shot of Bao saving his life might have been going to end up on the front page of The New York Times. As a vampire grabbed him and showed him his fangs, the photographer ran screaming.

Piers Anthony found himself backed up hard against a building, defending against multiple attackers. One blade cut open his right bicep, exposing the muscle, and it hurt more than he thought possible. When Dracula notices, he deflects the blade that would have taken the author's head, pushing them away from Piers before killing them.

"That was excruciating!" Piers shouted.

Margat knocked the sword out of the hand of one of the skinny bald guys; they looked to be identical twin brothers. She bit him, took a drink, and spat out the tainted blood. She disposed of him and his brother, making it look easy. Margat was like a tornado in how she twisted and turned, every move faultless; even her pauses appeared to be perfection. Dracula stopped for a moment to watch her fight.

After everything had ended, the sight of skeletons scattered everywhere was a haunting reminder of the chaos. Several ambulances showed up to treat the wounded as police officers shook their heads at the sight of such a horrible scene.

CHAPTER TWENTY-EIGHT

ALASTAIR ENTERED THE GARDEN AREA in his burgundy-color robe. Annie thought he walked like royalty. He had an air of importance to him, not that he acted as such. It was simply the way he appeared. Not everyone had style, but Alastair did. The scents of all the beautiful flowers surrounded him, and he thought she looked like an angel sitting amongst them because he saw her as young and beautiful. The sight of Annie always made him smile; he was so quiet that Annie hadn't noticed him until he was almost upon her.

Annie smiled back at him, as it was nice to be loved. "Watch out for the spider."

The vampire looked down and then bolted at the sight of the tarantula, blurring right through the door and sending it flying off its hinges into the kitchen. She laughed at Alastair. She didn't think a vampire would be afraid of a spider, although she had been and continued to be a little wary of it. But now she considered it wasn't an actual spider but a spell. In the kitchen, she found Alastair looking ill-at-ease as he stood in the corner now with an awkward smile.

"I fear spiders."

"Well, I can see that. I am, too, but not quite like that. Look what you did to your door. Anyway, it's not a genuine spider; it's a spell."

"What do you mean?"

"It's a spell. It came out of that yellow box."

He considered what she was saying, but he wasn't convinced. "Maybe so, but I don't want it around me. You should kill it. It might be poisonous."

Annie went over and gave him a hug and a kiss. "I killed it, but it came back to life. I think it understands what I'm saying. It's a magical thing."

"Really? It understands you?"

"Why don't you come back into the garden, and I'll tell it to sit somewhere else so you can sit beside me."

Alastair wanted to show his bravery because of Annie, but it wouldn't be easy. He didn't want her to think of him as a wimp, even if it was only with spiders. "I'm not getting close to it."

Annie walked up to the spider on the bench and stared down at it. It looked up at her and waved. Alastair took his time returning to the garden, but he wasn't about to get close to it. "Hairy, Alastair is afraid of you, so you must get off the bench and go over there. And don't jump. It'll scare him."

The spider crawled down the right leg of the ornamental bench and went about five feet away. Annie indicated with her hand for it to keep going, and it did, reaching just more than a dozen feet. It stopped and watched as Alastair sat down. He gave it the stink eye. "So, you killed it, and it came back to life?"

"Yes, I flattened it like a pancake, yet there it is. Guts came out of it and other stuff."

"If it comes close to me, I'm going to pick up this bench and smash it."

"Don't you dare. I like this bench. So why don't you tell me the story?"

"What story?"

"The story of why you are so frightened of spiders. Many people fear spiders, but not quite like that. Although when I was younger, I was entertaining this young man. I turned my head at something my cat had been doing, and when I turned back, he was gone. Later, I found out that he had seen a spider and bolted."

There was an awful story, but he didn't enjoy reliving it. Annie waited patiently for him to spill it. "Okay, Annie, I was frightened of spiders when I was a human boy. I awoke one morning to find a daddy-long-legs spider crawling across my face. That was the beginning of my arachnophobia. I used to hang around with a group of friends, and unfortunately, they discovered my fear; they tied my hands and legs and put spiders all over me. It was a horrific experience."

"Not superb friends."

"There definitely were not my friends." The spider remained in his spot, but Alastair couldn't take his eyes off him. "You actually believe that the spider can understand you?"

"Watch this. Spider, do a little circle for Alastair, but don't come any closer."

Alastair watched in awe as the spider skillfully spun its intricate web in a small circle. It was clear the arachnid possessed intelligence. Perhaps Albert Einstein had returned as a spider, but he knew it was magic. "You better tell it to stay out here. I'll freak out if I see it in the house."

"I'm sure you heard that, Hairy. You cannot come into the house."

Hairy felt sad at the news that he wasn't allowed in the house, but he made himself as low to the ground as possible and found it pleasant in the garden. He turned around, crawled under the variegated flax lily, and began digging out a hole. He would make his own if he couldn't go into the house.

Alastair got close to Annie. "Look what he's doing. He's digging a hole in my garden."

"He's making himself a home."

"Annie, take him two hundred miles away and drop him somewhere."

She put her arms around him and gave him a big kiss. "Give him a chance. If he bothers you, we'll get rid of him."

"He's already bothering me. Look how ugly he is."

"He probably thinks we're ugly, too."

"Maybe so, but he won't wake up with me crawling around in his bed. You want me to make a hole through the wall?" His cell phone rang, and he pulled it out of the right pocket of his robe. "Hello? Yes, alright then. See you there."

"Who was that?"

"That, my dear, was Dracula. The ceremony is tomorrow night at midnight."

"I'm going to be a red sheriff. You'll have to help me pick out a sword."

"Annie, I really wish you wouldn't. Besides, he gives a sword to every new sheriff."

She looked into his eyes and saw he was concerned. "Alastair, life is for living, not watching others live."

Hairy exited his hole and waved at Alastair. "Is that thing doing what I think he's doing?"

"He's waving at you. Wave back to him."

The vampire gave the arachnid the middle finger.

"Alastair!"

"He started it."

CHAPTER TWENTY-NINE

ARYM WALKED THROUGH CENTRAL PARK, wearing a beautiful black and brown embroidered front top with black pants. She was with her blonde friend Lucy. The day was pleasant enough because the heat no longer bothered her as a vampire, but being a biter had turned her life upside down. She may have been walking in the clouds with no reference points.

She felt better about herself and was learning the way of the fang, and because she had a talent for fighting, it helped to change her outlook. Playing with those weapons at Alexander's had boosted her self-esteem, which she needed, especially after discovering she was skilled with most weapons. The guy that had turned her had been a weapons master and had transferred a significant amount of talent.

"Isn't that a beautiful fountain? If only those pigeons would leave it alone. Too bad the angel wouldn't come to life and swat them away." Lucy laughed at the thought of it.

"My father used to call them rats with wings."

"I don't know why, but I love the sound of flowing water. Heavy rain at night will put me right to sleep. We used to go camping, and I loved the sound of rain on the tent."

Arym stared at the Bethesda Angel Fountain with the pigeon on the angel's head. It flew off as another took its place. She had flown, in bat form, for the first time yesterday. It had been an enjoyable though perplexing flight; she had felt awkward and ill-at-ease, but with some happy moments too. She looked at birds differently now that she had flown. Arym felt using the particular muscles it took to take flight as such a mammal was taxing. It had been no fun when she ran into the power line and spiraled down. Yet she would take to the sky again tonight; she wanted to experience flight under her own power again. Bat radar was a lot easier said than used.

"Do you think that Justin Bieber is a vampire?"

Arym pictured him with fangs. "I don't think so because he's growing and changing his looks, but he is so cute. The older he gets, the more handsome he is. Imagine having him as a boyfriend. Driving around in fancy cars and having enough money to live anywhere. You could fly to France for dinner."

That life sounded great to Lucy, with perhaps a few drawbacks. "Everyone would be dying to meet him. They would try to steal him too, which wouldn't be so cool. We'd be invisible; they run over us to get to him. Oh, that's right; you will look like that forever. Even when you are a hundred, you'll still look the same. When I'm a hundred, I'll be in a box in the ground and won't look so marvelous. My father says that all the time, *marvelous.*"

"That's if somebody hasn't chopped my head off by then."

"Don't say that."

Arym had the strangest look on her face. She dropped her cell phone but caught it before it touched the ground. It was the first time she felt it like a vampire, and it startled her. Her new life was like visiting a foreign land. Everything was so strange.

Lucy noticed that something was amiss. "What is it? What's wrong?"

"My heart just beat for the first time as a vampire."

Lucy's mouth dropped open, and she had a puzzled look on her face. "What are you talking about? Vampires don't have heartbeats; everyone knows that."

"We have heartbeats, but it's like once a month."

"I didn't know that."

"It scared the hell out of me." Arym had kept a single friend after the transformation, although she could tell that Lucy now looked at her with fresh eyes. At first, Arym's new state had impressed her, but now there was a level of trepidation. She had asked Arym to pick up a car, and when she did it, it put her strength into perspective. Lucy's parents didn't know about Arym, and no one could make her spill that information. She wondered if her vampire friend wouldn't suck all of her blood out of her neck one day, but she knew she was the same old Arym. What would it be like to be a bloodsucker just like her? Lucy had had a dream about it and had awakened screaming.

They spent more than an hour talking about boys and the best makeup. It was one of those lazy summer days enjoyed by many, at least until the vampire blurred into the area. Everyone noticed the vampire dressed as if he had come out of Medieval Europe; he wore a knee-length purple tunic and an ancient-looking sword on his side. If it weren't for the vampire thing, people would have laughed, but they quickly left the area.

Lucy was scared. There were so many attacks lately that she considered most vampires a threat. "Arym, let's get out of here before something bad happens. His eyes look weird."

Arym was getting bad vibes. "Let's go to a different area of the park."

But it was too late to avoid seeing something nasty happen. He grabbed two women in their fifties; one he fed on as the other let go with a scream that would elicit pity from just about anyone. He had her by the wrist. No matter how hard she struggled, she couldn't break free. Although Arym didn't want to get involved, she couldn't help it. She knew it was foolish and dangerous to tackle another vampire at her stage of development.

"Lucy, run!"

"Arym, no! Come on!"

She blurred and bit into his arm, forcing him to let the woman go. She knocked it out of his hand when he went for his sword and grabbed it. He kicked the girl and sent her flying as Lucy covered her eyes and screamed. Rowan let the other woman collapse as he focused on Arym, but she now had the sword. He rushed to kick her in the stomach, and she moved and cut his foot off. As he screamed, the foot regenerated, but she cut the other one too. She wasn't sure why, but it felt right to fight, as delightful as painting to an artist. As tempting as it was to let the fight continue, Arym knew it would be risky. Although she had talent, he was likely a lot more experienced; she took his head and watched as he turned to dust, realizing that was how she would end up one day. She was in shock as she gazed down at the skeleton.

Lucy ran and hugged her. Arym thought she didn't feel as bad as she should have. She had taken a life, her very first, but she knew he deserved it. She was surprised that she received applause for killing another vampire.

"Arym, why did you do that? You could have been killed!"

"I don't know why I did it. I couldn't stand to watch him torture those women."

"Do you know how stupid that was?"

"I know."

"How the hell can you fight like that?"

"That I don't know."

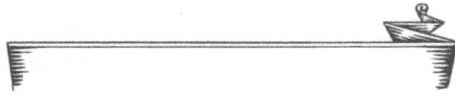

CHAPTER THIRTY

J ENNY STEPPED OUT OF HER PROTECTIVE BUBBLE
and fired a shadow arrow at Achak. It took her aback that it
penetrated the magical energy that had her trapped. Then she
unleashed two more. He dodged two, but she caught him with the
third in the chest. He pulled the arrow out of himself, including the
shadow that had taken over his body, and threw it on the ground. A
fair amount of blood exited, and the wizard looked hurt. Achak
paced several times before stopping and staring at Jenny with daggers
in his eyes. He wasn't at all happy as he blurred off out of sight. He
had been counting on the girl's age and inexperience to get the upper
hand, but now he wasn't so sure.

Jenny cut the head off the giant white snake and then kicked it
aside. She stooped and shook the lifeless lion, with her tears falling
onto Sarah as she listened for a heartbeat but found none. Jenny
cried as she petted her lion, kissing and stroking her face. She didn't
know what destiny would bring, but it didn't look promising. Jenny
stood up and had never felt so alone. The forest seemed so big and
empty now. Her heart fragmented and might never be whole again.
She looked down at Sarah and couldn't bring herself to leave her
out here for the forest to claim her, the bugs to consume her.
Emotionally, she was a wreck.

"Oh, Sarah."

She took several steps away from the lion, stopping and rubbing
her tears away. Jenny exhaled because she didn't know what to do
next; she felt like giving up and heading back, but she couldn't.
Something deep down inside wouldn't let her give up. She couldn't
think straight even though it would be necessary before proceeding;
getting herself together wouldn't be easy. Jenny couldn't face that
son-of-a-bitch in her current state. The girl needed time to mourn
but didn't have it. She wished she could wake up and find it was all a
dream. That book had damn well been worth it.

What was that? She heard something, but she couldn't make it out, whatever it was. It was a mind thing, not from outside, but from within. She listened intently and focused on it. Jenny's step closer to Sarah increased the volume. A lion's roar she heard in her mind. It was even louder when she got down on her knees near the cat. Jenny read Sarah's mind. She wasn't dead, but somehow paralyzed from the snake poison. Jenny stroked the lion and told her to fight it. She shook Sarah once more, but it didn't help.

"Sarah? Sarah, can you hear me?" The cat might not be dead yet, but she could go anytime. Again, she listened for a heartbeat, but that heart wasn't pumping. How could she be alive without a heartbeat? Of course, she had magic flowing through her veins. A silent heart was the worst kind of silence. She wished she could talk to her father. Too bad she couldn't mind Dracula from this far away. A skilled wizard for a friend would be invaluable, and one by her side even more so. But she was isolated. All the decisions were hers and hers alone. The wizard stood and stared off as she thought, rubbing the back of her neck.

Jenny's hands itched, and when she examined her right palm, she could observe a small patch of green luminescence swirling there; it was the same on the other side. That automatic thing was kicking in; was her desire for a solution answered? She began rubbing her hands on Sarah. It was strangely painful, almost like the sharp glass was coming out of her and into the cat. The lion lit up a beautiful gold color. The animal was radiant, and then the gold essence became solid. All the cat's features were completely gone, the gold now so bright that it cast rays of light on the trees as if she was a golden lamp. Jenny shaded her eyes as if blocking the sun.

"Oh, it's so fun not understanding one's powers. I should have come with a manual."

She knocked on the cat; Sarah now appeared to be solid. Placing her ear to where her heart should be, discovered that the lion's heart was beating again. That made her smile. The golden covering, whatever it was, had a slippery and shiny surface. It was cold. Felt more like plastic than metal. At first, she hit lightly at the shield, then a little harder, and finally, she punched it and hurt her hand. "For Pete's sake, how is being trapped there any better than being dead? Don't worry, Sarah; I'll get you out of there."

Jenny stood up to think things over. What if she was healing in there? Maybe Jenny just had to be patient. Sarah might break her way out when it was time, but she was getting restless after an hour. She had walloped it but not her hardest, but if she hit it again, she knew it would hurt. Jenny jumped ten feet in the air and smashed it hard with her fist and broke it. She broke her fist but didn't do any damage to the gold covering. She jumped around from the pain, wondering what to do next. Then she noticed that the cat's tail was white, or at least the covering over her tail. Had it been white before? The wizard sat down and watched the tail; the whiteness was expanding, so something was happening. In less than a minute, it dripped a white liquid from the end of her tail, like a candle burning off its wax only faster. It was likely that the poison was being expelled from her system.

Jenny watched the lion until her tail finally stopped dripping, and the cat's covering cracked. She was worried that Achak would soon return, hoping that Sarah would revive before that happened. When Sarah stood up, it broke and fell off her; she shook and then sneezed, making Jenny laugh. She laughed with tears of joy as her lion returned to life. Apparently, none worse for having had the experience.

They moved forward again in search of the nasty wizard. She formed an energy ball as big as a snowball and threw it far into the air in what she thought would be his general direction, and wherever it landed, there was quite an explosion from it. She hoped it scared the hell out of him.

CHAPTER THIRTY-ONE

MOON DIAMOND VISITED THE AMERICAN MUSEUM OF NATURAL HISTORY, spending most of his time on the fourth floor of the Hall of Saurischian Dinosaurs. They attempted to remove the Siamese cat from the premises. They left Zacharia alone when he hissed and showed his fangs, but only after they called a red sheriff. Informed that he was one of the good vampires. He circled the Tyrannosaurus Rex several times, examining it, thinking what a monster it would be as a vampire. The size of those fangs would have been something to see and feeding on other dinosaurs. He imagined a scene playing out with one vampire Tyrannosaurus Rex attacking another.

A five-year-old girl ran away from it crying, fearing that it was about to come to life.

Outside, the crowds were thick, and the sidewalks crowded like ants on a hill. But being a vampire, he had no problem zigzagging through the horde, anticipating their every move. He thought that someone had opened the zoo gates. What a bunch of animals. A drizzle begun, but it was sunny again within minutes, with big puffy clouds filling the sky. Moon Diamond hated the rain, but Zacharia had always enjoyed it for as long as he could remember. It was depressing when he thought about how he looked and what he used to be. Zacharia tried hard not to think about it, but it didn't work, and if anything, it made it worse. At least in his dreams, he could still wield a sword.

Moon Diamond was enjoying New York City. He pointed out to Zacharia every mouse and rat in the area, wanting him to leap at a starling flying by, but he refused. They were strolling by the front of the Bank of America Tower on 6th Avenue and W 42nd Street when he spotted a walking skeleton. The thing was on fire, and people were running in the opposite direction from it. It had an impressive-looking sword that was also on fire.

Zacharia had heard about its nefarious deeds and followed it. He wasn't sure what to do with such a creature and wished that Dracula was with him to take it on. It was a hell of a lot scarier in person than on television. He assumed the Master would have no problem destroying it, but he couldn't be sure. Magic had more sides to it than a hecatommyriagon. He didn't have to follow it far when it abruptly backtracked. He sat and watched it with his tail flicking side to side; apparently, Bones was pacing back and forth.

Moon Diamond showed Zacharia a mouse on fire, making him laugh. He missed having the Siamese on his knee for company; he knew it wasn't the cat's fault for his predicament.

The skeleton stopped, turned around, and looked down at the feline. The aura the animal was producing was perplexing, vibrant, and powerful. It scratched its head as it considered what to do next. As long as it didn't interfere with him, he wouldn't bother with it. Still, Bones was getting a strange vibe from it, some animosity. He could not only hear but feel it growling. It was an odd critter.

The pull of the wizard that Bones had been following was waning; he had escaped to the top floor of the building, just far enough away to confuse it. When a male jogger came around the corner, staring to his left at people fleeing, he almost ran into the creature. It swung its sword at him, but Moon Diamond pushed the fellow out of the way and engage the fiery thing. The cat had to dodge swing after vicious swing; sparks and embers flew as the sword hit the sidewalk. They paused the battle momentarily to give each other a menacing stare, with Moon Diamond growling with such ferocity that it would have frightened most humans.

Even though it had limited life experience, it knew that it was no ordinary cat but a thing of enchantment. The skeleton wasn't amused by the animal, which was taking up time. "You cannot defeat me! Run and save yourself." It spat fire at the cat, missing it, with hot embers bouncing on the sidewalk out of the flames. It came down hard at Moon Diamond with its blade, missing him and striking the sidewalk with the sword, sending more embers across the sidewalk and street. The sword broke off at the guard, surprising the skeleton and the cat.

The Siamese jumped in his face and scratched at the eye sockets. Although he made contact, there was no visible result, except the cat ended up on fire, with all its fur burning off. It jumped around from the pain, and its fur grew back as the fire extinguished. The skeleton attempted to form another blade, but it didn't work. Then he realized he was being summoned by Achak, disrupting its concentration.

He could hear his voice commanding him to return to help him. Although the thing wasn't supposed to be able to refuse orders from its maker, it could now, in fact, do so. Not only was Achak summoning it, but he was interfering with it as well. The wizard was temporarily lowering the skeleton's ability to fight. The walking bones were angry at the interference, but decided it might be best to return to the wizard. It took off so fast that Zacharia couldn't keep up with it.

CHAPTER THIRTY-TWO

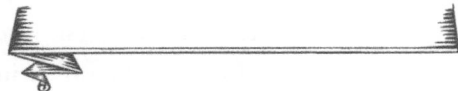

THE TIME WAS FOUR IN THE MORNING in the Calvary Cemetery in Queens. The wind was light but had brought in the scent of strong coffee from a pedestrian more than half a mile away. Such was New York. People were always present, regardless of the time of day or night. The moon shone through light clouds as an owl observed from a tree, intrigued by the movement.

Lemuel had encircled ninety-seven gravestones with an inch line of sulfur, ground-up vampire bat, and the most essential ingredient, wizard's blood. The powdered bat was over three centuries old, and it had come from a vampire that they had killed while in bat form; they had stalked her for hours before finally being able to take her down. The world was so different now.

Dorian had misgivings about what they were about to accomplish, but his brother was insistent. Once he got something into his head, you couldn't blow it out with dynamite. Zombies were unpredictable creatures; most would follow orders well enough, but bringing forth someone evil in life made them more likely to go out on their own, seeking human brains in death. Occasionally, one would have a mind of its own, more or less, and would wander off on its own adventure. But Dorian wanted increased power, even though they were two of the most potent wizards, especially when they were together; it was like a wealthy person never being satisfied. No matter how much money they had, they always wanted more. Lemuel was also greedy for power and was desperate to command an army of zombies. Just being around zombies would slowly increase their levels of magic. It was a well-known fact, yet most had no interest in raising them.

"Lemuel, it's not too late to stop this. Plenty of other ways exist for us to become more potent. No one will respect us if we do this."

"I do not seek respect. Well, I guess I seek respect, but the kind that comes from being a ruler. I want to be the Julius Caesar of wizards."

"They stabbed Julius Caesar to death," Dorian smiled. Dorian smiled. "What will your spider think of you if you do this?" He would say just about anything to dissuade him from it.

Lemuel paused as he thought about it. The spider was missed, but it was necessary to get on with his life. He gave it serious consideration for an entire minute. "He won't mind. Now give me your hand."

Even though he knew the effort was useless, Dorian would give it one last attempt. "Once we bring them forth, we'll have to kill them to get rid of them. Some will eventually wander off, you know that."

Lemuel gave his brother a stern look. "What the hell are you, an old woman? Have you lost your bite, brother? This is only the beginning. We're going to have a zombie army a million strong."

As soon as their hands touched, the cemetery lit up with an eerie green glow inside the circle; the light went straight up for hundreds of feet. The sight puzzled a pilot in the plane overhead. Black ghouls floated around in the pale green substance; evil souls that had long ago been tossed into the nether regions of darkness. Lemuel hit the circle with a lightning bolt that burst into flames of the reddest fire, with no yellow, orange, or violet variations of red. The smell was of rotting flesh burning, releasing its acrid smoke. Then a sphere of black fire larger than a basketball originated from a bony hand that opened and released it. Hovering inside the green glow were emanations from the globe that fell to the ground, having the viscosity of drops of blood, slowly spreading, making their way around, and saturating the area.

More than a dozen pale yellow eyes appeared from out of nowhere, hovered and watched, with no mouths to give warning, but still seemed to communicate with one another. They turned this way and that, their movements silent and mysterious, as if performing an unknown ritual in their otherworldly dimension. They moved around, and one approached too close for comfort. Dorian swatted it away like an annoying fly, telling it to back off. Then the eyes floated down into the ground one by one, a few glancing at the wizards before doing so. Other sets of eyes appeared and did the same. Lemuel found it to be a fascinating process; his eyes were wide with wonder.

"Dorian, isn't that amazing?"

As it struggled to escape, the first zombie made a dull sound from inside the earth, indicating that it was escaping its coffin. Scraping, scratching, and then pushing nails apart. With immense strength, it escaped, overcoming both wood and compacted soil. It loosened enough earth to stand, and then a hand with only patches of skin pushed through the ground.

It took a minute for it to dig its way out, appearing greenish because of the eerie light, and had half a face covered in maggots. Only remnants of eyes remained, dirt-covered with a worm or two. It shuffled but then blurred about ten feet. That was how the creatures got around. After they shuffled ten feet, they could blur ten feet.

Another zombie burst through the earth, this one being nothing but bones. It would eventually grow some skin for it to absorb more energy and brain tissue. However, that would take time, and it would have to consume several brains to accomplish it. They thrived on the neurons within the mass. Zombies in skeletal form regularly consumed part of the spinal cord to facilitate skin growth.

More skeletons emerged. One swatted at the black sphere of fire as it stood up. One recently buried skeleton appeared, which made Dorian wonder why there would be such variation in an old part of the cemetery. Had the recently interred been a recent murder victim buried in the graveyard? It was peculiar, but he could think of no other answer. Then two other recent victims dug their way out, making him even more puzzled. They had dirt partially covering them, but it was evident that they had probably been in there less than a month.

"Aren't they magnificent, brother? Just look at them! As different as snowflakes."

Dorian shook his head in disgust. Why on earth had he agreed to be part of this? His mind seemed to be fuzzy as of late, and he was getting a headache. "Magnificent? They are disgusting. If you look like that, you should be in the earth. Don't touch me!"

"Yes, Master," said one skeleton before he tripped and fell over.

"This is an abomination."

"This is the justification of our power as wizards. We must do what can be done. Wizards and their creations are part of the big picture."

"I smell brains," said the zombie with the most skin. And for zombies, brains smelled as good as a meat lover's pizza to a meat lover. It took in a deep breath, sniffing Dorian's brain.

"You're going to smell my foot in your ass if you touch me!"

"Yes, Master."

Other zombies agreed brains smelled wonderful, with one measuring the size of Dorian's with his hands from a distance. Dorian gave it the finger which puzzled it, making it stare down at its own bony hand, slowly lowering other fingers until it had also displayed its middle finger. The zombie was proud that it had accomplished it. It tried to smile at Dorian.

"I smell brains, too," said another zombie. "Smell two brains and ... some coffee?"

"Oh, shut up."

More and more of them extricated themselves from the earth and hung around, waiting to be told what to do. The first woman appeared. She looked down into her hand at a piece of skin that had come off of her face. The maggots puzzled her, and she ate a couple of them and made retching sounds as she tried to vomit.

Dorian shook his head in disgust. "Oh, that's nice."

The sun wasn't too far below the horizon, inching its way up as the last of the walking dead emerged. Lemuel and Dorian started to lead them toward the nearest section of the forest and into Central Park. Tomorrow night, they would bring them deeper into the woods, where they would be less likely to be discovered.

CHAPTER THIRTY-THREE

MICHAEL RETURNED TO CONSCIOUSNESS and looked up at Lauren, who was now standing over him, rubbing her stomach. She felt and looked a lot better. The severe pain that she had had was gone. Her precious smile lifted his spirits as he stood, but he continued to be concerned. He made it to Lauren and now believed that there was something wrong with the baby, and not being human, there would be no easy fix. If the baby were a wizard, it would complicate matters even more. Lauren looked as though she had fully recovered.

"Are you okay?"

"I'm okay for now. Whatever it seemed to have passed."

Michael sat on the sofa. "Do you think you're going to lose the baby?" He asked the question even though he knew there could be no logical answer.

"No, I don't think so. She's kicking up a storm in there."

"If you have such severe pain, something must be wrong. That can't be normal."

Lauren knew he was concerned, but she nonetheless gave him a little attitude. "Michael, I was fine until I was set on fire."

"Don't get mad at me. I didn't do it."

The doorbell rang, and they both looked a little puzzled and annoyed. They were dealing with the importance of their first and perhaps an only child, and they didn't need an interruption. Lauren sprinted to the door and peeked through the peephole, her excitement surging. She opened the door to reveal Dracula and Piers Anthony. "Master, come in, come in!"

They were both dressed in black suits, and they reminded Michael of FBI agents. Dracula hugged Lauren in greeting. Lauren also recognized Piers instantly as she had enjoyed his books. Michael stood up, not knowing what to do or say. His mouth hung open. He was in the flesh, larger than life, and in their living room. Now would not be the proper time to faint.

Dracula examined the loft and found it quite exquisite. The place had a woman's touch. "Lauren, I hear you're pregnant. Congratulations."

"I am Master, but something is wrong. I fought that crazy skeleton, and it set me on fire, felt sick and then got severe stomach pains. Is there anything you can do?"

Annoyance crossed Michael's face. "You just said you were fine."

"I heard about that thing. Nobody seems to know what the hell it is. Oh, where are my manners? This is Piers Anthony, the author."

"Nice to meet you."

Dracula put his right hand on Lauren's stomach and poked inside her with his mind. He went into her mind and then into the baby. "Oh, my. It's a girl, and she's okay. She will be a wizard-like my daughter Jenny, powerful too. She won't be a match for Jenny, but perhaps close. And like Jenny, some of her magical energy is automatic. She's already protecting you and herself. She's not doing it deliberately, but nonetheless."

Michael fainted and hit the floor like a cement block but ignored by all, although Piers raised his eyebrows. Michael got up and sat on the sofa, not saying a word for about a minute. "Lauren, what did he say?"

"He said it's a girl, and she will be fine."

"No, I mean the wizard part."

Dracula looked down at Michael and smiled. "The baby is fine, but Lauren's a dead duck."

"What!"

"I just wanted to see you faint again. She's okay. The baby will be here before you know it. She's already a fair size in there."

She turned her attention to the Master. "How is that possible? I'm not that far along."

"It's an accelerated pregnancy that sometimes happens with vampires, especially when they are a wizard. You'll have her in about three months, I would say. Perhaps even sooner. Jenny was born at four months."

Everyone looked for a reaction from Michael.

Lauren smiled. "Where are my manners? Would you like some blood?"

"That won't be necessary. I've just eaten a couple of girl scouts."

Michael's eyes widened. He assumed Dracula spoke in jest, but he couldn't be sure. He stood up and extended his hand. "I'm Michael." He also shook Piers Anthony's hand as well.

"Are you ready for the ceremony, Michael?"

"I don't know. I'm nervous."

"Glad to hear how confident you are about becoming a red sheriff. You two are getting married, and you'd like me to perform the wedding ceremony?"

It baffled Lauren. "How did you know?"

"I read Michael's mind. Of course, I'd be happy to do it."

Michael was beaming because of how utterly unique. Being married to Dracula and having a baby. It was all moving a little fast. Suddenly, he was feeling sick. "I don't feel so good."

Dracula could feel the heat radiating from Michael from the sofa. He walked over to him and extended his right hand. "Take my hand and let me in deep." The Master went deep into Michael and circulated inside him until he found the source of the infection, and even though it was something he had never seen before, he concentrated and killed it. "How do you feel now?"

"Better. Thank you."

"He had what I had?"

"I suspect as much."

"Master, what brings you here?" Lauren glanced at Michael, and he was trying hard not to think of anything that would embarrass him in front of Dracula. Enough that Lauren could go into his mind whenever she wanted. It wouldn't be much of a secret if he were a serial killer.

"What brings me here? Just visiting. As for what brings me to New York City? Let's just say that the shit is getting ready to hit the fan."

"I know I can feel it." Lauren yawned because the baby initiated it.

Michael looked away from Dracula's imposing eyes.

"I assume you wanted a bouncing baby boy?"

"Yes, indeed."

"Well, it's going to be a biting baby girl."

"And we'll be changing diapers in about three months?"

They could hear a commotion down on street level, and when they looked out the window, another hundred vampires were out there killing people. They all blurred out the door preparing for battle. Piers was regretting having Dracula as a friend.

Nine people had already been killed as they began killing vampires. The sounds of blades clashing were loud and music to Dracula's ears; although he felt sorry for the humans, it made him feel alive; he should have been doing this all along. Dracula kicked a muscular black guy so hard that he put his foot through his stomach before taking his head. Piers got the second kill when he stabbed one through the heart. After decapitating him, he hit the skull with his sword's pommel, sending it flying. Although the author despised the killing, he knew it was for the greater good. Dracula had given him a few fighting lessons, especially with judging his opponent's next move, which worked well. He also knew that becoming even a little overconfident would have his head rolling on the ground.

Michael fought with his eye on Lauren, a challenging and dangerous way to fight; Lauren had saved his neck not once but thrice. She scolded him, telling him to smarten up. She side-kicked a fellow wearing a Mexican flag on his chest into the air, and before the

Mexican hit the ground, she took his head. Michael sliced through a young-looking vampire's neck that appeared to be only eighteen. It wasn't deep enough and it healed, so he had to do it again.

Then it happened: a sword went right through Michael's stomach and stuck there, and the pain made him vulnerable to attack. Lauren was too busy and couldn't get to him. Piers removed the sword and took a deep slice to his chest for his effort from a short bearded fellow in a Navy Blue suit. Dracula grabbed him and pulled his head off, the blood spurting straight up like a fountain. That sword had been excruciating, and the Master had warned Piers that after enduring such a painful thing, he would have to fight through the emotional part of it. New vampires could become frightened of receiving more pain and often would make mistakes because of it. It had cost many biters their lives. Piers realized what Dracula had been talking about and now felt scared of being cut again, which led to him being sliced two more times.

After eliminating all the vampires, Lauren rushed to Michael. "Michael, don't you ever do that again. Don't try to protect me when I'm twice the fighter you are! I don't want you getting killed. Protect yourself and don't worry about me. I had to save you three times!"

Dracula smiled and nudged Piers, who was covered in blood. "Get the popcorn."

Piers returned the smile and shook his head.

"Michael, are you going to take that from her? Go on, tear her a new one." The Master tried to keep the fight going, but it didn't work. Michael shrugged because he knew she was right.

Piers nodded. "That shrug accomplished with lots of conviction."

"Absolutely. Let's see that shrug again, Michael."

Lauren shook her head.

CHAPTER THIRTY-FOUR

THE TWO WERE A BIT OF AN ODD COUPLE but appreciated one another's company. It was the same for both, because having someone to engage in conversation was pleasant. Bernie and Keith were sitting on the Sting bench overlooking an empty baseball field in Central Park; the bench had a small silver plaque that read *FOR STING AND TRUDIE STYLER, IN HONOR OF THEIR DEDICATION TO THE ENVIRONMENT AND SUPPORT OF MILLIONTREESNYC.* It was just a little before noon, and already the humans were uncomfortably hot. A small plane flew over, making a racket, carrying a banner with a wedding proposal. Even with all the turmoil, life went on as best it could. At the end of the bench, there was an old man in a pinstriped suit. While Keith stared at the fellow with the bird, Bernie drank a bottle of Italian wine.

"Bernie, that guy has birds coming out of his head."

Bernie turned to stare at the guy with the bird on his hat. "How does he do that?"

Keith shrugged. "Must be one of those magicians."

"Oh yeah. I, I. I knew one of those magic guys a long time ago, but, but, but he just disappeared!"

They both laughed like two maniacs released from the insane asylum. Eli had to laugh as well, not at the joke, but because of the funny way they were laughing. Both were indeed acting crazy, and it

180

was one of the most amusing things Eli had ever seen or heard. It was hard to stay depressed around those two clowns. His wife had been gone for six months, and he didn't think he'd ever get used to being without her.

The old fellow with the short white beard had endured them because he liked the bench and believed Sting might show up one day and sit beside him. He was reading the New York Times and had tried to ignore their banter, but that was impossible. Initially, he gave them dirty looks, but because he didn't move, they considered him an acquaintance, even though he hadn't responded to their remarks or questions. The newspaper was all vampire this and vampire that.

Bernie took another drink and stared at the bird as the bird looked at him. "That bird is giving me the stink eye. Bird, why don't you fly away?"

Keith leaned over and waited for an answer. "Maybe he's glued to that hat. What did he say?"

"He won't talk to me. He's a stuck-up bird."

"Oh, I guess he thinks he's better than us."

Bernie thought about that. "I, I, I know he's better than me. He is living on that guy's fancy hat."

Keith swatted at flies that weren't there.

All three noticed a young black couple strolling by hand-in-hand because they were so affectionate with big wet kisses when suddenly a little vampire grabbed the woman and bit her, and no matter how hard her boyfriend pounded on him, he wouldn't let go. He screamed and cried for help. Blood ran down her neck onto her beautiful yellow dress.

Bernie got up and accidentally hit the woman in the head with his wine bottle as he tried to catch the vampire. "Keith, help me! Get him!"

Keith grabbed the little vampire by the neck and choked him. He shook him fiercely. The sound of bones snapping filled the room.

The little fellow put up a serious struggle, and the vampire had difficulty holding onto him. He repeatedly punched Keith in the head, crushing part of his skull. He gouged chunks of skin out of his face with his long nails, and blood flying everywhere, making the scene gruesome.

Keith choked him so hard that his head finally came off, and Bernie caught it. Now being nothing but a skull, he threw it in disgust, also throwing his bottle by mistake. And by the time he reached it, he had lost a lot of the precious liquid. The beautiful young woman had lost a bit of blood but was otherwise okay. But they were never to return to Central Park; they would be on the next plane back to Australia.

Bernie the Bum cried at all the blood. He picked up his bottle and sank the rest of it. "Keith, are you okay? Please don't die!"

Keith was touched. "I'm okay. I'm all healed, see? Us vampires are tough."

"That guy's not so tough; he's got no head."

They returned to the bench and noticed that their friend and his bird had departed. Then they watched the burning skeleton walk by. They looked at one another and couldn't believe what they were seeing. It headed through the baseball field and continued. Keith gave Bernie an unopened bottle of wine; he opened it and took a drink before he commented. "Boy, I, I, I knew it was going to be hot today, but that guy's on fire."

Keith remained puzzled. "Yeah, and he's got no skin."

"Suntan lotion is not gonna help him." Bernie continued to shake his head.

"New York is getting crazy, but I love it."

Silence filled the air as they savored each other's company. Keith swatted at an imaginary bee.

"You know, you can drink shaving lotion, but you can't drink suntan lotion. Too damn thick."

"I didn't know that."

"Oh, yeah." Bernie continued with his slurred speech. "Stick with me, and I'll teach you lots of stuff. Like, don't throw up in front of a police ocifer. They don't like it. I, I, I don't know why, but they don't. When I throw up, I'm not doing it on purpose."

Keith nodded and then drifted off to sleep, but that didn't stop Bernie from continuing the conversation.

CHAPTER THIRTY-FIVE

ACHAK WAS BACK BESIDE HIS WIGWAM, searching urgently in his Blood Book for a spell that would destroy Dracula's daughter. But it was odd because the book didn't want to cooperate with his requests. He could only guess that Jenny was already influencing the tome. Not sure how, but it wasn't good.

He cursed her, but unfortunately for him, it wasn't magical, only emotional. Achak didn't know how such a thing was possible because the book was supposed to be attached to him. Did it show she was perhaps a lot stronger than him? Should he consider fleeing? Whatever it meant, it was making him nervous to the point he couldn't think straight. She and that stupid lion would soon be upon him, and he had to be ready. A spell was ruminating in his mind that would take care of her.

"Come on, you son-of-a-bitch!" Achak scanned the forest. Even so, there was no sign of it. He had summoned his skeleton multiple times. It should have complied with his every command. What was the point of creating such a thing if it wouldn't listen? It had taken a hell of a lot of magic to create the damn thing. He assumed it could take care of the girl and make him King of the Mountain. He knew it could hear him, so why didn't it comply?

The large raven flew down from the tree onto the antique table to observe, squawking several times, walking around with its wings spread. It stared up at the wizard and then examined the table's contents. Cocking its head, it stared down at the book and received a small electrical shock for its noisiness. The bird flapped its wings several times but didn't take flight. It pecked at the book and got another zap.

He spoke to the raven. "I wasn't talking about you; I'm talking about that stupid skeleton of mine." The bird nodded several times to show it understood.

Achak went into his wigwam, cursed several times, finally emerging with three pouches of transformation dust and a two-inch long red-eared slider turtle. If he could change her into a turtle, the most straightforward animal to transform a wizard into; he could let her wander into the forest and forget about her. He'd like to kill her. However, changing her would be just as good. The spell would endure for seventy-five years, and he would add a concealment enchantment so that even Dracula wouldn't be able to track her. It gave him the briefest smile to think of the Master's daughter as a turtle. She would retain her mind, but that would drive her crazy. Her magic wouldn't work. He would kill or transform the lion so it wouldn't carry her back home.

The wizard re-entered the wigwam, came out with another turtle, and placed it on the table beside the other one. The wizard wasn't sure what would happen to the lion because the spell was designed for a wizard. Using magic for something other than the designed enchantment was unpredictable. Sometimes it worked, and sometimes it didn't.

"Damn it. She's on her way. Where the hell are you?"

Achak took the three ingredients out of the pouches, placed them in a small beaker, and then put a cork in it. He shook it, studying it through the glass, exhibiting a nasty smile. Each pouch contained the essence of rare caterpillars. Then, from a small bottle, he placed a single drop of his own blood into it. Most wizards used their own blood to form enchantments. He shook the beaker with super speed. The friction turning the glass red hot, fusing the ingredients into a new magical element.

He poured the magically infused yellow Saffron dust onto both turtles, and they began to struggle and shrink until they became small ornaments the size of a thumbnail. He pocketed both and would use the second one to tag Jenny if he missed with the first, as she would be more trouble than the lion.

Achak stood entranced in his thoughts, and not even noticing as the raven landed on his left shoulder. His eyes had that faraway look. He had come a long way in his journey as a wizard, boosting his power significantly. The wizard had felt confident until now. The skeleton had taken something out of him, and while his magical abilities were recuperating, he was unsure of the battle to come. Long ago, he fought another powerful wizard, and both ended up near death. It took him months to return to his old self. Luck had been on his side that time; he wasn't so sure this time. Achak had been righteous back then. Now he was only a shadow of what he had been, maddened by the evil enchantments he had created. Evil spirits played with him daily.

Jenny walked past the maple trees, determined to get this fight over with. It was time to finish it. She knew good didn't always triumph over evil, but she was determined it would this time. Jenny hoped that being Dracula's daughter would pay off like hitting the biggest jackpot. She would attempt some bravado to scare him off. Doubtful it would work, but what the heck? The lion waited impatiently for her command to attack, butt wiggling like a house cat ready to pounce. Being brave wasn't the lack of fear in battle but fighting despite it.

His heart jumped when he saw the girl wizard; he had never seen such a complex aura. It swirled around her, changing colors, whites, pinks, and purples. He had hoped that she wasn't all that special.

"Don't take another step closer! Do you foolishly approach your own demise?"

Jenny slowed but continued to approach with the lion at her side. "I'll take that book, and then you can go! You know who I am?" She knew she was supposed to kill or capture him, but the book was more important to her, especially now. She would be more than happy to see him run. It would be a significant relief.

The raven attacked her, but she hit it with an energy ball. It exploded into nothingness, with only two feathers floating down to the ground. She would have preferred not to kill it, but she couldn't afford the distraction. Besides, she did not know what the bird could accomplish. Dracula had told her of one wizard that had trained crows to attack; they would explode near a wizard, weakening them to such a degree that they wouldn't be able to defend themselves.

Achak hit her with a bolt of black lightning, driving her back against a tree, and it hurt; she hit him with crystal daggers that vanished as soon as they struck him, making his left arm so numb that he could barely move it. He had broken something in Jenny's back, and she could feel it fusing back together. She didn't know how long her reflex magic would hold out against him, but so far, she could fight back. Both wizards put up defensive shields. The energy of powerful wizards in such proximity was unpredictable. Old tales spoke of two wizards who self-destructed upon approaching each other.

"I have something especially nasty for you. You are going to be one sorry little girl." It was crucial to wait for the right moment before striking Jenny with the turtle. A miss would leave him with a single one, and they wouldn't be easy to retrieve on the forest floor in an ongoing battle. His timing had to be accurate.

The lion was ferocious in her attack, but unfortunately, she didn't make it to Achak; just before she was to chomp down on his leg, he hit her with one turtle, and it looked as though the cat vanished. He hadn't wanted to use the spell on the lion first, but those canine teeth scared him, and she would have taken advantage of the lion's attack.

Sarah was now in a confused state as a turtle. Everything appeared too tall; Jenny was a giant, and the entire world was askew. The cat couldn't understand what was going on. She felt so peculiar.

Jenny somersaulted into the air, striking him with marble-sized balls of energy. However, he deflected them with his hands as if he were some martial arts master, taking down two trees with the deflections. He threw waves of ice at her. She dodged most of them, but one hit her left hand, turning it to solid ice. Achak laughed at her but stopped when she didn't transform into a solid block of ice, which was supposed to happen. Jenny broke the ice against a tree, but her hand remained chilled to the bone.

"Girl, run before it's too late. There are worst things than death."

"Yeah, like your face."

Achak blurred into his wigwam, returning almost instantly with his Katana swords. And they went at one another. He was, of course, looking for the perfect moment to hit her with the turtle. His blade went through her hair as she ducked, slicing off a tree branch. Jenny stared down at a piece of her hair on the ground, which pissed her off. Swords met, forming a T; she kicked him in the stomach and drove him off his feet. In anger, he threw one of his swords at her, and she deflected it, sticking it into the ground behind her.

Jenny hit him with a sphere of light that sent him flying ten feet in the air, up and against a tree; the turtle fell out of his pocket. He hit the ground hard, and when he reached for his spell, he realized he had lost it. His pocket was empty, and for a moment, so was his mind. When he crawled around on his hands and knees, Jenny knew he was frantically searching for something. She wasn't about to wait to find out as she attacked him with her sword. But before she could take his head, he located the turtle and hit her with it.

Jenny looked up at Achak, who now resembled a mighty giant.

CHAPTER THIRTY-SIX

ANNIE AND ALASTAIR WERE HAVING LUNCH at Le Bernadin restaurant while her rose was prominently displayed on the table. The butterfly hadn't yet appeared, and she didn't want to miss it. She was in a good mood enjoying the day. Although she didn't have to eat anymore, she continued to crave food, as satisfying as a hug from a best friend. The ambiance was beautiful, and the food was excellent. With each passing day, she appreciated Alastair more than the previous. They both had oysters and crab salad to begin, and then for entrees they also both ate the crispy sea bass. Then they had red snapper and warm lobster "Carpaccio," ruby red grapefruit and heart of palm. It was surprising how much vampires could eat. Annie also had a Vietnamese Cinnamon ice cream for dessert, and yet she was still hungry.

Alastair even had a rare filet mignon beef fillet Au Poivre with vegetables.

Annie took a drink of her red wine: Chateau Clos Cannon, Merlot Blend, Saint-Emilion, Bordeauz 2007. She had to laugh. "Alastair, we've eaten so much the waiter is going to think that we're pigs."

He picked up her rose and smelled it before placing it back on the table. "I know him, and he's aware of how much I can eat. He's a vampire as well. He eats more than I do."

She scented her rose as well, glancing around for a butterfly but didn't see any. "I didn't know that. We'll have to come here more often. I'd like to try the charred octopus, but I've already eaten so much. I've never had an octopus."

Alastair spotted a butterfly out the window, but the day-flying insect was an ordinary one. "Get the octopus it if you want it. The texture is like eating chewy chicken. It has a delicate sweetness like crab, but of course, it depends on how it's prepared."

"No, I think I'll wait until next time. You look so handsome in that suit."

"And you look exquisite in that cocktail dress."

Both wore black attire, and Alastair even sported a black tie. It was good to get out at least once a week, to mingle and enjoy the atmosphere of people, and she liked to see Alastair all dressed up. She was listening, off and on, to a couple at a nearby table talking about their taxes; she thought that they could have found a better topic of conversation. It appeared the woman was getting angrier as time went on.

"This black dress is for a young woman with stuff to show off." Although Annie felt young and vibrant, she knew she looked like a 90-year-old to everyone except Alastair.

"Well, you know how I see you, Annie."

"Yes, but you're the only one."

"The only one that counts."

Annie reached into her purse and pulled out the little yellow box. She placed it gently on the table and smiled, raising her eyebrows. "I don't suppose you'd stick your hand into it and see if there's anything else in there. I'm so curious that I could bust."

He returned the smile. "The last thing you pulled out of there was that crazy spider, and you want me to stick my hand in there to see what I get? What if it's something that's uglier than that spider?"

"You won't be my hero? My knight in shiny armor? My champion, who's more than willing to stick his hand in there."

"What happens if I pull out a Bao constrictor, and he eats everyone in here?"

Annie smiled and touched his hand. "Bao constrictors don't eat people, they constrict, and then they swallow them whole, so I suppose they do eat them."

He stared into her expecting blue eyes. With a flirtatious flutter of her lashes, she elicited a hearty laugh. He knew he was going to acquiesce but delayed the inevitable. "Annie, what do you suppose is in there? What treasure would have you risk my hand?"

"Because of the magical properties of the box, I suppose it could be just about anything. Your hand would just grow back."

Alastair pulled the box closer to him and looked down at it. He was a little apprehensive about the whole thing. What if he pulled out another tarantula? If he screamed like a little girl, he could never show his face back there. "I'll do it, but here's the thing. If I touch something down there that feels like a spider, I will not pull it out. People here wouldn't be impressed if I went through that window."

"Everyone would have such an interesting story to tell for weeks."

"Maybe I should ask the waiter to do it?"

"Oh, give it here."

"No, I'll do it. If I don't survive, I leave all my worldly possessions to the spider."

"You hate that spider."

"You didn't put it back in there, did you?"

"Of course not. Hairy is home in the garden."

He saw her excitement. It was almost as if she was a little girl again. Alastair liked to see her like that. If there was something else in there, it would be a spell crafted by Freder. "I'll do it, but why don't we wait until we get home?"

"If you don't do it right now, I'm going to do it myself."

Alastair removed the lid and cautiously put his right hand down into the box. She tried to read his expression, but it was one that she hadn't seen before. "Annie, oh no, something's got me! It's eating my hand!"

She jumped up, frightened for him, but then he laughed. She knew it was balderdash. "That is not the least bit funny. Scare me for nothing."

He pulled scissors out of the box, and they were familiar.

"Oh, those are mine. I dropped them in there to see if I could hear it hit bottom. Try again."

He reached into the box once again and had a puzzled look on his face as he felt something hard. Out came an antique broach. Six diamonds surrounding an impressive red beryl emerald in the middle, not small diamonds either. Alastair placed the broach in the center of the table. Annie's eyes lit up at the sight of it. Annie stared at it before picking it up, examining it and thought it was one of the prettiest things she had ever seen. It clearly looked expensive.

"It might have magic attached to it." He was trying to warn Annie there could be something nasty fastened to it. In any case, they were dealing with the unknown.

"What do you think it does?"

"That's just it; with Freder frozen, there might be no way to tell what it does. But it is beautiful."

"What a beautiful gem in the center. It looks like it cost a fortune."

"It does."

"Do you think there's any danger of me putting it on?"

Alastair shrugged. "I couldn't even hazard a guess. Enchanted things make me nervous even though I have used plenty of magic."

Annie thought about having such a cute broach and not being able to wear it made little sense to her. She imagined it was probably a pleasant magic attached to it. She held it to her breast and thought it was so pretty. Annie fastened it around her neck.

Alastair stood, horrified. Annie had vanished into nothingness.

CHAPTER THIRTY-SEVEN

ORIAN AND LEMUEL WERE CAMPING OUT in Central Park. It was a temporary location to hide their zombies until they could make better arrangements and formulate their plans. Over four million trees were in the park, and Lemuel hoped to produce almost as many zombies one day. Although the zombies remained standing, the wizards were prone on the ground, pushed up against trees, relaxing. Two zombies had one another by the throat, but otherwise didn't appear to be fighting.

"What a sad-looking bunch," said Dorian. He was staring up at the undead creatures, regretting that he had raised them. He was staring at a nightmare come to life. Nevertheless, he would play it out. His brother appeared to have control over him when it came to decisions. He never considered it before, but perhaps there was some sort of magical influence occurring. The power of magic could be a difficult thing to detect. When two wizards stayed in proximity for an extended period, their magic could entwine in peculiar ways and not always good. They enhanced one another, but there could be other things going on as well.

"I think they're most impressive. Just wait until we get a million of them." Lemuel could picture it, an army of zombies standing before him, willing to do anything that he commanded. He considered putting them in uniforms, but then dismissed it. They were more terrifying as they were. One fellow had his intestines hanging out. "You, do some push-ups."

"Yes, Master." It had accomplished eleven push-ups before he told it to stop. When it stood up, it had leaves hanging from its intestines.

The ninety-seven zombies were all gathered in one area, most looking puzzled why they were there, and all of them hungry for human brains. They examined one another with the curiosity of a child. Some pushed against others so that they could have their own comfortable space. One tall zombie that had been a basketball player in life stooped to pick up a piece of his face that had fallen off. He held the chunk of skin and stared at it, smelling it, and then showed it to others that cocked their heads with inquisitiveness at the rotting flesh. They were quiet now, but all it would take is for one of them to mention the word *brain* to get them all going. They were thinking zombie thoughts, and all but one imagining eating a juicy brain. And that one was visualizing killing a human before removing his brain.

A zombie in a tattered suit covered in soil was examining the brain of another zombie; a large section of his skull was missing, and so he could peek down into his skull. There wasn't much left of it, but he stuck his finger in it and tasted it. But being a decayed brain, it had a poor taste, a little like licking snot. "Bad brain?"

"That zombie brain."

"Zombie brain taste bad."

The wizards listened to the chatter because of the entertainment value. Occasionally, what the zombies were saying made them laugh. Lemuel was thoroughly enjoying it. He considered them his children. Lemuel was proud that he had raised them and was enjoying being out of that damn box, although he continued to miss his spider. It saddened him to think that he might never see it again. His children were helping him forget and get on with his life. The wind felt like kisses on his skin. Even the trees were wonderful after having lost his freedom for such a lengthy period. The sky itself had a beauty to it he would never have thought possible, as appealing as the most beautiful painting accomplished by the most talented artist.

"I smell brains."

"Hungry for brains."

"Brains good for zombies."

"Master got brain?"

"Can't eat that brain."

"Brains smell good."

"Now that is a one-track mind." Dorian had been annoyed by the zombie banter and aggravated by the situation. Perhaps he should have left his brother in that coffin. Unfortunately, he knew in his heart that he could never do that. He was as responsible for the situation as Lemuel. "You zombies be quiet."

Three zombies had gathered at the edge of the group, having a conversation about Dorian's and Lemuel's brains. They had formed camaraderie in death because one had existed in life. They had perished in an automobile accident, and all had been inebriated. Lemuel and Dorian's brains were giving off a delicate but delicious scent. The zombie pointed his bony hand at Lemuel. "He got bigger brain."

"Other brain smells better. I like eat that one."

"I like eat big one."

They were in an invisible bubble of sorts, a magical creation that wasn't portable, unfortunately. The enchantment allowed them to remain invisible to humans unless they entered the immediate area. They would need to set up a camp of sorts, but in a different location, away from people. They were in a temporary situation with few magical ingredients at their disposal. A canvas backpack beside Dorian contained the Blood Book.

Lemuel had been asking plenty of questions about the new world that he found himself in, being fascinated by the automobile. With no horses pulling them, he couldn't believe that they weren't a product of magic. It was surprising how women were so scantily dressed, and some were practically naked in their bathing suits. But the biggest bombshell was the number of people that now existed. He assumed people had spent most of their time in bed. How was it even possible to have so many people? After placing Lemuel in the box in 1710, of course significant changes had occurred in the world since then, but the greed and maliciousness remained comparable. Humans had been incredibly busy during the last three centuries.

All the zombies turned to the west, with the sounds of their necks cracking in unison, synchronized as well as any swimmer. They all sniffed the air at the delicious scent. It looked like a feast was being delivered to them. A better sight could not exist for a zombie. Those brains smelled and tasted as scrumptious as bacon to a starving dog if they could get their hands on them. There was a group of men and women, all different shapes and sizes.

They whispered in unison. "Brains."

"Un oh. Do you see what's coming, brother? Those people will die if they get too close." Dorian could imagine all those poor people being torn to pieces.

"We don't want any of them to wander off, and they have to eat. That's what they do. What the hell did you think they were going to eat?" Lemuel was happy at the sight of so many people heading for his zombies. It was going to be incredibly satisfying to watch. He couldn't wait for the action to begin.

It looked to be a little over a dozen people, nature lovers between the ages of twenty and fifty. They were examining trees and had stopped to ogle a blue jay that was screeching at them. They were admiring the bird as it was telling them to get lost. Although they were now only about a hundred feet away and heading toward the zombies, the monsters remained invisible for now. But if they were unfortunate enough to enter the bubble, it would not be the pleasant morning that they had planned. The end of their lives would come in a most horrific manner.

"Here they come, brother. Watch."

All the zombies were shaking with excitement. Some salivated, others emitted small whimpers. They were like rabid dogs in anticipation of juicy bones. One could have pitied them had they not been about to accomplish such evil. As soon as the first one broke the barrier, the zombies were upon them, scratching their flesh from their bones and causing them to let out awful screams of horror.

Most died rapidly from blood loss, and one had his head literally pulled off. The old-looking zombie with patches of white hair remaining on his head was eating the poor fellow's face, trying hard to get at the brain in the severed head. He finally broke the skull open against a tree, savoring it as if it was the best tasting food on the planet.

Insufficient brains resulted in occasional conflicts, although it was rare for them to fight each other, leaving the exact reason unknown. One reason could be that ninety percent of their concentration was on brains. Lemuel commanded them to share the brains, and they did, but never sharing more than a single bite. The nourishment began growing chunks of flesh, making them more robust looking, though no less scary.

There was one zombie that appeared to be smarter than the others; he used a distraction to get more bites than most of the others. "Look over there!" They always fell for it as he chowed down.

Lemuel laughed. "They sure love their brains. They look like you eating pizza."

CHAPTER THIRTY-EIGHT

MICHAEL AND LAUREN SNUGGLED UP IN BED, he couldn't help but notice that her stomach was extending unusually fast, she looked to be at least six or even seven months, perhaps even further along than that. The rate at which her pregnancy was progressing was a little freaky. They were naked and just enjoying the conversation of what the baby would be like. He placed his head on her stomach, and the baby kicked him harder than he thought possible as if to say *Don't crowd me, Daddy.*

He looked at Lauren. "A baby shouldn't be able to kick that hard."

"One day she's going to be a red sheriff, just like her mother. She's practicing her kicks."

"Breaking hearts and chopping heads? Our little girl is going to keep us busy."

"That's right Michael, a miniature me. Just imagine her terrible twos. I've been looking at some girl's names. What do you think of Shilin?"

He looked into her eyes; his eyebrows tightened. "Shilin? Is there something that I should know? Are we having a Chinese baby?"

Lauren laughed. "I just like the sound of it. How about Adisa?"

"Or how about a regular name like Lauren?"

"We're not calling her Lauren. *Lauren, get your head out of that garbage!* See what I mean? Which Lauren has her head in the garbage? What about Mulan? I believe it's also Chinese."

"Let's call her Bruce Lee."

Lauren had a bewitching laugh. "I think one has been taken. Naming a baby is hard. We're giving her something that's going to stick to her for the rest of her life. Let's give her something pretty." She picked up a piece of paper from the night table where she had written some possibilities. "Tanesha? Alexa?"

"Alexa's not bad. Or let's call her something that means swords of death! Or something that means: *My father will kick your ass if you even look at me!* Maybe we should just wait until we see her?"

Lauren rubbed her stomach, and he could see that she was in a bit of pain. "I'm getting false labor again."

"If I could take the pain away from you, I would."

"Here, take this!" She punched him in the shoulder, and it hurt like hell.

"Ow, what was that for?"

"You said you wanted to feel my pain." Again, she hit him in the same spot.

"Stop that. That's not what I said. You are progressing way too fast. Am I going to wake up tomorrow morning with you holding the baby?"

"Anything is possible. I'm craving strawberries and pickles. My mouth's watering at the thought. You should go get some."

"And how will you reward me if I do?"

"I'll reward you with so many kisses that you won't be able to count them."

"Could count pretty high. I should probably get dressed first." They shared a passionate kiss.

"If you must."

Lauren watched as Michael got dressed, admiring his naked behind. After Michael had left, Lauren had a contraction that was unlike all the others. It was so painful that she thought that maybe the baby was coming. The contractions were now almost back-to-back, wave after wave. She tried to grab her cell to call Michael, but it fell, and she couldn't get up to get it.

When Michael returned from the Food Emporium, he couldn't believe what he was seeing. Lauren was on the floor and now looked to be nine months pregnant, and she was in labor. Dracula had guessed that she might deliver at four months but was he wrong. The baby's head was crowning.

"Michael, I'm in labor! Get some towels."

Michael hit the floor like a watermelon, his head split open and then almost instantly healed. The baby girl was coming, and nothing could stop her from getting out of there.

CHAPTER THIRTY-NINE

NINETY-YEAR-OLD ANNIE WAS A SPECK IN A SEA OF SAND, finding herself in the middle of a desert with wavy sand dunes and the sun beating down on her. The dune in front of her was huge, and she couldn't see past it. Some unknown desert with no features to orient on, no structures of any kind that she could see. Nothing but sand all the way to the horizon behind her. The air was so hot compared to the air-conditioned restaurant that she had been inside only moments earlier. Being a vampire, she quickly adjusted to the heat but remained confused by her location. She had never been in such a place and impressed by its beautiful exquisiteness.

"Where the heck am I?"

The desert lines had a style all its own. Mother Nature's flowing and creative art. That color of Earth-Yellow sand was perfection. The wind had a mighty brush and was a master with its strokes of perfection; such beauty was both impressive and inspiring. She stooped and scooped up a handful of sand, allowing it to slip through her fingers, confirming its authenticity.

Annie didn't think that she would ever forget the sight upon which she was gazing, so majestic. She noticed that her tracks in the sand were only five feet behind her, which is where she must have appeared. She raised her head up and to the right. The sky seemed to be a darker blue than normal. Some sort of bird flew toward her in the far distance, nothing that she had ever seen before. She followed, realizing it wasn't a bird at all. A large red dragon appeared to be heading right where she stood, the beating of its wings slow and deliberate. It landed within a dozen feet of her, and she was unsure of what to do next.

The dragon stared at Annie as she gazed at it. If it was a dream world, was it possible to get hurt? "Good GOD, look at the size of you! Alastair warned me about the possible magic attached to that piece of jewelry. I can be too stubborn for my own good. What if I'm stuck here?"

The red, scaly dragon cocked its head, curious about whom he had found in the desert. It nodded its head with slight movements. He snorted, and the heat that hit Annie from out of his huge nostrils was hotter than the air itself; they were so big that her head would fit in there. It sniffed her, with the air from its nose being so powerful that she was momentarily stuck to his face before he again snorted, sending her flying head over heels into the sand.

"What the hell do you think you're doing? Keep that nose to yourself. Go find another dragon to play with and leave me alone."

The dragon reached out with its massive claws and delicately took the broach between two mighty claws and stared at it with a single red eye. The broach remained attached to her as it stared, fascinated by it. It had been drawn to her because of it. It flicked its tail, sending sand flying.

Annie slapped the dragon's claw away from her. "Get your paws off me!"

The beast looked saddened by the rejection, spreading its wings and flying off in the same direction from whence it came. Adept at flying for such a huge thing. The wings had disturbed the sand as it had taken flight, getting sand into Annie's silver hair and blue eyes.

Her mind continued to be a bit fuzzy, but she remembered Alastair being in the restaurant with her. How would she get back?

She wouldn't be at all happy if she were stuck here forever. Could her own consciousness be trapping her? She could guess all she wanted, but she did not know what was going on.

What had been a pretty sight was already troublesome. She could still see the dragon getting smaller and smaller in the dark blue sky, wondering if it could breathe fire. But that was something she didn't want to find out in such close proximity. It hovered in mid-flight and turned toward and let go with a blast of orange and red flames, as if it had heard her thoughts. Turning, it eventually disappeared from view.

A horse whinnied from somewhere. She listened intently and there it was again. It took a while to climb to the highpoint of the dune, couldn't seem to blur in the soft desert sand. Her feet went like hell, but they only dug a hole. Finally, on top of the dune, she saw a massive tent surrounded by camels with a single black stallion. Annie descended to the tent, which was the same color as the sand, and as she approached a handsome sheik exited. He was tall with a dark complexion and very attractive.

Tahnun approached Annie and smiled at her. "My queen, we found it, but have to move quickly as the infidels will be upon us. Come, come! It is as you have said. Fantastic!"

Annie looked over her shoulder, believing he was talking to someone else. In this world, she was some sort of queen? She thought he had features of Johnny Depp and Emile Hirsch, a distinguished fellow with mischievous brown eyes. What had he found? He opened the flaps for her to enter, and inside, at least twenty men were pulling what looked like a treasure chest out of a large hole. Why such a thing was in the middle of the desert was beyond her imagining.

They pushed the chest, causing it to swing, and one man grabbed it and pulled it down to the ground. Whatever was in there, it was heavy. He hit it several times with the hilt of his curved sword until it finally burst open. It sparkled with treasure, jewels, gold coins, rubies, pearls. It made almost everyone in the tent gasp, which she found amusing. Annie was in a B-movie.

Suddenly, one infidel appeared dressed in black, and the fighting started, sword against sword. A sword tossed to Annie as the fight spilled outside. Dozens had shown up to steal the treasure. People were killed left and right. One of the bad guys had his beard cut off by Tahnun and his chest sliced open at the same time. He fell into the sand, dead. A towering fellow prepared to attack Annie, and she was not ready, so he waited for her to notice him before he attacked. Annie stuck her sword in him, and he also fell dead. More of the infidels showed up on horses. One second they weren't there and then they were.

A sword cut the antique broach off Annie's chest, and she caught it, suddenly finding herself back in the restaurant, both hands raised over her head as she had been prepared to strike, only now there was no sword just the broach was in her hand.

"Annie, what happened to you?"

"The broach brought me to some sort of fantasy world, with lots of handsome men and even a chest full of treasure. And a dragon. It was huge, could have eaten me with a single bite. Not an ugly man in the bunch. Felt as real as you and me. How long was I gone?"

"Less than a minute, I would say."

"Incredible. It certainly felt a lot longer."

"Whatever you do, don't put that broach back on."

Annie smiled. "I might try it again, but not today. This thing is amazing."

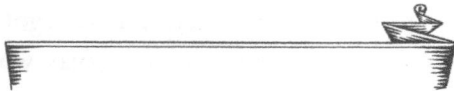

CHAPTER FORTY

I T WASN'T EASY BEING A TURTLE and perhaps even worse was that she knew she was a turtle. If the situation remained unchanged, she would be miserable. Life would be maddening. What the hell was she supposed to do as a turtle? She wanted to scream, but she couldn't even accomplish that. She discovered that her eyesight sight was excellent, but it was so weird being in that body. Looking up at Achak, she scowled as he looked down at the reptile and laughed.

It was satisfying having attained victory over Dracula's daughter.

Jenny pulled her head into her shell, trying to think. She thought hard on launching a spell, but she had nothing. Jenny was now a magical being, devoid of magic. She stuck her head out and looked around. Jenny ate a leaf she found without even realizing what she was doing it, and so delicious. Being low to the ground was unpleasant. A small branch blocked her vision, and it wasn't easy to get over it. When she went around it, her slow and deliberate movements felt like she'd been at it for hours. The girl, already discouraged by her new lot in life, would have preferred to be something like a hare. At least she would have had some speed to her movement. Never in a million years would she have imagined ending up in this mess. The only positive thing she considered was that she was alive. Jenny would like to turn Achak into a hare and herself into a wolf.

"I told you to run." Achak picked up Jenny and stared into her shell as she pulled her head inside and wishing she could give him an uppercut. "I told you that there are worse fates than death. Your magic won't work for you with this enchantment. You are stuck." He placed her on the ground and stared down at her.

The wizard tried her best to hit him with a lightning bolt. Her unconscious magic had been absolutely no help to her, and because she could think of no solution, it was disturbing. Now she really felt for Zacharia. It could take her a decade to walk home. Jenny also realized she did not know which way home was. Adding to it was anyone could simply pick her up and take off with her.

Jenny felt disheartened, just like anyone would in her situation. Seeing from her diminutive point of view, how would she recognize even a familiar area? Help appeared to be improbable. Every tree looked to be a thousand feet tall. A hill would become her Mount Everest. Nightfall would be scary. What if he kept her as his pet? Her mind was haphazard, with no positivity to propel her forward.

Jenny cried.

Then she met the other turtle and realized that Sarah was also a reptile. Jenny rubbed her turtle head against Sarah's, seeking comfort. Having company didn't cheer her up at all. If anything, it made her more depressed. It was indeed a fate worse than death. Jenny saw his big hand approaching, but couldn't escape. Achak picked up both and placed them on the table. He was silent for quite a while as he considered what to do with them. He strummed his fingers on the table, and they found it disconcerting because it was so loud. The victory was sweet for him. "I like turtle soup. Yes, I believe I shall make turtle soup out of the both of you."

Jenny got close enough to his hand and bit him.

"Ow! Still feisty, eh? You won't be belligerent for much longer, little wizard. The trouble you have caused me. I'm going to have to abandon this place before someone comes looking for you." The thought of moving to another location angered him.

Was this how her life would end, being boiled alive? If only her father were here. Being Dracula's daughter was turning out to be more trouble than she was worth. Her mother was going to be frantic when she didn't return home. Losing a child destroyed many couples, with both grieving and being angry in their own ways.

Both turtles watched from the table as Achak made another fire beside the magical one, taking a rope and hanging a pot from a nearby branch. It was as disturbing as watching an executioner tossing up a noose knowing that your neck would soon be in it. Jenny dropped off the table when he went inside the wigwam for water. She ran her fastest, but of course, she was about as fast as molasses. Her top speed wasn't far more quickly than standing still. Achak poured some water into the pot and heard Jenny fall. He picked her up and placed her inside the pot. And then Sarah joined her in the shallow water.

The girl minded the turtle. "Sarah, I am so sorry. Look at the mess I have you in."

They both scratched the sides of the pot to escape a terrible fate. When the water began boiling, Jenny closed her eyes.

CHAPTER FORTY-ONE

KEITH CARRIED THE UNCONSCIOUSNESS BERNIE past the James Hotel. His mood was light, and he was thoroughly enjoying having a friend. He enjoyed having conversations with the beggar, filling his hours with something to do, becoming quite fond of him. Keith ran at the speed of a human, trying to kick a Red Admiral butterfly without waking the vagabond. He followed it down Thompson Street until it flew up and out of his reach, narrowly missing smashing Bernie's head on the side of the building, but Bernie was oblivious to the world. The largest earthquake wouldn't have wakened him.

"I'll get you next time, you little bastard." He watched the butterfly until he couldn't see it, being disappointed that an insect had gotten the best of him. He had briefly considered using Bernie as a flyswatter.

Keith came to a basketball court surrounded by a high fence and watched a basketball game in progress. Lots of energy and perspiration inside that fenced off area. He watched both sides struggle for dominance, but it seemed like they were evenly matched. One fellow had the ball knocked out of his hand, and then fisticuffs erupted. After someone broke up the fight, Keith wandered off. He turned down the Avenue of the Americas and continued to walk. Bernie looked as comfortable as an infant as he was being carried, holding onto an empty wine bottle instead of a baby bottle. He had been someone's cute baby once, but now there was nothing cute about him. The people that walked by could smell his unpleasant odor, and one woman had to cover her face. They turned down Broome Street and stared up at a Chinese therapy establishment that advertised back and foot rubs. Rubbing Bernie's feet might be deadly, succumbing to the stench of athlete's foot and sweat.

Keith was now quite hungry and could both hear and smell the blood pumping through his buddy's veins. He turned away from the Chinese establishment walking, but he was aware of that available neck, ready for the taking. He stared and stared at it. The vampire licked his lips, and then sniffed the neck, snorting like a dog. It was simply too much to resist.

Keith took his sharp fingernail and cut Bernie's neck until a trickle of blood became visible. Bernie stirred but didn't awaken. He licked the vagabond's dirty neck, and the blood tasted delicious. He tasted a little more and then a little more. His fangs jumped out as fast as a switchblade opening, sinking them into his neck. Bernie's color drained when the vampire bit him. The wine bottle fell to the ground but didn't break. It bounced and then rolled.

When Bernie lost all his blood, Keith let go with a massive belch. His hunger satisfied, but at a cost. His best friend no longer had a heartbeat, Keith had gone too far, and Bernie was dead. He felt pounds lighter with no blood in him. Keith felt sorry for the little guy, but only to a degree. He stared at his face, and he looked peaceful. Perhaps he had done him a favor.

Bernie's soul pulled itself out of his body and floated near Keith. His ghost stood beside the vampire and looked rather happy; he could see his family waiting for him in the bright light, and he ran to them with open arms. Bernie was so happy he cried tears of joy. The big vampire was confused. He listened for a heartbeat, but there was only silence. Was he dead or playing possum? His mind slid sideways as he attempted to concentrate.

"Bernie?" He shook the dead man, easy at first, and then violently. Keith forced his eyes open, but they were, of course, lifeless. He continued to walk with the corpse for almost an hour, finally depositing him in a round garbage can with both his head and feet sticking out. He glanced one last time at Bernie the Bum, and then the vampire went off in search of another friend.

CHAPTER FORTY-TWO

IN NO TIME AT ALL, Lemuel and Dorian had raised over ten thousand zombies. They had a good time gathering the ingredients, reminiscing about different parts of their childhood, though not always accurate, and about just being brothers again. It was impossible to tell Lemuel everything that had happened during the last three hundred years, but he did his best. Dorian thought Lemuel continued to be a little off, but in time, he would hopefully return to his usual self.

Sharpton had an extensive network and had heard about the zombies, initially being very curious. But when he researched their capabilities, he became more than curious. He was interested in obtaining such an army. And so the brothers joined the mastermind with the stipulation the three of them would run a large section of the new New York. A place where nightmares would be an everyday adventure.

There would be zombies and vampires side-by-side in the carnage. What a fantastic arrangement. And to give the city an even more dreaded atmosphere, Sharpton already had plans to knock out the power to the entire city. He envisioned the city after dark, and it brought the biggest smile. Vampires and zombies running around in total darkness.

Sharpton walked around the buildings with his hands behind his back, like a four-star general observing his troops. The zombies massed in clusters, so many of them that some were now in the nearby forest as well. Most of his troops didn't know what to make of the zombies. They were told to get along, but of course, there was tension. A zombie approached a vampire, and the vampire slapped him, and then several zombies were on him. They were formidable, forcefully pulling the head off the biter, but to their disappointment, he turned to dust, including his brain. The sight was incredibly disturbing to the zombies and processing it was disturbing and challenging.

The zombies looked simultaneously puzzled and saddened. "Where brain go?"

One zombie, who had his left eyeball hanging out, picked up the skull and smelled it. He detected the slight odor of the remnants of the brain. He shook the skull. "Brain gone?"

"You eat brain?"

"Me no eat brain. Brain gone before me eat it."

"That awful sound."

"Worst news me never heard."

"Where brain go?"

Entertaining to listen to the zombies, better than any TV show. However, it taught the biters that they were nothing to fool with, as dangerous as any vampire. Most had heard tales of zombies but had never seen one. Some had considered them to be a myth. They were an incredible sight, freaks of nature and magic.

Sharpton's plans were getting a lot more interesting.

CHAPTER FORTY-THREE

MICHAEL PLAYED WITH HIS NEW BABY GIRL, and although she was only a day old, she was already the size of an eight-month-old. She stood on her legs on his knees and bounced. The baby, dressed only in her diaper, was the center of attention. In the cute department, she was exceptional, round face and big bright blue eyes, the product of such an attractive couple she couldn't help but be adorable. She laughed out loud at Michael's faces and *ba ba ba boo*. They were both glad to have the birth over and done with. Neither had known what to expect because they were both vampires. The baby had come way too soon, but for the child, it was all systems go, and now came the hard part of raising an exceptional baby.

"Alexa is growing so quickly that she will be potty trained in a week." Michael noticed the baby staring at him with an almost knowing look, as if she had some secret that she would not spill. "Look at the way she looks at me. This kid is smart."

Lauren turned on the vacuum cleaner, and that took the baby's attention, not knowing what was going on with that. The noise confused but didn't scare Alexa, even though it was loud and hard on the ears. She laughed when Michael tickled her belly, grabbing him by the hair and pulling out a chunk.

"Ow!"

Lauren made Michael lift his feet so that she could vacuum under them. "I like Alexa. It means defender of mankind." She shut off the vacuum. "Thank god she wasn't that big when she came out of me. She's growing so fast it's crazy. Did she pull your hair out?"

Michael took the hair from the baby's hand and showed her. "Look at that. That hurt." He put the baby down to stand against the coffee table, continuing to hold her, and he saw her growing almost another inch. His mouth hung open at the sight of it. The baby picked up the coffee table and threw it. The glass part of it went to pieces on the floor, and the baby found it to be so funny. Her machine gun laugh would have made them both laugh if they hadn't been in such shock, but Michael had to smile. Was she already as strong as a vampire? He grabbed the baby so she wouldn't get into the glass.

"Michael, do you see how strong she is? That's not good. Alexa, no, we don't throw things!" Lauren blurred and cleaned up almost all the glass instantly, then continued vacuuming up the small splinters. The baby watched closely at how fast her mother was moving, and it puzzled her cute little face. Her eyes were jumping from side to side as she tracked her.

"What are we going to do? We can't let her play with any other kids. She'll pull their arms off. It is so freaking dangerous to be that strong at that age."

Lauren shook her head. "Yeah, well, at the rate she's progressing, she'll soon be able to understand us."

"Not soon enough. But this cannot be normal?"

Alexa struggled to get out of Michael's arms, and it was all he could do to hold her. Those little feet were going more than a hundred miles an hour. It was like holding a cat that didn't want to be held, and s he accidentally slapped him in the face while struggling, loosening several teeth, and the sound of the impact bounced off the walls. "Don't kill Daddy!"

"Here, give her to me."

"Watch out for her right hook."

Lauren took Alexa into her arms to settle her down. "Alexa, no, be gentle. Like this, see?" She gently stroked her hand.

"No!" said the baby defiantly.

"Oh, my god she can talk! Our baby's a genius. That right there comes from my side of the family. Take that Albert Einstein. I'm gonna teach her to say, Daddy. Alexa, can you say Daddy? Say, Daddy."

"No!"

"Put her down and see what she does."

After Lauren put her down, the baby started walking alongside the sofa, enjoying the freedom that had been granted to her. But it wasn't long before she yawned. All that effort had tired her out. Lauren picked her up and rocked her, and soon she was asleep.

Michael gazed at her in wonder, the most precious thing that he had ever seen. "Look how beautiful she is when she's sleeping. Who would think that she could kick a hole in your head?"

"Not funny Michael. We'll have to hire a vampire for a babysitter."

"Or somebody we don't like."

Lauren put the baby in the bedroom in her crib and returned to Michael. They snuggled and kissed as they got comfortable on the sofa. They stared tenderly into each other's eyes.

Lauren looked pensive. "Michael, there's so much death and violence. How are we going to shelter her from it?"

He looked sad at the thought of it. The world was going to hell and if it continued to slide, it would be a terrible place for all except the bloodthirsty vampires. Soon enough, she could look out the window at the carnage below. It was depressing. If the scales of justice didn't tip soon, they might never recover. People wouldn't have to worry about going to hell they would be in it.

"If she wakes up while we're still sleeping, she could destroy the place."

Michael thought about it. "Yeah, you better hide your swords."

"Don't think she has the dexterity to pick up a sword."

"Are you kidding? If she can throw the coffee table, she can throw a sword."

Raising Alexa was going to be a formidable challenge. That cute face was going to change their lives forever.

After the baby's nap, they found their daughter the size of a 2-year-old standing in the crib.

CHAPTER FORTY-FOUR

MOON DIAMOND WAS SITTING ON A BENCH in the Conservatory Garden with the scent of flowers all around him. A few puffy white clouds added atmosphere to the beautiful summer morning. Zacharia was daydreaming about a long-lost love, and how they often danced and shared one another's hopes and dreams. Constance had been human and had refused to be transformed; he had stayed with her until the end as she had perished of natural causes. Even after four hundred years, he continued to remember her beautiful spirit. Her goodness and zest for life had been something to behold. Everyone had loved her. Her light had outshone most others, indeed a gift to humans, he thought. Zacharia had had many loves, but Constance had been magical to him. It seemed he would miss her forever.

A young man on the opposite end of the bench was wearing shorts and a white shirt; he was holding an eBook reader reading a Dean Koontz novel, occasionally staring at the Siamese with inquisitive eyes. He thought there was something peculiar about the animal the way it looked at him. It was quite unsettling.

Zacharia was having fun batting the cat's eyes at him with the occasional wink. From the corner of his eyes, had he observed Moon Diamond sticking his tongue out at him? The feline got up and sat closer and closer to the fellow until he finally got up and left, giving Moon Diamond one last look before he departed.

Zacharia appreciated the ambiance and the day as he continued to be happy about not being a ghost. What would he be experiencing now if he had entered that inviting light? Would he have again gazed upon Constance's face on the other side? Or would she have been on a level beyond his reach? That thought saddened him. Had he considered her being in that light, he might not be here right now? He imagined that his heaven would have involved battles with fantastic sword fights, but who knows? He would find out one day, and there was no point dwelling on it.

Knowing there was indeed an afterlife brought satisfaction.

Suddenly the funniest feeling came over Zacharia, or rather Moon Diamond, but Zacharia could feel it nonetheless. A feral cat named Molly, who had been confined to her apartment before she ran off three years ago to the day, was in the area. She was enjoying living off the Big Apple's vermin, and there were plenty of rats and mice to go around. There was nothing unusual about Molly being feral, but now she was in heat, which got Moon Diamond's interest. It was the best scent in the world, and might as well have been an inviting index finger summoning him to her. He jumped off the bench and searched for the sexy feline, and Zacharia couldn't stop him. The cat was now in control of his own body. In less than a minute, he had found the beautiful tiger-striped black and gray cat. Molly flicked her tail because she knew what was coming; she had had a litter two years ago.

Zacharia usually had control of the cat. He fought for domination, but it was just out of his reach. The primal urge was not to be denied. He screamed at Moon Diamond to forget about the other cat, but those shouts went unheard. The cat was now fixated on mating, and a brick to the temple wouldn't have dissuaded him, a brick in the testicles, perhaps. He was going to get some, no matter what.

"Moon Diamond no! I said no! Bad cat! I know where there's a big juicy mouse!" Zacharia tried to run away, but the cat's legs wouldn't move. He showed him a delicious mouse, but he didn't care, as there was something more appetizing in front of him. The call of nature was stronger than the mouse, at least for now. That stripped cat was a thing of beauty.

Another cat showed up, a gray British Shorthair. He was a big one and could handle most cats, but of course Moon Diamond wasn't most cats. The gray feline didn't look at all happy that it was going to have to fight for the female, but he couldn't deny nature's call. They arched and prepared for battle with wicked growls, deciding on the proper moment to pounce. The fur started flying, and the Shorthair quickly realized that he was outmatched. It ran off as fast as it could, smashing into the bench as it did so. Fortunately, it scented another female in heat about a mile away.

Molly ran off at the start of the battle, but Moon Diamond soon tracked her down.

Zacharia knew what was coming, but there was nothing he could do about it.

Moon Diamond grabbed Molly by the nape and held on. She protested but was receptive to the mating. Zacharia told Moon Diamond to be gentle because its strength could have easily killed it. When the event began, the look on Zacharia's face would have been priceless if others could have seen it. If Dracula would have walked by, he would have perished of embarrassment. Life inside a cat was not something to be desired, and he sure missed his own body right about now. He might be better off had he never purchased the Siamese.

With the mating finished, he found he had regained control, but the cat talked him into a nap on the bench. Slumber took him to a naked Constance waiting for him, her smile so precious.

"Get that stupid cat!"

They both awoke as a Doberman Pinscher on a long leash attacked them, with a teenage jackass encouraging the dog to kill the cat. But both the dog and its master were soon sorry as Zacharia forced the large dog to submit, jumping on and digging into Alec, tearing chunks out of his skin. That idiot had never screamed so loud or felt such pain. The Siamese climbed up one side of him and down the other, digging into his calves, his thighs, his back, his shoulder, his chest, his stomach. No matter how hard he pulled on the cat, he couldn't get him off. He would never again dare to sick his dog on a cat, and they would both end up with phobias because of it.

Then Zacharia let the teen escape and went back to sleep.

CHAPTER FORTY-FIVE

I T'S A KNOWN FACT THAT TURTLES CAN'T SCREAM, and that was unfortunate for Jenny because she wanted to scream her loudest. She tried, but the endeavor was pointless. The girl closed her eyes and hoped the end would come quick, that the boiling water would deaden all their nerve endings, delivering them to the land beyond the living. The water in the pot was boiling energetically at just over 212 degrees, definitely not a place for anyone to be sitting. A hand would be scalded in no time, and yet Jenny and Sarah were stuck in it with no means of escape. Steam rose and out of the pot and into the forest, smelling like turtle soup.

Achak was in his wigwam checking on the reliability of his transport spell. He knew Dracula would show up eventually searching for his daughter, and he didn't want to be around when that happened. He didn't feel strong enough to take him on yet. If caught there, the Master would delve into his mind, and that wouldn't be healthy. All the ingredients glowed their proper hues, indicating that the spell, created years ago, was fine. The enchantment would transport him up to three thousand miles away; he had decided on an area north of the Polar Bear Provincial Park in Northern Ontario. He had spent almost a year there in 1904, knew the area well, and would be happy there while he solidified his plans. All his belongings would go with him, including his magical fire. The skeleton could track him if ever the damn thing decided. Whenever he pictured his creation, it now enraged him. He wanted to strangle it.

Achak heard scratching from inside the pot, figuring that they were suffering their last twitches of life. Almost everything alive on Earth suffered at one time or another. It was simply the way of things. Jenny had opposed him, and she deserved her fate. He was going to enjoy chewing on the turtle's legs. The moment he finished with Jenny, he would be off to his new location. Achak would leave a spell behind so that he would be impossible to track.

It would be interesting to see how the area in Ontario had changed over the years, if at all. So far out that it was rare to see people there, and he had never seen a single one in 1904. It would be harsh winter conditions, but his magic would surround him and keep him comfortable.

Achak danced a native dance, summoning energy from evil spirits. Achak placed his feet at particular angles to get their attention, stomping twice with his right foot in a rhythmic pattern. The chant was melodic, and his voice had a beautiful timber. A few clouds swirled above him but gave him next to nothing. Some days, they were more generous than others. Today they weren't giving him much at all, as if the spirits had given up on him. He chanted and stomped and changed his voice to a high pitch yelp but soon realized that it was pointless. Whatever the reason, they were ignoring him.

The reptiles were uncomfortable in the boiling pot, but only because of the cramped space. They watched the water boil around them, and Sarah tried to hit the bubbles. No pain involved whatsoever. Perhaps they couldn't be killed? Having been in there just over an hour when Achak checked on them and he was not happy. They could feel the water, but that was it. They were turtles, and the wizard had no way of transforming herself back into a girl. It annoyed and frightened her. She couldn't use her abilities.

He stared down into the pot at them. "What have we here? No effect, eh? Oh well, I'm sure that you must have gone through some mental anguish waiting to die." He kicked the pot, upsetting it, and watched as Jenny and Sarah were released. The girl didn't know what the hell to do. Living as a turtle would be especially torturous. It was probably a fine condition for a turtle, but not for a wizard. "Don't worry Jenny. You'll only be a turtle for seventy-five years or so."

There was no satisfaction in that news. Her mother would be gone unless she let her father transform her into a vampire. Jenny guessed that because of her disappearance, her mother would most likely opt to stay a mortal. The idea of never seeing her face again was one of the worse thoughts that she had ever had. Without hope, Jenny's state of mind was sinking fast, no solution to the predicament that she found herself in.

Jenny was worse off than Zacharia. He could still blur with the strength of a vampire, but she was stuck at a turtle's pace. Jenny was an ordinary turtle. She might accomplish a mile every four days? All her thoughts were negative, but there was nothing positive to grab onto. Always important to look for the positive and to keep on fighting, but she had nothing to fight with.

"Well." Achak was thinking aloud. "I believe I shall take you two with me. I'll let you go up there, and then you can just wander off. Probably take you the full seventy-five years to get home, if ever. That's what I call a long walk. Good exercise, though."

Jenny tried to blur, but it was pointless. A cat could try to fly, but it wasn't ever going to happen. If she could find the ocean, perhaps she could swim most of the way home. But she did not know in what direction that would be, and then which way to swim? She never felt so alone and so disheartened, even with Sarah by her side. Achak picked them both up and placed them on the table. She tucked her head back into her shell, defeated. He took a piece of branch and poked her in the face with it, but she didn't feel a thing. Would she be more turtle than a girl in a year or so? If she ever got back to being a girl, she would fix him. She would turn him into a turtle with a thousand-year spell and keep him in her bathtub!

Sarah saw it coming through the woods like a walking fireball with the black smoke rising through the trees and into the air. She cocked her turtle head as best she could. The flaming skeleton had finally arrived, and Achak was furious when he saw it, picking up a piece of branch and throwing it at the blazing bones. Jenny watched as he jumped up and down like an angry chimp. At least that made her smile. He was calling it down to the lowest, cursing at it. Achak was its master, and it had to listen to him. It just stood there, offering no resistance. But then it crossed its arms defiantly as the belittling continued.

He wondered where the skeleton had picked up the sword it was carrying. "I could have died, and if I had perished, so would you have. You let me battle Dracula's daughter by myself! What is wrong with you? I made you, and I can destroy you! You son-of-a-bitch! Maybe *I should* destroy you! Now give me what energy you have and be quick about it. You are the reason I had to turn the girl into a turtle, and now her power is lost to me!"

What happened next caught Achak off guard. The skeleton backhanded him so hard that it sent him cartwheeling into the woods; he couldn't believe that it would dare attack him. It shouldn't have been able to do so, but the wizard's own evil emanations had altered it, which now floated around the globe. The sorcerer didn't know as much as he thought he did. Jenny would have clapped if she could have done so; he was indeed getting what he deserved. Achak blurred back to the bones and hit it with a bolt of black lightning, knocking it backward, but otherwise didn't appear to have accomplished much. Was his creation already stronger than him? He demanded the energy that it had stolen from other wizards. It swung its sword several times at the wizard, just barely missing him. It saw Achak was forming a ball of energy and so threw fire at him, but the wizard was expecting it and eluded the flames which went over Jenny's head. Multiple embers fell off, starting small fires that extinguished themselves.

"Come on, kick his ass!" Jenny screamed in her head.

"I can smell a deer nearby," thought the lion.

It rushed the wizard, and he almost tripped backward. He received a powerful punch in the mouth from his own creation, knocking his head back and setting him on fire. He screamed in agony, rolling vigorously on the ground, but there was no putting that fire out. The skeleton stood him up, facing away from him, entered him, pushing Achak's own bones out and killing him. The wizard's bones smoldered on the ground. Now it looked as if Achak was burning, but it was only his likeness that remained. The skeleton was now hidden inside the wizard's vanquished body. Jenny watched as it rushed off. Soon it was almost out of sight, with its fire burning brighter than ever.

Jenny stared at her hand because she was a girl again. The death of the wizard had released them both. She gave Sarah a big hug, and the cat reciprocated with a face lick. When Achak perished, it had destroyed some of his magic. Even the wigwam had vanished, but the Blood Book remained on the table. The skeleton, not being a wizard, had no use for it. The book lit up a florescent green as she approached it. Sparkles of light floated from Jenny into the book as sparkles of gold flowed into her; they were now bound to one another as the book's cover turned a bright white.

Dracula's daughter had been fortunate, but Achak's downfall was entirely his own doing. He now danced with the evil spirits and wasn't at all happy to be there. He sealed his fate long ago when he turned away from the light. Jenny was so glad to be back in her own body she danced. She would never have considered that it could feel so divine to be normal. She couldn't wait to see her mother and father again. "Come on, Sarah, let's go home."

When Jenny got home, her mother told her that her father wanted her to rush to New York for the ceremony of the red sheriffs.

CHAPTER FORTY-SIX

TWO DAYS AFTER ALEXA WAS BORN, she was walking and even blurring to the chagrin of her parents. She had put a hole in the wall when she had lost control of her little feet, and it was a good thing that she was as tough as she was fast. Baby proofing the place was out of the question, and even covering the place in cement wouldn't likely do it. She had already pulled one leg off the sofa, which was now held up with books.

The terrible twos might only last another day or two, and that was all right with them. They were looking forward to the baby understanding right from wrong and listening to them. Her progression was nothing short of miraculous. She was the cutest thing, with blond hair and a smile that could melt both their hearts, but an uppercut that could knock them off their feet.

They had talked to Dracula on the phone, and he told them it was more or less normal, that vampire babies progressed differently, although he had only known about a dozen others that had progressed at her pace. He said that he couldn't wait to see the little princess and that he would see her at the ceremony. They were unsure of how safe it would be to even take Alexa to the ceremony.

Michael rolled over in bed, slowly opening his eyes and staring at the baby and her crib; his pupils expanded. Alexa had such a cute and angelic little face, determined, too. They had brought her into their room last night to monitor her. She had picked up Michael and tossed him into the wall in the living room, where his imprint remained. The baby was sitting on the floor beside her expensive crib, which may now as well be a pile of rubble. And as Michael watched, she was snapping one of the few unbroken rungs as if it was a piece of uncooked spaghetti. She had such a cute laugh and was getting such joy out of destroying her bed.

Michael sat up. "Alexa, where are you going to sleep tonight?"

"No!"

"That's right, you won't be sleeping in that crib because you know what; it's not a crib anymore. It's a pile of lumber. Don't throw that!"

The rung stuck into the wall about two feet above his head. He shook his head. "Lauren, get up and deal with your baby."

Lauren turned over and sat up, still half asleep, instantly noticing the crib. "What happened to her bed?"

"What do you think happened? Termites? Alexa happened, that's what happened."

The baby laughed the cutest laugh and then blurred out of the room, falling on the way out. It sounded like she was moving the sofa around in the living room. "Michael, go get her before she rips the door off of its hinges or something."

Michael rushed out of the bedroom and then right back in with Alexa, with her feet kicking so fast that they were a blur. He gave her to her mother, and she struggled to get free. "Here's your little tornado."

"Alexa, be gentle. Like this, see?" She touched Michael's face.

"No!"

Michael blew a raspberry on her belly. She laughed as she pulled two chunks of his hair right out of his head. "Owwwww! What is it with you and my hair?"

"No!"

"Can you say yes?"

"No!"

"Can you say no?"

"No!"

Michael put his face close to the babies but had to pull back as she tried to hit him, and what a hit it would have been. "Aha! You just said it. Can you spell Mississippi?"

"No!"

"Is Brad Pitt better looking than Daddy?"

"No!"

"I didn't think so."

Lauren was unable to keep herself from laughing. "Don't hurt Daddy! Daddy's gonna be bald."

Michael shook his head. "Lauren, laughing while saying it is giving her mixed signals."

Lauren held the baby up. "Look how beautiful she is Michael."

"She's as bad as she is beautiful, and that's pretty bad."

"She's not bad, she's mischievous."

"Yeah, like Hitler was naughty."

"Michael, look at that cute face."

Michael made cute faces at the baby, and she scrunched her face. Jumping up and down, she hit him in the forehead and driving him right off the bed against the wall. "Look at that. She made me put my head through the wall. Alexa, can you say goodbye to mommy's damage deposit? Can you?"

"No!"

"Lauren, do you know that she can already mind?"

"No, she can't."

"She can. She was in my mind running around, and it sounded like baby steps inside an empty room."

Empty, huh? You can't let your guard down for a second. How come she's so rough with me and not with you?

Alexa had a growth spurt right in her mother's arms. She was suddenly the size of a 3-year-old.

Alexa turned to her father. "Sorry, Daddy."

CHAPTER FORTY-SEVEN

Twelve minutes past midnight, the church was bursting with attendees, every nook and cranny occupied by vampires, wizards, and even a few crow-shaped namuhwoorks perched on the rafters. It was an atmosphere of remembrances of days gone by, minds drifted as they awaited his arrival. Those that had met the Master recalled previous encounters and how his energy had been so overpowering. His presence so impressive.

All had been anticipating the ceremony for quite some time, a rare event that wouldn't soon repeat itself. The press had eagerly anticipated the chance to get in and take a photo of the ceremony, but no such access was allowed. And none would risk crashing the event with so many vampires. Besides, it would be Dracula, they would have to face.

Outside at the back of the church, a gentle wind caressed Dracula's face. Staring up at the crescent moon he could see craters on the lunar surface that no human could observe with the naked eye. He stared at the Piccolomini crater. What would be like for a vampire to walk up there? How would lunar gravity affect a vampire's speed? He thought it would likely be an amusing sight. He could sense a myriad of minds inside the church, all anticipating his arrival and Jenny minded him. *Are you coming in or what?*

I will appear soon enough, daughter.

Alone time could either be satisfying or lonely or even disturbing, with unpleasant memories flowing like waves in the ocean, crashing with unstoppable power, relentless. Dracula was thoroughly enjoying the night air. He reflected on how far his state of mind had come in such a short period of time. Allison and Jenny had changed everything. The days were no longer cumbersome. The nights were no longer torturous. He wanted to suck every bit of joy out of it.

Inside the church near the altar was a beautiful wooden throne fabricated from African Blackwood, inlaid with several red diamonds and solid gold bats pressed into the carved-out wood. The back of it stood eleven feet tall, exceptionally carved swords on each armrest, with a diamond in the blade of each. It was a thing of exquisiteness, and most couldn't take their eyes off it. Red velvet covered the seat. It was a striking piece of furniture even without the Master sitting in it. Tall and regal, any king would be proud. It had a slight magical red glow to it, which added to its stateliness.

The church was as quiet as a daycare at midnight. It was an anxious atmosphere. Some vampires had never laid eyes on the Master. Those who had never seen him were both apprehensive and eager. They could detect his irresistible attraction from outside, and it was disconcerting. Seconds were a lot slower than they usually were, like drops of water from Chinese water torture. The invitation was exclusive, and more than a thousand biters felt disappointed when they didn't receive one.

Alexa turned to her mother. "Mom, where's Dracula?"

"He'll be along soon." Lauren was a little nervous for Michael, but tried not to show it.

"Why are there so many people here?"

"Alexa, you need to be quiet."

Lauren and Michael sat in the front pews, along with their daughter Alexa, who now resembled a 5-year-old. They had noticed that her rate of growth was at least slowing somewhat. Michael, dressed in a one-button notch black tuxedo with a silver tie, and Lauren in a beautiful white strapless floor-length wedding dress, looked stunning. They smiled affectionately at one another, and she knew Michael was nervous, but she also knew that he'd do fine. She felt naked without her swords, but soon would be sufficiently distracted.

Moon Diamond sat on the end wearing a red collar, and the small badge he would receive would be pinned to it. Those who didn't know about the feline were puzzled as they saw it enter. They would be even more confused when it was transformed into a red sheriff.

"Mom, how come Dracula is so strong?"

"Alexa, we'll talk about that when we get home."

Jenny, Allison, and Piers Anthony also sat in the front, awaiting the arrival. Jenny, upon discovering that Dracula was her father, knew that life would never be normal, and that thought couldn't have hit the bullseye more accurately. The way they perceived her father made her smile, especially knowing the things that she could get away with.

"He's late." Jenny whispered to her mother.

"Fashionably late."

"Late is late."

Alexander, Abbey, and Arym sat beside Piers Anthony, and beside them sat Wei and Bao dressed in fancy Chinese garb. Wei was in a modernized black Mao-style suit with black pants and a silver dragon on his left breast. Bao was sporting a colorful style dress which was last worn by a scholar-bureaucrat from the Han Dynasty. It had a Hanau style crossed collar. Vincent was the only one wearing his weapons; with permission from Dracula, he had his pistol and sword. He was getting looks as some thought he might be defying Dracula, also wondering if there would be a death at the ceremony. Annie and Alastair sat beside them. the 90-year-old was happy to be able to see him again. Alastair had been surprised at the invitation.

They could sense Dracula's approach as the hair on the back of their necks stood up.

The church doors swung open with a thud, seemingly magically, and everyone's head turned to face him. The resonance of Dracula's footsteps walking down the aisle broke the silence. Sounds of his slow, deliberate footsteps echoing throughout the church. Some felt scared, although they would never admit it. He was wearing a black Armani suit that appeared to repel the light. A black tie with a small white bat on it. On top of that, an impressive red cloak trailed on the floor.

Jenny thought he overdid the dramatics and would talk to him about it later.

It took time for him to reach his throne, which was by design, the sound of his black Testoni shoes continuing to reverberate off the walls and ceiling. It was unsettling to some, as most knew he could read just about anyone's mind, except for Jenny's. He wanted to give those who had a change of heart time to get up and leave, but no one did.

Dracula reached his throne, removed his cape and throwing it over the back of the chair he sat. Someone coughed. The Master lowered his head and concentrated on the ceremony that was about to begin. When he brought his head up, all eyes were upon him. He brought both hands together, finger to finger, thumb to thumb. He winked at Alexa, and she reciprocated.

Jenny spoke to her father in his mind. "Father, there are so many in here that are frightened of you."

"They may be frightened of you one day."

"Yeah right. You look like a king up there."

"And you a princess."

"Don't make me barf."

Dracula nodded towards Michael and Lauren. "Michael, Lauren, you may approach."

Michael and Lauren approached Dracula and stood before him, both a little nervous but also eager. The pause before he spoke seemed longer than it should have been. They held one another's hand. Even this late in the game, Michael was unsure if he wanted to become a red sheriff or not.

Dracula nodded and smiled at Michael and then did the same to Lauren. "Michael, do you take Lauren to be your wedded wife?"

"I do."

"Lauren, do you take Michael to be your husband?"

Her smile couldn't have been larger or more radiant. "I do."

Dracula nodded. "Then, by the power invested in me, I now pronounce you man and wife. Michael, you may kiss your bride."

They exchanged a brief but passionate kiss as they noticed the applause. Their personal photographer took several photos for posterity. Michael touched her face, and she touched his.

"What GOD has joined together, let no man or vampire tear asunder." Dracula had conviction in his voice.

Even though it was the briefest of ceremonies, it meant the world to both Lauren and Michael to be wed by the Master. As they returned to their seats, someone wheeled a sword rack forward but left it behind his throne. Jenny went up and stood beside her father as they smiled and nodded at one another. The Master nodded toward Michael, and without hesitation, he returned to kneel in front of him. Jenny placed her hand on his right shoulder and read his mind. She would decide whether he was righteous enough to become a red sheriff. She met her father's eyes and gave him a simple nod. A single tear ran down Lauren's cheek.

"Do not take this oath lightly, for I may show up to remind you of your duties as a red sheriff. You wouldn't like that. Michael, do you solemnly swear to join our circle of light? To defend the defenseless and to wear the red badge courageously? Do you promise to be honorable in your deeds, and to give your life if necessary?"

"I do Master."

"Then I now pronounce you a red sheriff of this ancient order." Dracula placed his hand on top of his head and Michael lit up with a purple luminescence. Dracula transferred energy to Michael, and he felt the heat. "Michael, stand in the realm of red sheriffs for truth and justice. Receive your badge and sword. Every single life that you save will light every one of us."

A little red-haired girl that looked to be about 8 years old came forward with a red badge. Michael stooped to allow Rukiya to pin it on his left side. Although she looked like a girl, she was a powerful vampire that was over a thousand years old. Dracula took the most inspiring sword off the rack and handed it to Michael. "Behold your sword of justice. Wield it with impunity against those who seek the darkest night."

Michael returned to his seat with his sword and received applause and a big kiss from Lauren. She had never used the sword that Dracula had given her, but she knew Michael intended to use his.

Dracula nodded at Annie, and she blurred next to Dracula. "Annie, you are looking well. Are you absolutely sure that you want to become a red sheriff? So much danger."

"Mister Dracula, dangers abound for everyone these days. Do I get a sword?"

"Indeed."

"Is it enchanted? Will I automatically know how to use it?"

"The only spell on the swords is one that makes it indestructible. Seek someone to become proficient."

"Will you teach me, Master?"

He didn't expect that question. "We'll see. Perhaps I can give you a few lessons."

Moon Diamond ran and jumped on the throne. Zacharia was excited, more than he thought he would be. The cat puzzled most. Jenny had been instructed that it wasn't necessary to delve into Zacharia's mind because Dracula knew he was a good-hearted vampire. Upon finishing the ceremony, he was given a tiny red badge that hooked onto his red collar. Zacharia felt supercharged and raring to go kill some vampires.

Before Dracula was finished, he had meticulously made seven hundred and one new red sheriffs. Moments after completing the ceremony, New York City went eerily dark.

CHAPTER FORTY-EIGHT

NEW YORK CITY WAS A DIFFERENT PLACE AFTER DARK. Towering skyscrapers were nearly invisible in the blackness. Abandoned streets were devoid of the sounds that should have permeated the air. Day or night, the Big Apple was never meant to be silent. In some areas, the echoes of bats flying were the only sounds or the shuffling of zombie feet combined with their low moans. The vampires cut the power and received instructions to kill any human caught attempting to restore the electricity. They sent an army platoon in, but all of them got killed. The government was having trouble deciding on the next move.

Glowing red eyes were all over the place. They were in the windows and on the roofs, in doorways and on crosswalks. Vampires seized control of the bars. Some alleys were filled with ecstatic vampires, boasting about their accomplishments and sharing tales of their numerous kills. Four went across a crosswalk reminding a senior looking down from his apartment window of the Beatles.

The New York night was now more sullen than it had ever been. There was no escape from the summer heat and the screams in the night, at least every minute or two were terrifying. Weapons were plentiful, but not as comforting as they used to be. Some people wielded crossbows with wooden shafts, while others carried guns with wooden tipped bullets. The city would soon be overrun by zombies and vampires, and over two million people had fled, but that still left plenty of people behind. Police directed traffic during the day, but now the night belonged to the ghouls.

Occasionally, a colony of vampire bats would descend upon a stupid human that dared to go out into the darkness; they would remain in bat form and rip him to shreds, nonetheless. It was a fun challenge, and other vampires would stand around and watch. Carnage had high entertainment value for the evil monsters.

"Kill the humans! Suck them dry!"

New Yorkers were gathering and traveling in groups. Some had automatic weapons supplied by the government, figuring that if the city was going to hell that they might at least have a chance. A lot of teenagers made up their own militias, some so stoned that they walked right up to groups of vampires and begun firing. Unfortunately, the guns didn't save them. It was simply more screams for the night to absorb.

Many people had gone through various stages during the vampire uprising, the first being denial, then anger and depression, now acceptance. The millions that remained were single-minded in defending their turf, but the more they witnessed death, the more they had wished they would have run away with the others. Now more than a hundred thousand zombies were on the streets as well as the vampires. Soon many would run low on food.

An old man carrying a shotgun exited the Chrysler Building, smoking Peterson's Old Dublin pipe tobacco in his pipe. He was so upset and couldn't even recall lighting the pipe, didn't realize he was smoking it. Palmer had been wandering in the dark, being lucky so far. He had just lost his wife of thirty years to a vampire, and he was in shock. He inhaled deeply, taking long puffs. A vampire came out of the sky in bat form, morphing as he dropped in front of him. Palmer blew his head off and watched as he turned to bones. He cursed it as he kicked the bones onto the street, telling it what he thought of their kind. The senior puffed and puffed until he observed three vampires with their glowing red eyes approaching him from across the street.

He then calmly reloaded his weapon and killed himself.

On the corner of Lexington Avenue and E 50th Street, eleven zombies had gathered as they had been stalking a group of teens carrying guns. The young group of males full of testosterone and bravado was unaware of the strength and capabilities of those monsters. And they could only move at a slow pace, and so they were teasing them. They encouraged them to follow, aiming their guns at them but not shooting, with the idea that after they had their fun, they would kill them all. The zombies were calculating their distance so that they could soon blur and at least get some of them.

"Brains," said several zombies in unison.

"We're gonna shoot you in your ugly brains. Come on! Damn, those son-of-a-bitches are ugly." They shot four zombies in the head. Flesh and skin flew, but they continued to move forward, getting ever closer to the launching point. Shooting a zombie in the brain could indeed destroy them.

They all stopped and aimed their guns. Two had Baby Desert Eagle handguns, three had Beretta M9's, and three others had Versa Max Tactical shotguns. Two vampires seemed to come out of nowhere, pushing them all into the zombies, and that was it. Heads were torn off. Their screams went into the night as the faces were eaten. A shotgun blast went off, taking a zombie's leg off at the knee, but it reattached, and she continued.

The vampires laughed as the zombies pigged out on the humans; it was as good as any Broadway show. They smashed multiple skulls while anxiously sucking out the brains. Every zombie there had taken at least two or three bites when more than a dozen of the new red sheriffs showed and began swinging their swords. The red sheriffs quickly dispatched the two vampires and all the zombies, but it was too late to save the foolish mob that had run out of luck.

CHAPTER FORTY-NINE

A T HALF PAST NOON Jenny was in her new bedroom in New York, sitting on her bed being annoyed. She had her arms crossed, and she was giving the book a stern look. The room was entirely white with a large painting of the Mona Lisa above her queen-sized bed, only the painting was from a different angle than the original. How strange? The room had an antique dresser and her own bathroom, and she could get used to that.

Life was moving so fast it was starting to become a bit of a swirl. Too much was happening in such a short period. One could look out the window, and it wouldn't be long before you'd see a zombie or two shuffling around down there. It was fun to run them over, but not so pleasant to be caught by one. A club had started where each zombie that was run over and caught on video would gain you ten points, with the monthly winner receiving the money that was pooled.

The high stakes and overwhelming stress made her reluctant to be an integral part of it. She had the occasional nightmare about failing, and always an end-of-the-world scenario, more or less. Life continued, but for humans, it just wasn't worth living. After conquering the Big Apple. They spread throughout the world like a virulent virus. What an awful dream.

The acquisition of the Blood Book aggravated Jenny, because for now, it only wanted to show her one page. She had fought with it, trying to hold it open to the page that she wanted, but even with her strength, she couldn't do it. Jenny had slipped and had received the mother of all paper cuts. The book was supposed to help her on her journey, but at the moment it didn't seem to be. Perhaps things had to be done in a particular order to save the world. It annoyed her, nonetheless.

Her father stopped at her bedroom door, and he was looking as handsome as usual. Dracula never seemed to have a bad hair day? Not a single strand of hair was ever out of place. Too bad that she hadn't inherited that. Dracula observed her frustration. Her mind was tired, and she needed to rest, but time appeared to be compressing like a pair of pliers on a rotten tooth.

"How's my little turtle?" Dracula investigated his daughter's bedroom.

Jenny felt like throwing the book at him. She turned and gave him such a look. "Are you trying to be funny? Believe me when I say that you do not want to be a turtle. How can Zacharia stand to be a cat?"

"Your mother and I are going out, so don't just wander off. I have important business to attend to."

"This frigging book is useless!"

"What? Why?" A Blood Book was what every wizard wanted with few of them to go around. In 1179, a wizard named Maccutcheon the Great created the books. No one knows why or how he built the tombs, but reportedly less than ten exist. According to legend, he animated them with parts of his soul. More than a dozen vampires set upon him and killed him in 1201. Many battles have taken place over the Blood Books. Not a single collector on the planet has one, but it was a desire and a dream. A Blood Book was worth its weight in rhodium.

"Watch this." Jenny opened the book to page 31, observing several spells highlighted in green. However, the book quickly flipped, opening itself to almost the halfway point where a hologram of an impressive wand slowly circled about four inches above the page. The instrument turned and turned, occasionally pausing as if unsure. "No matter what page I turn to, it opens itself to this wand."

Dracula slowly nodded. There was an awkward silence as Jenny raised her eyebrows at him. "Oh, you're one of those wizards. I should have guessed. My mind has been quite full lately, like dumping too many popcorn kernels in a small pot."

"Why is it I know I will not like what comes next? It's always something. I'd like to just lie down and read a comic occasionally but noooooo. Or relax with some Justin Bieber music, but noooooo."

Dracula sat on the bed beside her. "There is only a handful of wizards that can use wands, the reason being only the most powerful can handle them. As strange as it seems, a wand will kill most wizards. The power contained within is extraordinary. I've only known two wizards that have wielded wands in all my years, and both have been dead for over 700 years, no, 800 years? They destroyed one another, and it was quite something to see, a little like a nuclear explosion. The blast blew me right off my feet."

Jenny produced a deep sigh. "It is beautiful, but how am I supposed to find it?"

The wand was indeed beautiful, with an impressive round red diamond at the bottom of its handle. Unknown characters and symbols lit up on the striped ebony. It looked so real. She showed her father that her hand went right through it. Jenny noticed the diamond seemed to have a bit of extra solidity to it. Jenny touched the space where the diamond would be and was surprised to see a cascade of glimmering red sand flow out of it, paused near the ceiling and then out the window it went. She ran to the window and watched as the sand flowed down over the street and, of course, she knew she would have to follow it to find the wand. Something always complicated matters.

"And there it is! I must follow the red sand to find the wand. It just couldn't be simple."

"Red sand?"

"You don't see that red sand flowing out the window?"

"I do not."

"Really? Why don't you come with me this time? You can help me find the wand." Jenny figured it would be an easier quest with her father at her side, and a lot safer.

Dracula stood up, desperately wanting to say yes. "If you can wait until tomorrow morning, I can join you."

Jenny considered it, but there was no time like the present. She could feel the pull of it. "I think I need to go now. I don't believe that it's just going to hang in the air until tomorrow morning."

"Then you best tell your mother."

"You tell her."

"Oh no, she'll blame me."

Jenny smiled. "The indestructible Dracula scared of my mother."

"You already said that. She might not have fangs, but she still has quite a bite."

"Uh-huh. Would you like me to hold your hand?"

"No, but I'll take a hug."

The wizard sighed. She rubbed her head as she had a slight headache. "I guess I better get out there and follow that thing. I suppose there's some sort of monster waiting for me at the end. Maybe I'll be transformed into a cockroach this time, so don't go stepping on any bugs." She was disappointed as she blurred past him.

Jenny followed the red sand until she got to Times Square and then lost it when a gust of wind blew up, dispersing it. When she found it again, Jenny followed it all around the city. It doubled back at times, and she wondered if it wasn't taking liberties with her. What was the point in going north, only to turn around and go south? It seemed unlikely that the enchantment was having trouble locating the wand? Or was it? When the sand took her all around Central Park, she was getting more than a little annoyed, especially when it took her right back to the Bethesda fountain. It paused above the fountain before adopting a sharp right and then continuing.

"What the heck are you doing?"

Jenny saw a woman who looked to be in her sixties, although her hair was black, long and down to her backside. Her appearance reminded her a little of a witch. She had an old and stern face with a pronounced nose. Jenny did not enjoy thinking it but she was homely. Of course, it was only an opinion and not a nice one.

She was a skinny little thing, just over five feet tall. Jenny had been blurring to follow the magical sparkles of sand, mostly staring up into the sky as she pursued it, not paying too much attention to the surrounding people. And she got a few looks. Jenny had observed the woman in another location, which meant she was also moving swiftly. No mortal would have been able to keep up with her. She must have had a concealing spell because she couldn't sense her energy. And then she caught her looking up; she could see the sand even though her father couldn't. Was she another wizard? Was she also seeking the wand?

When the girl wasn't looking, a bolt of gray lightning hit her, but Jenny's shield came up automatically and blocked it. Elsa was indeed a powerful wizard and was surprised by the result. Jenny turned, now realizing what the spell had been doing; it wouldn't lead her to the wand while another wizard was also pursuing it. She hit Elsa with an energy ball and it blew her into the air, and she landed hard. She attempted to get up multiple times but couldn't, so Jenny was off once again. It had depleted Elsa so much that she wouldn't be able to walk for days and had to suffer the indignity of being taken to the hospital.

Jenny followed the trail all the way to the Adirondack forest. It had ceased its evasive tactics and now only surged forward, increasing its speed drastically. At times, it had to wait for Jenny to catch up. It took her to the waterfalls in Keene Valley where the sand begun to accumulate on one particular boulder. Soon it was almost an inch thick. The sand marked the spot. The conclusion was that the wand was located inside the rock.

"Who would put a wand inside a boulder?" Jenny cleaned the sand off the rock, and strangely, the texture of the grains was soft, melting and disappearing as she touched it.

Was the wand really inside that rock? Would it be okay to hit it with an energy ball or a lightning bolt? That would break it open, but would it also damage the wand? Might have a protective spell on it, but it might not. But how would she get it out of there? She supposed she could go back and find a sledgehammer. Jenny didn't yet know of any transportation spells to bring it home to work on it. The wizard stood back with both feet in the water, trying to hit it on the side. However, a shield came up and deflected her magic, sending it into the sky before exploding like a crack of thunder.

"That answers that question. I guess that would have destroyed it? Now what? I must take a freaking sledgehammer to it?"

Jenny blurred off. Now that she knew its location, she could always come back to it. On the way, she returned to the Blood Book. Because she knew the location of the wand, perhaps it would show her how to get it out of there. It was worth a try.

Jenny stared at her Blood Book displaying a transportation spell and showing a likeness of Jenny with the boulder magically appearing beside her room. On a loop, showing it to her over and over. The cartoon of herself made her chuckle. The spell was in some strange language, but then it turned into something that she could at least pronounce, even though she didn't know what the words meant. "Dontomah soca dachomi foralso?" And with saying it, the boulder appeared in the room beside her. "Wow, that was quick."

She heard her mother's footsteps approaching from down the hall. Allison looked in at Jenny. "I thought I heard you in here. You're back already? We're leaving. What the heck is that? What on earth are you doing with that rock in here?"

"I guess there's a wand stuck in it. Tell Dad to come here for a second."

Dracula blurred into the room and furrowed his brows at seeing the boulder. "Rock collecting, are we?"

"Can you break this thing open? The book is showing you punching it. You can't argue with the book. Believe me, I've tried."

"Stand back. I'll try." He smashed it hard with his fist, breaking it open pretty much right down the center. The noise was deafening when the rock hit the hardwood floor. The wand glowed in the center of the boulder.

"Okay, I can take it from here. Move along."

Dracula took Allison by the arm. "You best consider that wand as dangerous as a gun. Don't point it at anyone you don't want to kill."

"Can I point it at my baby brother when he's born?"

"If you must."

Allison slapped him, hurting her hand.

Her parents departed, and it took Jenny almost a minute to pry it out. It had a pleasant weight to it, feeling like it belonged in her hand. When she rolled it in her hand to examine it, she saw them. Her mouth hung open as she observed it had three circular holes in it. Where one could place three more precious stones? Oh no. She had a sickening feeling in the pit of her stomach as she let herself fall on her bed. She slapped her mattress several times. Jenny could hear the pages of the book turning; she lifted her head off the pillow to stare as it stopped but now emitted a yellow glow. Of course, it wanted her attention.

The wizard whined. "No, I don't want to look. You can't make me. I'm not looking."

The book jumped almost a foot in the air and landed with a thump on the antique dresser. She sat up and glared at it. She was going to be bossed around by the book? The thing had a mind of its own. Again, it jumped, this time higher than the first. She pointed at it, telling it to stop, but then surrendered. Jenny got up as slowly as she was able, dragging her feet dramatically as she approached. She didn't want to look down at that page. But when she did, the book showed her the Great Pyramid of Giza. "Are you serious? Egypt!"

CHAPTER FIFTY

J ENNY AND HER FATHER ARRIVED IN EGYPT at the Mena House Oberoi hotel at ten in the morning. The place was already as hot as hell, approaching a hundred degrees Fahrenheit. She thought the hotel deserved a rating of six stars out of five. What beautiful style. The hotel was in the shadow of the Great Pyramids at Giza, embraced by 40 acres of gardens, and a little over two thousand feet from the towering pyramid of Cheops. Being there was magical. She would have loved to have gone for a walk, but as usual, she had pressing business. Egypt was begging to be explored, but New York City was at stake.

A handsome young man went by on a camel and nodded to her; she watched until he disappeared around the back of the hotel. Dracula had to pull her, and although the heat didn't bother her or her father, other tourists were running inside to escape it. As one would hurry to avoid the rain. But the beauty of Egypt was undeniable, even from the air it had been captivating. The desert was as fascinating as she was dangerous and would claim anyone that wasn't prepared for her harshness. The pyramids charmed tourists like fish attract fishermen. What an adventure it would be to explore such an ancient land.

They ate on the balcony with the pyramid in view past the palm trees. Jenny felt thrilled to go on an excursion with her father, even though they deemed her mother too dangerous to tag along. Though Dracula had been there many times, it was surreal for his daughter. Her eyes couldn't have opened any wider. It felt like being awake in the most beautiful dream. Even the shapes of the doorways were exotic and, to Jenny, fascinating, like stepping back in time or stepping into an old but excellent movie. Such an overload Jenny knew she wouldn't remember all the details. Staying at the hotel expanded her horizons.

"Father, this place is unbelievable. Photos don't do it justice, that's for sure."

"Nothing can replace being here in person. It's definitely one of the most picturesque places on the planet."

The artistically crafted interior impressed Jenny with filigree fretwork, exquisitely carved paneling. Beautiful murals, gilding, and inlaid mother-of-pearl and mosaic tiles. Dracula informed her they built it in 1869, and it would indeed cost a fortune to construct it today. Replete with antiques and genuine works of art, it was more like a royal palace than a hotel. The vampires that worked at the hotel bowed to him, and their eyes almost bugged out as they did so. They wondered what the Master was doing in Egypt. Outside, the royal residence drifts into its historical setting, a bit like walking around inside a beautiful postcard. It had domes, towers, colonnades, and minarets juxtaposed among the palms, jasmine, and the bougainvillea flowering plants.

It was an oasis of opulence in the desert landscape.

Regrettably for Jenny, they were there on business. Life was all business lately, which made Jenny irritable. She longed for carefree days of just being an ordinary girl, or as close to that as she could get. Her father promised her that after it was all over, he would take the family there for a month's vacation, and that lifted her spirits higher than they had been in a while. How amazing would it be to have lots of time to explore Egypt, especially being able to share it with her mother and father? She couldn't wait to return after the battle was over, and so now she was even more determined to survive. Egypt awaited the 12-year-old wizard.

It wasn't long before Dracula and Jenny were inside the pyramid. She had the Blood Book and the wand inside her backpack. She could visualize the Egyptians building it all those years ago. How would it feel to experience being there right after it was built? It looked to be as tall as a 40-story building, making Jenny feel small. Once inside the King's Chamber, the book jumped in her backpack.

"Father wait; the book wants me to look at it."

"I'm waiting. The air is hot and stale in here. It would not be a place for someone who was claustrophobic."

Jenny removed the book, and it opened to a page showing the area they were in, a map that highlighted two narrow shafts in the north and south walls. The map showed two separate sections of the walls, with moving arrows showing the basalt blocks should be pushed simultaneously. "We need to push in two stone blocks at the same time. This place is almost like being inside a video game."

"We have permission to be in here but not to destroy the place. This one?"

"Not that one, the one beside it."

"This one?"

"No." Jenny went over and touched the location that she wanted him to push. "Just wait. We need to push them together."

"That's not beside it. That's above it."

"Whatever. Okay, push it now."

They pushed simultaneously and the floor of the south shaft lowered as the right wall also expanded. The book jumped again, and it showed an area to press inside the shaft. She placed her book and the wand back inside the pack and climbed up inside the shaft. Only God knew what she would find in there, but Dracula was both impressed and fearful of her lack of hesitation.

"Follow me. What are you waiting for?"

Dracula followed her by shaking his head, with 2000 years of dust at their feet. He watched as she searched the wall, assuming that Jenny was hunting for a particular location. It took her almost five minutes, but she finally pushed a section of wall, and it slowly opened, with rock grinding against rock, revealing narrow stairs that led down into darkness. They could see perfectly in the dark, which was a good thing because no light existed down there. Jenny could see a sarcophagus at the bottom of the narrow steps, but she couldn't see anything else.

"Look a sarcophagus!"

"Jenny wait!"

She headed toward the sarcophagus, so eager she tripped and fell the last few steps. Dracula followed, and they both stared at it. Was it possible that they had discovered something that no one else had? If it weren't for the Blood Book, they would have never found it. There was the sound of grinding stone. However, the echo prevented them from identifying the source until it was too late. They believed it to be another passage opening, but unfortunately, it was the same one closing. The passage had sealed behind them, and even the stairs had receded.

Dracula stared at Jenny. "Oh, that's not good."

"Holy shit!" said Jenny. They were in an undiscovered tomb surrounded by riches. Much to their dismay, they found themselves trapped with no way out.

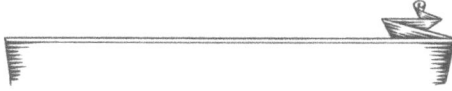

CHAPTER FIFTY-ONE

ALEXANDER AND TESSY were called to the 453-foot Lipstick Building at 885 Third Avenue because of zombies. The building looked like a giant lipstick because of its shape and color. The morning brought twice as many calls as red sheriffs. Things were going downhill fast, and every couple of minutes there was more *breaking news*. New York City was looking a lot like a war zone. The bodies were piling up.

When they turned the corner on East 54th Street, they discovered four zombies and two vampires hanging around outside the entrance of the building. As soon as a zombie attacked a person exiting the building, Tessy bit the zombie, pulling its leg off, allowing the woman to pull away and run. Alexander sliced its head off and stomped its skull flat, killing it. The two vampires attacked the sheriff, forcing him to deflect multiple blows from their swords; his style showed that he was an expert at it. He had expected other sheriffs to be there because of the ceremony, but the Big Apple was a big place to defend.

A zombie jumped on the shepherd and flattened her to the ground; her legs went out in all directions as it prepared to take her head. That was one thing about zombies: they were as strong as hell. The dog realized it had pinned her. The zombie smelled her brain through the top of her head and licked it, ending up with a tongue covered in dog hair. A piece of its skin, covered with mucus, fell off. Alexander took the head of one vampire, blurred and threw the zombie off Tessy into the street, where a yellow taxi ran over its head and kept ongoing.

Taxi drivers had their own game going called Zombie Kill. Ten points for each kill, but only five if it survived. The vampire cut the dog's hip open, and she squealed. Then she turned and lunged with her fangs out, grabbing him by the throat and with a couple of bites decapitated him. When it was needed, Tessy could become savage. She grabbed the skull by a piece of loose skin and tossed it onto the street. The head attempted to make its way back to its body, rolling awkwardly before a food service truck ran over it, causing a loud crunch.

The two remaining zombies had a conversation. "He kill zombies."

"Dog kill zombie too."

"Run!"

The two zombies attempted to make a run for it, but because they could only blur ten feet at a time, they were caught and killed. In less than a minute, five of the new red sheriffs that had formed a pack for protection showed up; they arrived a little too late for the fight.

Tessy barked a quick greeting as the German Shepherd and her master blurred off.

CHAPTER FIFTY-TWO

Jenny and her father found themselves trapped in the undiscovered tomb of an apparently undiscovered king. Because of its secret location, no one had found it in over two thousand years. The walls had sections of gold covering them. It looked like layers and layers of gold, and whoever had painted it all those years ago had talent. At the bottom of the rendering was the king being carried as the sun shone down on him as a dust storm approached.

Jenny kicked her legs as she sat on a large throne made of wood and overlaid with sheets of gold. The throne had a cobra's motif, which made it comparable to what people had discovered in Tutankhamun's tomb. It had front and back cobra legs with two cobra heads for arms to rest one's hands on. On the back of the chair was a likeness of the king in ivory and gold. She wiped some dust off the cobra heads and was captivated by the carving. How long since anyone had laid eyes on it?

In the corner was a tabernacle, close to being a cube, fabricated from ebony covered with gold, and four golden cobras appeared to dance on top. It had four small coffins that slid into it to hold the king's internal organs. Everything in there was irreplaceable and deserved a spot in a museum. They both felt fortunate to see such treasure.

Dracula scratched his head and raised his eyebrows. He never considered that they would have discovered a tomb. Of course, it wouldn't do them a bit of good if they were stuck in there forever. Thank goodness that Jenny wasn't prone to panic.

The sarcophagus, a work of art that represented the Sun God Ra and resembled a man with a falcon's head, was made of solid gold. Neither Jenny nor her father were experts on Egyptology, but any archeologist would be ecstatic in that chamber. It seemed like the tomb had been abandoned, resulting in a bit of a haphazard appearance. Did the Egyptians get spooked? Someone had scattered several impressive necklaces on the floor. The throne wasn't straight.

A dagger was in the center of the chamber as if someone had dropped it and ran.

Jenny looked up at her father as he looked down at her. "Father, are we, like, oh I don't know, trapped in here forever?"

He didn't want her to worry, but the prospect didn't look good. "Too soon to tell." He picked up a necklace and gave it to her. It was the eye of a falcon and beautifully crafted. "Looks like you have discovered an unknown tomb."

Jenny liked the thought of it, but she was more concerned with getting out of there. Jenny was feeling more than a little anxious. If she had to spend even a week in there staring at the walls, Jenny would likely go stir crazy. "Yes, well, I'd be happy to discover my way out of here." Jenny placed her book on the golden funeral bed and watched it swing open.

"If only your mother could see us now."

"Hey, pretend you're my friend Jessica and ask me what I did in Egypt."

Dracula thought about that for a moment and then played along. "Jenny, what did you do in Egypt?"

"Oh, nothing much, I just you know discovered a tomb!"

The wizard got up and paced as Dracula sat on the chair, knowing that it might break under his weight, but at this point, he didn't care. "Tell me that the book is showing us a way out?"

"Father, it is not showing anything. I mean, it's showing the chamber we're in but not showing a way out. Game over. Why would it open just to show us nothing?"

There was silence for a time as they both considered the situation they were in and what to do next. Dracula adjusted his suit coat. It might be physically possible for him to pull those blocks out and tunnel out of there, but neither the Egyptian government nor the world would be happy with him destroying the pyramid, besides parts of it might collapse on them.

Dracula nodded as he deliberated. "Your mother is going to wonder what happened to us if we're not back in a thousand years."

"Oh, ha-ha."

"What does your instinct tell you?"

Jenny considered what they were doing in there. "That at least one of those gems for the wand is in here somewhere, and ideally, all three would be nice. But that still would leave the problem of us getting out of here. *Seek the book, Jenny*!"

"What do you think of this father and daughter bonding?"

"Ask me again in fifty years."

Jenny started searching the chamber for the gems; she began by examining the necklaces, but no such luck. She put one of them on, and it looked marvelous on her. Dracula checked the chair he was sitting on, even turning it upside down. They searched everything in there, and as Jenny felt along the walls, he did so as well. No sign of the gems. He turned into a bat and flew up the walls, which were about fifty feet high but couldn't see anything up there either. He morphed into his regular form and landed with heavy feet.

Jenny showed a look of unpleasantness. "Oh no, I just had an awful thought."

"What?"

"What if it is inside the coffin?"

"That could be unpleasant. Why don't you be a brave daughter and open it?"

She hesitated. "Listen, Dad, you're the adult here. You open it."

"I don't like coffins." There was something in his past that made him wary of coffins, something that he couldn't put his finger on, but they made him uncomfortable.

"Are you telling me that Dracula doesn't like coffins? Since coffins usually have dead people in them ... Oh, what the hell." Jenny took a deep breath and opened it. The situation took a turn for the worse when a snake emerged from it, causing her to jump back in surprise as she realized it was a small snake that swiftly disappeared into a crack in the wall. "There we go. I opened it so you can search it."

Dracula smiled at her. "I'd rather not. Look into my eyes!"

She had to laugh. "Shut up. I guess we'll just have to stay here forever. Is it forever yet? How about now?"

He searched inside the sarcophagus and under the mummy, but found nothing. When he moved it to one side, he could see a small leather pouch that came apart when he pulled it out. A small round stone fell out of it. It was unimpressive, but it looked to be the right size. Dracula was happy that he didn't have to tear open the mummy. It seemed like a round yellow jasper rock except it had the tiniest crystal in its center, about the size of a grain of salt.

Jenny took it from him and examined it. She placed it in the wand, and it fit, then a bright yellow flash bounced off the walls and made them see stars.

"I guess that's one. See if there's more in there."

"No, that's it."

Jenny began banging on the walls, searching for an unfamiliar sound that might hide a door or something else. Then she stomped on the floor, listening for a sound that might indicate a way out. When she got to the center of the chamber, she stopped. "Do you hear that?"

"Yes, it sounds like there might be something down there." He kneeled and detected a little air rising from somewhere below them. Dracula hit it with his fist and broke part of it and then pulled out the enormous block. It destroyed part of the mechanism which would have opened it by placing pressure on one side of it. A steep slide descended before him, its depth hidden by the angled wall. It went down and over a slight hill.

Jenny knew it could be dangerous, but what other choice did they have? "I guess we should slide down there?"

Dracula nodded. "You go first, and I'll be right behind you. I wouldn't be happy if we got separated."

They stared at one another before deciding to give it a go. They slid down into the hole, one behind the other, and astonished to discover the fall was over fifteen hundred feet down. They collided as they reached the bottom.

CHAPTER FIFTY-THREE

WHILE ALASTAIR WAS HOME DRINKING ETHIOPIAN coffee on the sofa, perusing the New York Times, Annie was on Broadway, the street not the show, battling vampires and zombies. She had already killed nineteen zombies and two vampires by noon. Annie appreciated the extra zest that Dracula had bestowed upon her as she cut through the miscreants. Even some vampires had learned to avoid the 90-year-old swinging her sword; it didn't look right getting beat by a 90-year-old. She was doing remarkably well

270

for someone that had no training with such a weapon. She had learned to anticipate their every move, which gave her a tremendous advantage. It was a new talent that she had developed right after becoming a red sheriff.

Annie helped an armed group across the street. Even though they had lots of weapons, they were smart enough to be frightened. They had five shopping carts full of food and were helping people that were running out of the essentials. Two Japanese vampires watched as the old woman kept her eyes on them. Speaking in Japanese, they said how they were going to enjoy cutting into that bunch of frightened Americans. They blurred, but so did Annie. She moved so fast that she threw her sword, raced it and placed the taller of the two in front of it. She grabbed the other one and flung him across the street. Having underestimated Annie because of her delicate appearance, they were paying the price.

Annie removed her sword from his throat, taking his head as the other attacked with his Shinogi-Zukuri Katana. Annie was so swift that it appeared as if his head had just fell off. The crowd cheered as she took a little bow.

"I wish that were my grandmother," said a young man with a red Mohawk that was actually a native. He had saved the lives of a senior couple that morning with his shotgun. These days, the number of heroes had greatly increased.

Annie blurred off and stopped at the Chrysler Building, where she saw the skeleton wearing Achak's skin, and killing a wizard in front of the Duane Reade pharmacy. It had him down on the sidewalk, and before Annie could get to him, it was too late. All that remained was a pile of ash.

"Hey!" It shot three balls of fire at her, but she dodged them all. A fireball crossed the street, setting a delivery truck on fire. The driver had to abandon the delivery truck. The fire was spreading fast.

Annie put her sword through it fifteen times, but it had no effect. Spreading flames from its fiery sword that covered such a large area, it caught both her legs. It rushed off, leaving Annie to burn. The flame engulfed her, and all her pain receptors exploded. She tried to roll and extinguish the fire but couldn't. Her energy and her life were ebbing away. She thought of poor Alastair as she burned.

Annie, carried by Vincent, and his speed quelled the fire. When he put her down, she thought he was so handsome; she loved the way he tipped his hat to her. Although she had survived, she felt weak and went home to Alastair to recover.

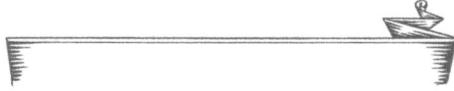

CHAPTER FIFTY-FOUR

D RACULA WAS UPSET that he had sent his daughter flying across the chamber. However, she reassured him by insisting it was an accident, which it undoubtedly was. His face had shown little emotion in over a century. How would he have coped with it if he had caused significant harm to his child? The tumble that she took would have killed a human, but she got up and dusted herself off. She stood looking down the steps that led even further into the pyramid. They would go down there, but not yet.

The temperature was lower in this place, and they were clueless about their whereabouts. It seemed to Jenny that they were in a pyramid under the great pyramid. How was that possible? But what a perfect place to hide a pyramid! She couldn't even imagine what treasures they would encounter. The memories that she could take back with her would be priceless. If they could escape, the entire world would hear about their exploits.

"Father, are we really somewhere under the Great Pyramid?"

"It would appear so. What a brilliant idea."

"I was thinking the same thing. Exceptional minds think alike." The dust made her sneeze. "And idiots get themselves trapped in a tomb."

The chamber was smooth walls with a glossy ceiling. The floor looked like blocks of pink granite. And the ceiling appeared to be about fifteen feet tall, with an interpretation of a hawk in the center. High on the right was Ra in a solar boat holding a cat. Dracula thought it might be some sort of gallery, with the walls covered in Egyptian art and amazing hieroglyphs.

In the center of the room was a solid gold table. Against the wall was an enormous statue of Ra with a cobra on its head. The figure took his attention. When he peeked behind the wall, he saw something hidden in the shadows. When Dracula pushed the heavy object, he discovered a rectangular hole with seven polished rocks. All stones had their own symbol. One looked like an eye. Another appeared to be a scarab beetle, and the remaining images were unknown. Jenny placed them on a gold table adorned with different animals.

Dracula didn't know what he was sensing, but it had an ancient feel to it and was not a pleasant one. Whatever it was, it was moving. Was there some sort of specter down here? What if something happened to Jenny? He had to alter his train of thought because it wouldn't do either of them any good.

Jenny opened her backpack, took out the Blood Book and set in on the table, discovering an unpleasant surprise. All the pages were yellowish from age and blank, as if the book had run out of juice. "What the hell? Not a single word in the entire book?" She continued to flip the pages back and forth. "What's happened to my book?"

Dracula was uneasy as he walked around. "I feel something down here. Counter-magic perhaps? See if you can conjure up a bolt of lightning."

The bolt of lightning worked fine, taking a chunk out of the wall, filling the air with more dust. "Whatever, it only seems to affect the book."

"We might need that book to save us."

"Believe me, I know."

They methodically explored the area. Dracula found another hidden chamber inside the wall with a hawk skeleton and a fantastic necklace, but the second stone for the wand remained undiscovered. Jenny took one of the polished rocks and put it in her backpack, the one emblazoned with the scarab. It would make a good souvenir of the adventure with her father.

"I guess the stone is not in here; we may as well go down those stairs." Jenny never thought that her first trip to Egypt would be such a quest.

They descended the steps and the further they went, the narrower it got. When they observed the sarcophagus, they realized it was probably the king's chamber. Dracula stopped at the entrance, and Jenny bumped into the back of him. He stuck his head inside and scanned the area; he couldn't see anything, but he knew that someone or something was in there. Whatever the hell it was he felt its aggressive nature.

"What is it?"

"Jenny, I can't see anything, but I know something is in here."

"I see nothing. Do you think it's a ghost?"

He continued to examine the contents of the chamber at the end of the stairs. A goddess of Isis' statue holding a scepter was in the right corner, looking heavenward. The sound of footsteps echoed throughout, catching their attention. "I don't know what to think, but I have the feeling that as soon as we go in there, we're going to be attacked. Why don't you wait here while I go in?"

"Someone's walking around in there."

"I know he's in that corner." She pointed. "I'm going in." She pushed past her father and was immediately hit with a punch in the face that crushed her jaw and knocked her unconscious.

"Jenny!"

CHAPTER FIFTY-FIVE

TWO TRANSLUCENT GUARDS MATERIALIZED. Although they weren't as tall as Jenny, their muscular frames gave them a powerful presence. Magical creations with but a single purpose: to keep anyone from entering the chamber. They were dark-skinned and handsome with stern faces, dressed in ancient Egyptian garb, white linen Shendyts, and short skirts with golden sashes. They had bare chests that somehow glistened even though there was no light in there. The Egyptians quickly changed and appeared solid.

Dracula rushed to Jenny but was lifted by one guard and thrown into the wall, crushing his frontal lobe. He healed and blurred into it with a punch that would have decapitated most, but all that accomplished was to jerk its head back a little. The Master had never seen such a powerful opponent, and that Jenny wasn't moving made him panic. He dodged a fist that came straight down toward his head, forcing him to take a step backward. The other Egyptian broke Dracula's neck from behind. It healed, but he had never, ever seen such powerful magic. What kind of wizard had created such potent entities?

Dracula was never so glad to see Jenny stand. She was rubbing her jaw, but there was no time to think during an ongoing battle. He had to sidestep several more attempted blows. He kicked one just above the knee, trying to break it. However, it was like a human kicking bricks. Dracula tried hard to read its mind, but it didn't seem to have one; it was in a loop to destroy and protect.

"What just happened?"

"One of those things knocked you out."

Again, one guard attacked her. She drove it high onto the wall with a mighty kick. Although Dracula was stronger than his daughter physically, obviously her magic was better suited to fighting the spirit guards and her blows much more efficient. It toppled hard onto the granite floor, getting up as if it hadn't sustained such a mighty blow. She hit it with a bolt that deflected off the top of its head, but it just kept coming. Both of the guards ganged up on her and held her down; she thrust one off with her foot as Dracula grabbed her and rushed out of the room back onto the stairs. They both watched as the guards stood in front of the sarcophagus with their arms crossed and then vanished.

Jenny felt her chin where it had been crushed. "Apparently, they can't leave that room."

"It would seem so." Dracula cracked his neck. He had never encountered a situation where he was outmatched, and it infuriated him.

She looked at him, studying his expression. "What is that look on your face? Are you actually angry? It's alive!"

"I've known no one who could best me in a fight. I am peeved."

Jenny smiled at the anger she was seeing. "It's a wonder you don't have smoke coming out of your ears. Father, do you think we missed another exit back there?"

Dracula stood with his arms crossed, staring into the chamber. "I don't think so, but I suppose it's possible."

Lots of dust in the air from all the rapid movements of the fight. Dracula sneezed loud enough to scare anyone.

"They probably heard that sneeze in China. I'm going back there to search one more time. You can wait here if you like."

"I shall do so."

When Jenny blurred off, Dracula went back into the chamber, and the fight continued. He picked up the guard with the golden sash and flung him hard against the wall, breaking a piece out of a block and narrowly avoiding the sarcophagus. The guards looked at one another and spoke words he couldn't understand, one being the ancient Egyptian word for vampire, and then simultaneously attacked. They tripped him and knocked him down when one pinned him, the other attempted to pull his head off. He was more amazed than frightened when he could not escape. He felt the vertebrae in his neck coming apart. Dracula kicked the Egyptian twice but couldn't budge him.

The guard couldn't pull the vampire's head off, so they tossed him out. Dracula stood up and dusted himself off; his Armani suit was now unkempt as Jenny returned.

"I can't find anything. Were you in there fighting with them again?"

"I was not."

"Are you lying to me?"

"Maybe."

Jenny sat down on the steps and considered the next move, but she couldn't come up with one. Took out her brush and brushed her hair. Not knowing what to do next was aggravating. She was aware not every problem had a solution, which made her nervous. She hoped that this wasn't a dead-end that would be the death of them. The way forward was most likely through the chamber with the guards. "So, what do we do now?"

Dracula stuck his head in the chamber and quickly pulled it out as one of the guards missed him with a mighty punch, catching the side of the doorway and breaking a piece off it. They had felt the wind from it. "Temperamental sons-a-bitches."

"Any human that stuck their head in there would be killed instantly." Jenny also stuck her head in, grabbed it by the arm when it tried to kill her and kicked it across the room.

"I don't know what to do." Dracula blurred into the room, punched one of the guards in the head and then blurred back.

"Are we having fun yet?"

"I actually broke my hand on his head."

They sat and talked about things, about the baby and how the adventure that was their lives was going to get even more interesting as time went on. Jenny thought that her mother would eventually let her father turn her; Dracula said that he hoped so but wasn't so sure. The conversation returned to the fact that they were at an impasse.

Dracula stuck his head into the chamber again but his timing was off, and Jenny had to go in and pull him out.

CHAPTER FIFTY-SIX

S atellite photos revealed nearly two hundred thousand zombies roaming the streets of New York City during the day, and there could have been even more at night. No one knew where they were coming from, although they suspected it was the work of a wizard. Most of the vampires appeared to be evil, and now they had to deal with zombies as well. The government had hired their own wizard, but so far Carlos wasn't much help. All he could convey to them was the prevailing presence of evil in the atmosphere, indicating an impending escalation. He had protected the president with a spell and a few others, but his abilities and levels of power were limited. He feigned being a higher-level wizard than he was because the money was so good.

The sun appeared to fall much too fast these days. The nights seemed way too long, and without electricity, darkness was also the enemy, as was the oppressive heat. More people followed the progression of the sun than ever, especially when it approached the horizon. They pressed their faces to their windows and watched the zombies and vampires on the streets below as they clashed with armed humans, but those confrontations were lessening. More and more people were being dispatched. It was like the scariest reality TV, with all of New York being part of the show.

Most of the vampires roamed the streets after dark, enjoying one another's company. They felt feeling like they were becoming a nation in themselves, and that was far from satisfactory news. Vampires rarely worked together, making the current situation even more terrifying. According to Carlos, the city's vampire population exceeded five thousand, with a constant influx of newcomers. To where the government didn't know what to do. They couldn't go in there with tanks and blow the place to pieces, which is what some wanted to do. Besides, the vampire's senses were so heightened they could get out of the way of the bombs.

The sun had been down for about two hours when it happened. The biters brought more than a thousand full-size trees to Times Square, having ripped out of the forest with their bare hands. They put them in the middle of the street, then set them on fire. It was a massive blaze, with the smoke choking the air in the area. Sharpton wanted to prove that he had complete freedom to do as he wished. The world was indeed paying attention because if they conquered New York City, the villains would almost certainly spread out from there.

In the Central Park West apartments, over thirty zombies had found their way in and were searching for fresh brains. They were looking a little more robust with their loose skin not being so relaxed, and some had grown new skin. More skin or not, nothing could stop them from resembling spawns from hell. One couldn't dress up a monster to look any better. A zombie had scared a senior to death as he had stared out his keyhole at the corpse that had one of its eyes hanging out.

A zombie wearing nothing, but a dirty white shirt broke down a door and stared down at two 10-year-old girls that lived with their grandmother. He cocked his head at the scent of such fresh young brains. When he looked up, a shotgun blast to the head ended him as he crumpled in the hall.

"Shoot him again Nanny!"

"Nanny doesn't want to waste any shells. You two go to bed now."

"Call us if you're gonna shoot another one!"

"I will."

It had been the third one shot in less than a week. A lot of brave souls out there now, some too brave for their sake. Some were luring zombies just so they could kill them, but there were always risks.

"Can we watch the zombies out the window?"

"For a few minutes."

When the kids went into their room, she dragged the zombie down the hall and left it there. She found it quite weighty for something that was mostly bones. It was time to get the tools and put the door back up before another one of those bastards came along. They smelled brains like a dog smelled bones.

Outside the building, A. J. Gallant showed up with his Beretta shotgun and killed zombies. He was a short man at just over five and a half feet tall, with black glasses and a salt and pepper beard. He was doing well, not allowing them to get too close before tagging them, until he ran out of shells. Two zombies jumped him, knocking the gun out of his hand. They tore his skull open and commenced to eat.

"Brain taste funny."

Almost the same number of red sheriffs attacked a hundred zombies. Wei and Bao were killing machines, and so was Arym. Moon Diamond was becoming adept at removing their heads where others would stomp them flat. Lauren and Michael were there as well; Michael noticed a vampire run, and they took after him. They killed him when he was about a mile away, only to discover that a baker's dozen of evil vampires surrounded them.

Alexander showed up with Tessy, and the battle continued. The shepherd flung herself at a tall black vampire and chewed his head off with two bites, but another pulled her tail off as Alexander took his head. Lauren was swinging her blades faster than anyone had ever seen, killing three in an instant. Michael was more confident than ever, taking two heads while sustaining a slight cut to his abdomen. They each killed another as Tessy stopped one from fleeing. Lauren threw her sword through one's chest as Michael took his head.

Alexander swung his sword, getting rid of its excess blood with the sound of it cutting through the air. "I don't know how we're ever going to kill them all; there's too many. Five sheriffs were just killed on Monroe."

CHAPTER FIFTY-SEVEN

J ENNY AND DRACULA had been sitting on the steps deep inside the pyramid, gazing into the king's chamber for over an hour. The guards were now invisible. Waiting for anyone or anything that dared to cross the threshold. They could not see beyond the chamber, it was their entire world. Dracula and his daughter could hear the guards whispering back and forth; Jenny would have loved to have known what they were saying. The ability to understand every language in the world would be a great enchantment. She wondered if she would ever be so adept as to create such a complicated spell. She had so much to learn, and it might take her a century to acquire such knowledge.

Dracula rushed back into the chamber, knocked one guard down, and then was suddenly on the steps. He took some satisfaction out of it not having been able to tag him. He smiled and raised his eyebrows.

"Is there any point in what you are doing?"

"I think they're getting weaker."

"Really?"

"No, not really. But it sounds good. I hate magic. I don't hate your magic."

"Yes, well, because you have a Blood Book, you know what that makes you? Otherwise, that book of yours would show you nothing."

"I know, but I don't practice.

Jenny stood up and examined every part of the chamber that she could see from her location. Her eyes moved slowly and meticulously, taking in every detail of the wall, inspecting even the ceiling for any sign that could assist them. She observed a giant spider web in the corner, but that was the most interesting thing she saw. Jenny let go with an exaggerated sigh when she discovered nothing new. Getting into that sarcophagus would be anything but pleasant, if it became necessary.

"Jenny, what do you see?"

"Not a damn thing. I see a spider web over there, but that's it. You know..." She paused for several seconds as she thought. "They might actually be a diversion."

"A diversion?"

Her face scrunched as she considered. Sometimes, magic was designed to be tricky. "Maybe they're trying to make us think the sarcophagus is the center of attention when it isn't. But if so, what the hell are they hiding? Oh, it's so frustrating!" She blurred into the room and knocked their heads together, then back out again.

They sat silent for a few minutes, both thinking about Allison. Dracula thought that had she been a vampire and not a frail human, she could have joined them. However, then she would also be trapped in there, resulting in one big unhappy family. Jenny imagined her mother curled up with a book, struggling to read but consumed by worry for them. Time appeared to be getting slower, like watching a truckload of sand flowing through an hourglass. She opened the Blood Book once again, but it remained lifeless.

Dracula's thoughts drifted off to the cave.

Now sitting on a lower part of the steps, Jenny just glanced at the wall near the floor behind the sarcophagus. She saw what looked like holes in the wall close to the floor. Not just holes, but deliberate shapes. She took the rock out of her backpack, rushed in and placed it in one indentation, and then hurried back to her father. The stone in the wall lit up briefly a spectacular purple, and with the chamber being in the dark, it was impressive. The guards, however, were not at all impressed.

"What did you do?"

"Those polished rocks fit into the holes. Look!"

Both guards now remained visible even though they were on the steps staring in at them. One was trying his best to remove the polished stone but couldn't. The second Egyptian pushed the other out of the way and also attempted to remove the stone, but couldn't.

They argued with one another. Briefly, their voices had inflections of anger.

Jenny was eager. "I think it's a little like a safe. Place all those rocks in their proper places and I'll bet something is gonna open. Probably a door, and we'll get the hell out of here before I go stir crazy."

Dracula returned with the other six rocks and placed them on the steps, and both now had smiles of anticipation. He took one and Jenny grabbed one. "I'd like to biff one of these off those hard heads."

Jenny shook her head. "Whatever you do, don't break it. Do you want us to be stuck in here forever? Look what they're doing now, guarding the holes. And they're visible. Here, why don't you take both rocks? I'll push them out of the way, and you place the stones."

"Be careful."

She ran in and kicked one of the Egyptians in the stomach, pushing him into the other one and sending them both flying. It wasn't difficult for Dracula to place the rocks because they were all a bit different. The trick had been to move that massive statue to get at them, which they had already accomplished. Back at the stairs, they watched as the guards desperately tried to remove all three rocks now, but to no avail. They were so desperate that it made her laugh. The stones had sunk into the wall to such a degree that they were now flat with its surface.

Dracula took the three remaining rocks, and when Jenny went in, he followed her. She attacked from the opposite direction, pushing them out of the way. Dracula placed two more, but one of the Egyptians knocked the last one out of his hand and grabbed it.

Jenny and Dracula paused briefly and looked at one another. If the guard broke the stone, they would be doomed. The Egyptian smiled at them and then vanished. She could hear his footsteps; she hadn't liked its proud smile either. Being unseen made him that much more dangerous. It might be possible for the guard to kill them.

Jenny had panic in her voice. "What if he breaks it?"

The invisible Egyptian laughed like a little boy with a tremendous secret, naughty and happy. The sound of it would have made her laugh if she weren't in panic mode. Jenny now appreciated the ticking clock of an ordinary life.

Dracula felt a powerful blow to the back of his head, causing him to stumble and fall. Jenny attacked the space where she thought it might be and kicked the Egyptian. Jenny sent him hurtling against the wall, where he dropped the rock, and it broke into two pieces.

"No!"

CHAPTER FIFTY-EIGHT

THE RED SHERIFFS HAD ORGANIZED and had moved into the city three hours after midnight, one thousand strong. Bao and Wei, Annie, and Alastair, Michael, and Lauren, Alexander, and his vampire dog, Tessy, Vincent and two of his Japanese friends. Arym was there as well with the beautiful Margat; they had met at one of Arym's vampire meetings and had become friends. Bodolf in wolf form was commanding his pack of wolves, and a hundred namuhwoorks in crow form were flying with them, ready to do battle.

Over ten thousand vampires and zombies clashed on Franklin D. Roosevelt East River Drive near the Fulton Fish Market with the Brooklyn Bridge in the background. It was a fierce battle that went on for almost three hours. Zombies and vampires were flying everywhere, heads were popping off. Margat kept an eye on Arym as they fought side-by-side. The girl reminded Margat a little of herself because she had such talent for fighting. She fought like a master.

It was like two armies clashing. Wei grabbed one vampire by the throat as he cut the head off a zombie and stomped the skull flat. He threw the Gothic style vampire at Bao, who rapidly took his head.

Annie was chopping zombies and vampires as good as any lumberjack cutting down trees. She was more than happy to do her duty to help save the world. Alastair was mostly holding his own, although Annie had already saved his neck twice. He was scared for Annie, but his attempts to talk her out of joining the fight had been unsuccessful.

Vincent was busy shooting zombies in the temple, and with his explosive bullets, it only took a single shot to the brain to do them in. He bit a chunk out of an evil vampire's face that had killed one of his old friends, slicing his head off and kicking it like a football. He sliced another in two, then in four as the two halves of the skull fell under his feet.

Namuhwoorks flew down, changing into human form, releasing poisonous claws that could take a vampire's head with a single swing. They jumped into the fray but soon dwindled in numbers, as they weren't as hardy as vampires. They refused to back down and continued killing, even as they themselves were being killed.

The wolves launched themselves into the skirmish, biting off zombie's heads with a single bite, and then crushing their skulls beneath their powerful teeth. The fur was literally flying. Abram, a nasty vampire from England, killed three wolves before Bodolf jumped and killed him. This was going to be a battle to be talked about for centuries.

Alexander and Tessy were both in kill mode. The dog was as vicious as could be because she had to be, ripping zombies to pieces, pursuing vampires that were frightened of her and killing them. Alexander fought with her, commanding her when necessary. She had already saved Arym from two attacks from behind. She barked twice and chased one of the vampires who attempted to run but had nowhere to go. Game over.

A wizard that was fighting the red sheriffs cast a spell that prevented any vampires from being able to turn into bats. And then the ambush launched. Over ten thousand vampires surrounded them, no escape. Behind them, almost a hundred and fifty thousand zombies inched into place. The sheriffs realized there were simply too many of them to come out on top. They would go down fighting. It was as inevitable as sunset. All the red sheriffs would soon be dead.

CHAPTER FIFTY-NINE

JENNY GRABBED THE TWO PIECES OF ROCK and rushed to the steps. Her mouth opened as she was horrified. Were they now fated to an eternity inside this chamber, with only her father and that spider for company? Things appeared to be going from bad to dreadful. It was one thing after another, like a snowball rolling downhill picking up more snow. She closed her eyes tight, and when she opened them, her father was standing there looking down at her.

"Perhaps we can still place it?"

"I don't see how, but I suppose we have to try." Important to keep going as they had no other choice. That book could have saved their butts, but it remained dormant, as if in a coma. She watched the guards, who were continuing to try to remove the other stones. Did that mean they still had a chance? "Let's try it. Here you place the pieces in the hole while I get them to move their Egyptian asses."

Jenny knocked them back with lightning bolts as Dracula put the pieces together and set the last stone, but it fell out. Her magic didn't hurt them much, but at least she could push them back. One of them hit her so hard that it launched her across the room, and she landed with an "oof!" He tried again, this time ensuring perfect alignment of the two halves, and he succeeded. All the stones lit up purple as the guards vanished. Even the air seemed more pleasant. A section of the wall lifted with a rumble, revealing a skinny door and the actual king's chamber. What a chamber!

"They were a diversion!"

But before Jenny entered the next chamber, she had to open the sarcophagus in this one and search it, but to her dismay, she couldn't. Her father tried to open the lid but couldn't because the sarcophagus was solid gold. Thieves would have loved to have discovered this chamber.

As they entered the chamber, they observed that the golden sarcophagus in there was three times larger than it needed to be, painted with symbols of the sun, but some had worn off. A foot-long black scarab was on top of it with a scarab ring that belonged to the king inside it. Rubies on the coffin formed a pattern of sorts, but they weren't sure what it was, some kind of bird. Hieroglyphics were on every inch of the wall and ceiling. Three wooden chests covered in gold were against the wall, each had nine solid gold statues of different animals, with eagles and snakes being repeated several times. A round circular table resembling a birdbath was in the center of the room.

"Wow, look at this place." Jenny's voice echoed off the ceiling.

In the right corner was a small chair and table. Perhaps the king had used them as a child. On the table were tiny animals, lions, camels, and giraffes. All his toys were solid gold. The lion reminded her of her lion back home; she picked it up and put it in her backpack. On the wall was an enormous sun with a red eye in the center.

"When we get out of here, do you think we'll ever find our way back in?"

She considered it and then thought it would be easy enough. "I think so. But this place is too dangerous for people to be wandering around in. I can feel the magic everywhere. It might be best for it to go undiscovered." Jenny examined two shafts, and both had small amounts of sand that had leaked out onto the floor. If they were under the sand, it would be impossible for his spirit to have reached the sky, but then again, why couldn't a spirit travel through anything and everything?

Dracula opened the coffin, and Jenny searched it. The king was lying on a white flannel blanket. She wondered what he had been like in life. Did his people quietly rejoice when he died? She even searched under him but found nothing, and because there was no obvious way out, they were stuck.

"Father, a queen's chamber should exist. So, there must be a way out of here, right?"

"This chamber has to be thoroughly searched first."

"Well, I know that."

They searched the chamber, even looking through the drawers with the king's organs. A rendering of the king on the ceiling fascinated Jenny. He looked so handsome that now she wished she could have known him. He was adorably cute. Dracula noticed and smiled at her appreciation of his attractiveness.

"Good looking, isn't he?"

"He reminds me a little of a young Elvis. Too bad he couldn't return back to life."

"The way things have been going down here, I don't think you'd want him to come back to life. Probably kick both our asses. Use the force, Jenny, find that stone."

"Be quiet, I'm thinking."

Silence enveloped the chamber. Dracula was rather fond of silence, as the world could be much too noisy. Quiet was a gift that youth didn't appreciate. The stillness of meditation could take one deep down into peaceful bliss like nothing else. He sensed the magic swirling in the surrounding air.

"Look at this!" she gazed at a painting on the wall of sixteen birds inside their own blocks of time. Each one a smaller painting which fit into a larger one. On closer inspection, the blocks had seams as if someone could push them in. She pushed in an Egyptian goose, and it remained so. It was a puzzle that probably opened something.

"Daughter, you have a good eye. I looked right at it but didn't see that."

Jenny pushed in an eagle and then a Sacred Ibis. Then finally she pushed in a Red-billed Tropicbird. All the square blocks moved back out on their own, and they let loose a hundred arrows. It had, of course, been the wrong combination. Dracula blurred and prevented them from striking Jenny, but one caught him in his right bicep. The arrows were small, only about four inches long, but red as fire. The Master staggered to his left and then fell over sideways like a ton of bricks, displacing dust and sand. He was lifeless.

Jenny ran to him. "Don't be dead, don't be dead, don't be dead! Dad!"

CHAPTER SIXTY

✕

"DAD!"

Dracula was lifeless, and Jenny couldn't revive him. He hadn't turned to dust and bones, but he looked dead. She couldn't tell if he was dead or in a coma. Being the king of all vampires, Jenny wasn't sure what his death would look like. If he was dead, were all the other vampires now gone as well? It was unsettling seeing someone so powerful, so motionless and unresponsive. Jenny was in shock and couldn't believe what she was seeing. If her mind consisted of gears, the progress would be slipping. Her mind struggled. Jenny didn't know what to do.

Jenny stood and stared at her father, looking for any sign of movement, pulling the arrow out of him and throwing it so hard against the wall that it broke. Alone in that chamber was not an option she wanted to deal with. She stooped and shook him hard, but there was no response.

Jenny experienced a cold sweat. Time appeared to be frozen. Minutes were now nonexistent. Her eyes blinked slower while her mind wandered. Her face showing more stress than it had ever shown. Now, what? Jenny tried to enter his mind, but there was nothing to penetrate, and that really frightened her. Was that proof that he was dead?

The silence was now deafening. Jenny refused to believe he was gone. Dracula, being immortal, couldn't be killed by an arrow. He just couldn't. He must be in a coma, yes that was it. In an hour or two he would awaken, but what if he didn't? No, he would come back to life. Jenny was sure of it. Only she wasn't. She screamed at him her loudest; it was an outburst that just happened, that snuck up on her. "Dad, get up!"

There was no response, no movement, no sign of his condition improving. He appeared to be dead. The chamber was now a lonely space, and all those treasures didn't mean a damn thing. Jenny would give away every treasure in the world if he would just get up. She pushed him again, and it was like trying to push an elephant. He was so solid. Jenny's mind was a jumble of anguish and panic. She wanted to be home with her father sitting beside her on the sofa.

Dracula's ghost floated around the chamber. It wasn't easy to move around with no physical legs because everything was accomplished mentally. Several minutes passed with him being up near the ceiling, trying to get to the floor. A bit like swimming, only it wasn't. He had to will himself around, and he discovered it took practice. Dracula finally got down to where Jenny was staring at his body. Even though he was dead, he found he could still feel pain, though not physically. Staring at his daughter in mourning was almost more than he could bear.

So, this is what it was like to be dead? After all those attempts, an Egyptian arrow did him in? It was clear they had had some powerful wizard working with them all those years ago. They probably had complicated enchantments lost over the millennia. Who knows what the hell was on that arrow? It clearly wasn't pixie dust.

He tried to console Jenny, but he was as silent as the air to her. Allison was going to be so disappointed in him. If they never returned, Allison would never know what happened. A search party would be sent into the pyramid, where the darkness and labyrinthine passages and magic made it nearly impossible to find them. What they had discovered had remained undiscovered for thousands of years. Time seemed different now; he couldn't tell if he'd been dead for an hour or a year. Dracula had gotten himself into a predicament where he couldn't fight his way out.

The Egyptian king's ghost appeared and was indeed young and handsome. He had dressed himself in some sort of white Egyptian garb with gold, and he carried a dagger on his side. Dracula could tell immediately he was conceited. He walked over to the Master and looked at him with derision, and even the way he shook his head was scornful. Dracula believed that his heart was tainted with a nasty disposition as he passed judgment.

There was just something about those brown eyes that were unpleasant. Then the Master realized he could go into the Egyptian's mind. Inside there, Dracula discovered he had been a horrible ruler and a torturer. When the king laughed at Jenny's tears, Dracula put his fist right through his face. No connection and yet the Egyptian king vanished. Whether or not he had hurt him, he couldn't say, but he wiped a bit of his essence off his knuckles.

Dracula tried to go to the far wall but found out that he couldn't. He could hear voices whispering he couldn't understand, but it sounded like inquisitive whispers. Were other souls curious why he was there? He got the notion that his strike on the king impressed them and now they were also getting ideas. They had not only feared him in life, but in death as well. Dracula imagined a thousand souls chasing that impudent king around the chamber, and it made him smile.

Jenny had cried loudly, and that caught his attention. If he had to watch her suffering, this place was going to be hell. Zacharia had spoken of a white light, but he couldn't see one. Perhaps none was to be had for the king of all vampires? He couldn't count the number of people he had killed in his life; most of them deserved it, but still.

The Egyptian king reappeared, not looking so happy, and Dracula put his foot through him. Others appeared with angry, twisted faces and pursued the king. No longer so smug.

It was strange to think that he now had proof of an afterlife, but should he remain confined to such a small area for the rest of eternity was a dreadful thought. Eventually, he would have to befriend the Egyptians. He thought that the afterlife should have had a single language.

Jenny's hands tingled. She stared at them, and they were glowing white, so bright they lit up the room. Her heart jumped at the possibility. She placed them on her father, and he turned white. Sparkles of light went up and down his body, swirling and flowing. She felt the heat rising from him, and then he turned over and sat up.

"What *are* you doing?"

Jenny half laughed, and half cried, and he got his hug all right. If he were human, she would have crushed the life out of him. She had never been so happy. He stood to return the hug and wiped away her tears.

An hour passed, and Jenny was again staring at the birds because even after all that, she still had to get the right combination. This time, they were going to be smart about it. As Jenny punched in another four birds, Dracula waited on the steps. After the third attempt, there were no more arrows. Apparently, it had run out of them, or more likely, the spell had only called for three sets of bolts because no human could have survived one.

After Jenny had attempted the 14th combination, she considered it could take a while. The only good thing was that within the combination of four, the same bird couldn't be pressed twice. Otherwise, it might be impossible. It was now a chore to get the right combination. With the passing of time, they made a game out of it. Her father would push one and then she would push one. Over three hours later, they were still at it. They took a twenty-minute break and then got back to it. They had become bored with it, but it needed to be done.

Finally, when Dracula pressed in the Eagle, all four birds remained inside the wall. A square section of the far wall commenced to open, but then halted. It was stuck. Dracula gave it a boot, and it fell into the adjacent chamber. Two thousand years of dust displaced when it revealed the queen's chamber.

"Father, we should be archeologists."

"Indeed."

They crawled into the queen's burial chamber and discovered a smaller version of the king's chamber. The sarcophagus was regular-sized, and her throne was impressive. On the back of it was a scene of the Queen sitting on that very throne. It had a golden necklace hanging over the top of it. The four walls featured scenes from Egypt, such as the queen walking behind the king on the banks of the Nile, and her crossing the river in a boat.

Small shafts were running parallel to the ground, and when Jenny investigated one, she saw an iron door. A small child could probably crawl in, but it was unlikely that she could. It proved hard to predict what might be inside, and she dreaded seeing one of the two stones she required. How did they put it in there?

Another Egyptian guard with a hawk on its shoulder stood near the coffin, but this one was made of stone. It made Jenny nervous. She hoped it would not come to life. It held a rather pointy spear with Egyptian symbols carved into it. Dracula shook it and shrugged. He knew it to be stone, but might some sort of spell unleash it?

"Jenny, should I break the spear off? If it comes to life, I would rather that it didn't have it."

"I say go for it. I wouldn't want that thing sticking in my head."

As he was about to break it, Jenny grabbed him and screamed at him, trying to frighten him, to make him believe it had come to life.

Unfazed, he broke it off and dropped in into the dust. She smiled at his lack of response to her effort.

Dracula blew some of the dust off the statue. "Another dead end?"

"Look how small those shafts are, and there's a door in there."

"I see that." Dracula tore apart the granite wall with his bare hands. The king of the vampires felt pain as it cut his hands, but as they healed, he continued as he could see no other way. They had to know if the stone was in there. He pulled the door off and discovered the queen's jewels, bracelets, necklaces, and seven rings. Was it her most prized jewelry? Had they considered the possibility that someone would rob the tombs? They searched through the jewelry but couldn't find a single stone to fit the wand.

Jenny put on a ring, a necklace, and one bracelet. "I'm keeping them."

Her father shook his head slightly. In time, he would convince her to turn them over to the Cairo Museum. Dracula went to a likeness of the king on the wall and saw he was holding a stone in his right hand. It gave him an unpleasant idea and told Jenny he would be right back as he went into the king's chamber and into the sarcophagus. He tore through the many layers of linen strips that covered the hand, staring at the jewelry and sacred necklaces that covered the body. And there it was, the second stone that would fit in the wand. It clearly looked to be the right size.

Dracula felt like giving the mummy a whack, knowing what the king had been up to in life, but he only went back to Jenny and gave her the stone.

"Where did you find it?"

"In the king's hand. There's a small likeness of him over there holding the stone."

Jenny placed the stone in the wand, and sure enough, it lit up and remained lit, even though there was still one stone missing. She opened her Blood Book, but unfortunately, it remained dormant. The girl waved the wand, releasing tiny sparkles of Mantis green color, but otherwise, nothing happened. Her knowledge of spells was lacking. She would have liked to have commanded it to locate the final stone, and she told it to do so, but nothing happened. Why couldn't at least one thing have been easy?

"Father, do you have any ideas on how to locate the last one?"

"Not a clue."

CHAPTER SIXTY-ONE

T HE CEMETERY WAS A SEA OF REPLICATED mounds of dirt from where the zombies had escaped their graves. So Dorian and Lemuel had to move to yet another section of the graveyard. The smell of fresh earth hung in the air. Sharpton promised Lemuel a large section of New York City, and he could visualize how he would run it, mostly with zombies as servants. Dorian was enjoying himself more than he thought he would, wandering the streets, commanding huge numbers of zombies. It was a little like a video game, but a lot more fun. Exciting to see a thousand zombies fight for a single brain.

They were preparing to raise another hundred thousand zombies when a murder of crows appeared in a nearby tree. Thirteen sets of dark brown eyes stared down in unison. Four of them begun nodding concurring nods as they were now certain that these were the two that they wanted. They were not common crows; they were namuhwoorks.

"Brother, there must be a dozen crows in the tree." He then noticed how they were all staring at them.

Lemuel turned and looked up at them. "Those are namuhwoorks, and they mean to attack. Best you form a level seven bolt."

He had just finished speaking when the birds attacked, changing into human form with razor-sharp, poisonous claws, landing hard when they hit the ground as they transformed. The wizards were both protected from their poison as they had had several confrontations with the namuhwoorks years ago. However, that didn't mean that those dangerous claws couldn't remove their heads. They had killed one in crow form almost a hundred years ago, dissected it and had come up with an antivenin that now flowed in their veins.

Suddenly, claws ripped open Dorian's face from the corner of his left eyeball to his right cheek. The pain knocked him down to his knees. It healed, but the poison would remain for days while his protective properties broke it down. A barrage of daggers that Lemuel conjured up killed the attacker. He turned and sprayed the others, killing two more.

"This is what you get when you raise the dead!" Dorian screamed at his brother. "Nothing but trouble!"

Although the battle was uncertain, the namuhwoorks had attacked the two high-level wizards on orders from the Queen. They knew the odds of success weren't overwhelming, but they were brave fighters. Dorian threw a ball of red light the size of a baseball at three of them; inside the sphere were thousands of jagged pieces of shrapnel that sliced through all three with disastrous results for the namuhwoorks, shredding them to pieces. Lemuel screamed as the shrapnel ripped open his back. One sliced halfway through his neck when Dorian dispatched them both with a barrage of daggers.

Dorian grabbed his brother and blurred some fifty yards, throwing an explosive white sphere that killed all but two. Two of them shifted back into crow form and flew off. Lemuel aimed his fist at them, extending his pinky finger for aim; he killed one with a lightning bolt, but the other escaped.

"Those bastards can fight."

"I imagine that they'll be back with greater numbers." Dorian wiped a bit of earth off his brow as he surveyed how they had decimated large sections of the cemetery.

Lemuel's back continued to burn. "Do we have enough to raise another two hundred thousand?"

"I think so."

"Let's do it then. Sharpton will be happier with more."

"We're going to have to go over that way to do it." Dorian noticed a regular crow flying over and blew it out of the sky with a purple lightning bolt.

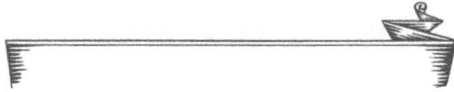

CHAPTER SIXTY-TWO

J ENNY AND DRACULA SPENT FOUR AND A HALF HOURS searching the queen's chamber for a way out. It would be easy to miss something that was concealed by enchantment. Jenny was now walking every inch of the floor, searching for a way out. Dracula was perusing the ceiling and upper walls, but he didn't have any luck either. She would be happy to breathe the outside air if they ever got out. The sun's light would be fantastic after all this darkness.

"Jenny, we're making progress, and with only one stone remaining, we're close."

They accidentally bumped into one another and stopped. "Father, we might be close to finding the last stone but getting out of here? It could be like coming to the edge of a cliff that's too far to jump, with the long way around being too dangerous a journey."

He stared down at her. "How old are you? Thirty?"

Jenny took the part of the broken spear and knocked on the floor as she made her way around. She was hoping to discover a distinct sound that would point to a secret passage. A simple doorway to the next chamber would have been nice, but no such luck.

"What do you want to do with your life when this is all over and done with?"

Jenny continued to tap as she thought about it. "I'm not sure of everything, but I know a couple of things that I want to do. I want to come back here as a family and explore. But before that, I want to enchant things and put them all over the world so the dangerous vampires will have no choice but to stay away from humans."

"So, you want to travel?"

"Yes, I want to explore every inch of England as well."

He was happy that his daughter was looking forward to exploring the world, and he couldn't wait to take Allison with them. It would be nice for the three of them to travel as a family. "England is a fascinating place to explore, and so is Italy."

"Hey, this sounds different. Listen." She tapped the floor. *Tink, tink, tok.* "It sounds like there could be something under here." She tried to push it down into the floor, and it moved a little, about three inches. "Dad, see if you can push it."

"Aw, she called me Dad."

"I can call you something else if you like."

And with two firm pushes, he moved it about five feet down, almost falling headfirst into it. The enormous block had become the first step down another set of stairs leading even further down into the Egyptian sand. Jenny jumped down, and Dracula followed close behind. They discovered a rectangular chamber with seven statues chiseled from limestone. They looked like guards of some sort. Their faces had incredible detail, so much so that Jenny thought they were a bit spooky. One statue had a falcon on its left arm and a spear on its right. Dracula thought the faces were so well done that he could pick them out in a crowd. He postulated real people had done them.

There was also a doorway with small steps that led into a lower chamber, but this one would have to be thoroughly searched first. The room was taller than it was wide, with a single shaft leading up at a 60-degree angle. Jenny looked inside of it but couldn't see anything, and it was the smallest one yet, barely big enough to accommodate a rat.

"These things are incredible. The faces are so lifelike, and that Falcon is perfection."

"Museums would fight one another for these things." He examined one from front to back and discovered a crack in one. "Look at this! Made in two equal parts and cemented together." He found a hole and peeked inside. "There's a skeleton in this one."

Jenny also peeked inside the statue. "Ew! Do you think these were the king's personal guards? Sealed alive to defend him in death as well?"

Dracula turned away from the statues to examine the rest of the chamber. "I do not know. It wouldn't be a pleasant way to depart this world."

The statues were in a straight line, and Jenny stared at the last one. "Look how handsome this guy was. He was gorgeous. What a shame."

Dracula examined a large painting of the seven guards in battle, protecting the king from five brigands. Was it a scene that had occurred in life? Or was it a rendering of praise to the guards that were entombed in the statues? In any case, it was excellent work accomplished by skilled craftsmen, evident in every intricate detail.

There was a large selection of weapons against the wall. Spears, shields, a bow with more than a hundred arrows. There was a dagger for each guard, but only two maces. Jenny didn't feel like touching anything in there. The fate of those seven men was too sad to contemplate, even though she knew her conclusion was only a guess. Then again, she thought it was probably a good guess.

As fascinating as that chamber was, she knew it was time to get down to the business of finding the stone; Dracula was already doing a visual search for it. Jenny examined the weapons and the statues. She concentrated hard on the wall paintings; she thought it would be easy to conceal such a small stone within a painting, and perhaps not so easy to find. Her father had the same idea as he scanned the walls as well.

"Father, what if the stone is inside one of those statues?"

"Great minds think alike. We'll revisit that possibility after we tackle all options."

After exhaustively searching the chamber, they proceeded into the smaller room. Empty except for a three-foot basin-like stone thing and a gigantic eye on the wall. But there was a hole in the seven-foot ceiling. She stood up on the basin, balanced herself as she prepared to look inside the opening. Jenny stuck her head up into the hole as an enormous sword swung at her neck.

CHAPTER SIXTY-THREE

DORIAN AND LEMUEL HAD RAISED another two
hundred thousand zombies, or at least they were in the process
of doing so. They cast the enchantment, and the zombies were
digging themselves out of the ground. Less than fifty thousand to go
as the others stood around waiting to be told what to do and where
to go. The undead emerged from the earth, with some headfirst, with
others it was hands digging their way out of the earth. Men, women,
and children came forth, skin hanging, bones covered in dirt. It was
an ugly army, but an army, nonetheless.

"Brains, I smell brains." They repeated that mantra over and over.
"Master, brain smell good."
"Smell brains that way!" He pointed his skeletal finger up into
the sky where a jet was flying over.

Lemuel told them where to go in New York City to wait for
further instructions. The zombies that knew the way guided those
that didn't. They were a sea of walking dead heading out. Some
jostled one another for more space. They usually got along, but in
such large numbers, it was frustrating. Some were already wondering
how they were all going to feed being so many in numbers, making
them irritable. The only thing that was on the mind of a zombie was
feasting on human brains.

A murder of crows three hundred strong spiraled out of the sky
and attacked. The namuhwoorks attacked in waves. The zombies
received orders to attack, and if it weren't for them, Dorian and
Lemuel would have been bones for sure. The zombies began feasting
on dozens of namuhwoork brains. Bolts of lightning began flying,
along with powerful energy spheres. The wizards stunned themselves
when one of the energy balls caught the zombies, launching a nearby
zombie into the air along with the namuhwoorks. Blowing it to
pieces and knocking down the two wizards.

The namuhwoorks were forced to pull back, transform and fly
away as the numbers that they faced were insurmountable. But they

would return when the odds were in their favor; they were determined to kill the two miscreant wizards that were causing such havoc.

CHAPTER SIXTY-FOUR

J ENNY LOST HER BALANCE AND FELL just at the right moment, with the blade cutting less than half an inch off the top of her head. She screamed and fell as Dracula caught her. She healed, but the blood was such a disturbing sight to the Master. When he saw she was okay, he blurred up into the hole and destroyed the mechanism that had been designed to decapitate. Dracula smashed the pieces into smaller pieces, and she could hear him cursing up there as he did so. Jenny blurred up beside him and observed as he continued to smash the already destroyed pieces. He even broke the blade into three pieces.

"Temper, temper. If I hadn't tripped."

They looked around and found that they were in a small corridor. It went for just over a hundred feet in front of them and only thirty feet behind them. All the paintings only used silver and gold colors. There was a miniature of the Great Sphinx of Giza against the wall behind them in perfect condition, only about two feet tall. It had the same composition as the big one, being made of limestone. The mythical creature with the body of a lion and the head of a human was puzzling. Why it was in there, they did not know. It was a replica of the one on the west bank of the Nile, except that the man's face had a perfectly formed nose. Was the Sphinx built from inspiration from the smaller one, or was it the other way around?

Dracula stared down at Jenny, who was smiling up at him. "What is that look?"

"Is that what you'll do with my boyfriends if you don't approve?"

He returned the smile. "Good luck finding a guy when they discover who your father is."

"I already have one."

He raised his eyebrows. "Really? Do I know the corpse?"

"Funny. No, I was just joking."

Dracula walked toward the far end of the hall and halted. He had never sensed such evil. There was darkness so dense that he took a step back. Then he moved forward and felt as if the life was being crushed out of him.

"Father, what is it?"

"I don't know what it is, but it feels like certain death if we go this way."

"I sense nothing."

Dracula picked up his daughter and placed her beside him; she took several steps back.

"Oh, I definitely don't want to go that way." She turned and saw a four-inch figure, the king, carrying the little Sphinx across the sand toward a crowd of people. "Look what he's carrying. Why the hell didn't I bring my camera?"

"Are we stuck yet again? And no sign of the third stone."

Dracula thought about the next move. The only thing he could come up with was to backtrack as far as they could go, hoping they had missed something. They went back and searched for several hours. They ended up back in the hallway beside the replica of the Sphinx no further ahead. Jenny tapped on the floor and then the walls as far as she dared go. However, she found nothing. They sat prone with their backs against the wall; Dracula drank a vial of blood, and she had several pieces of dried meat that she had brought with her.

She stared at the Sphinx. "You know, I'd like to take that little Sphinx home with me, that if we ever get home."

"Take it if you like; no one's ever going to find it in here, anyway. You know the handsome king had an evil wizard working for him."

"I thought that earlier."

"I'd guess almost as powerful as you, but wielding dark magic."

"I wish I had some dark chocolate right now."

Hours went by with conversation and thoughts and stories of past adventures that the Master had enjoyed, and others that he had endured. They were both worried at the prospect of being trapped in there and wondered what was going on in the world outside. They did not know how bad things were, and no inclination of all the zombies that were now roaming the streets of the Big Apple.

Jenny got up and picked up the Sphinx. "Look, Dad, I'm lifting the Sphinx."

Dracula stood up and grinned. His pupils widened. "You found it."

"Found what?"

He took his fingernail and pried the stone out of the Sphinx's right paw. "Look, that's it isn't it?"

She put the Sphinx down and took it from his hand. She took the wand out of her backpack and placed the last stone into it. The wand illuminated with such intensity that for a minute, all they saw was a blinding white.

"Dad, I can't see anything."

"I can't either."

They experienced temporary blindness until the light gradually dimmed to a moderate glow. The wand went back to normal, with the tip of it remaining bright white. Jenny circled the wand and observed as fine white particles flowed from it. The Blood Book now jumped in her pack. She opened the book, and it had returned to normal. It swung open to page 444 and showed her a spell that was highlighted in white.

Jenny spoke the words after she twirled the wand three times. "Coramathro dandor corisima dalto!"

Dracula and Jenny found themselves thrust into Jenny's bedroom in New York. "Well, that was fun, not! Damn it, I forgot the Sphinx. But I have two necklaces, a bracelet, and a ring. And ..."

Allison ran in when she heard them talking, and she hugged them both. Dracula was so happy to see Allison that he picked her up and kissed her. She now looked to be six months along.

"Mom, how did you get so big, so fast?"

"That's the way it works with vampires."

"Are you telling me that brat is going to be born ahead of time?"

"Allison, how are things holding up here?"

"Not good. Look out the window."

As Jenny and Dracula surveyed the street below, they witnessed a chilling sight: hordes of zombies and vampires lurking in every direction, with the fiery skeleton chasing Jenny. The street was shoulder-to-shoulder with zombies. The Blood Book jumped on the bed and opened to a page near the beginning of the book. It showed Jenny outside casting a spell, waving her wand toward the sky.

"Dad, come on, I need to do an enchantment. You're going to have to keep them off me until I do it."

Allison thought that there was always something to put her daughter in danger. "Be careful!"

Outside at street level, Jenny noticed that the wand had powered up. It was now pure energy. The flaming skeleton tried to attack her, but Dracula wrestled with it on the ground. She had repeated the spell in her head before she cast it. She wanted to get the words right. Zombies attacked them, but Dracula knocked them down by the dozens as if he was bowling.

Jenny stood and swirled the wand at the sky. "Teg tra mongoriatha." A tremendous surge of white light shot up into the clouds and spread out throughout the word. The blue sky fleetingly transformed into white. The flaming skeleton was the first to collapse and perish. All the zombies and the evil vampires dropped; the vampires turned to bones and the zombies now littered the streets of New York City. Over a million zombies would have to be carted away and disposed of in one massive grave.

The people that saw what happened came out and danced in the streets. Dorian and Lemuel dropped dead. They had too much evil magic in them, and the only way for the wand to destroy it was to kill them.

The nightmare was finally over. And to make sure Jenny was going to enchant objects which would keep any vampires with hostile intentions toward humans away from populated areas throughout the world.

Dracula smiled down at his daughter. "Whatever you do, don't point that thing at me."

Jenny gave her father a big hug. "Now to see if I can change that brat into a girl."

CHAPTER SIXTY-FIVE

ONE YEAR LATER JENNY was sitting on the sofa staring at her suitcases as her brother Drake ran in and pushed knocked them over. He had black hair and brown eyes and was a miniature version of Dracula, and so cute it annoyed his big sister. Even though he was only one, he looked to be about four. She pointed the wand at him and transformed him into a toad and watched him jump around. It had been the third time she'd turned him this week.

Allison entered the living and stared knowingly at the toad. "Jenny, you change him back."

"Oh, he looks better that way."

"Jenny!"

"Oh, all right." With a wave of her wand, he was Drake once again.

Drake jumped up and down. "Do it again. I like jumping!"

"I will not do it if you like it."

"Then I don't like it. Do it again."

Dracula entered with his suitcase. "The limo is here. Jenny, do you think Egypt is ready for us?"

"I can't wait. Mom, just wait till you see it. It's magical."

Drake sent a small lightning bolt at Jenny and singed the top of her head.

"Drake!"

EPILOG

ALEXANDER RETIRED FROM the red, at least for a while. The sheriffs married Abbey in a huge wedding ceremony that was talked about for weeks as the Master and Piers Anthony had attended. Arym and Jenny became the best of friends and went out on their first dates together. Dracula was waiting for them at the end of the movie, and Jenny's boyfriend had his very first panic attack.

Annie and Alastair also tied the knot and spent more and more time inside the magical world of the box having adventure after adventure. Sometimes they brought Hairy along. Alastair now allowed the spider into the house, with instructions that he stay out of the bedroom; he usually slept in a box in the living room, except for the nights that he liked to watch them sleep. They were happy. Annie was always ready to defend the defenseless, to fight for anyone that was in trouble.

Allison agreed and was transformed into a vampire in Egypt and, more than a century later, they remained together as a family in a mansion in Florida. They would visit Disney World every October.

After much cajoling and pleading, Piers Anthony convinced Dracula to let him write his life story, which became the bestselling anthology of all time. Jenny was the first to read it with a big smile at all the adventures that her father had been through.

Wei married Margat, and they ended up having seven kids, three boys, and four girls. In less than a year after Wei got hitched, so did Bao. He married a vampire from Texas. Wei and Bao now live across the road from one another in Savannah Georgia, occasionally going out on adventures.

Sheriff Vincent continues to travel and explore, but now he travels with a beautiful redhead called Big Red. She's tall and gorgeous and looking forward to Vincent meeting her father in Alaska. Both vampires are happy in their adventurous life.

Zacharia moved in with Dracula, traveling the world with him and his family. The Master journeys by private plane so Jenny can always bring Sarah along; the lion is never far from Jenny's side.

Keith is still wandering the streets of New York City searching for a friend.

Observing cats blurring in the Big Apple made Zacharia wonder if the union between Molly and Moon Diamond had produced kittens. One came up to him in Central Park and sniffed him before blurring off. The thought made him smile.

Zombies ate Sharpton.

The series was meant to be a trilogy, but it does indeed continue with more books!

Next in the Series. Dracula: Hearts of Ice Book FOUR

Don't miss out!

Visit the website below and you can sign up to receive emails whenever A. J. Gallant publishes a new book. There's no charge and no obligation.

https://books2read.com/r/B-A-QLJH-OHGPD

BOOKS 2 READ

Connecting independent readers to independent writers.

Did you love *Dracula Hearts of Glory*? Then you should read *Knights of the Dragon*[1] by A. J. Gallant!

An epic fantasy of dragons, knights, and wizards. A kingdom is in grave danger from a kingdom of conquerers. They have spelled dragons on their side. Their sorcerer is old and failing, and his protective shield does not have much life left in it. A search for a new wizard is in progress, but the odds of success are slim. Prince Marcus miraculosly befriends a dragon and they come up with the idea to hire foreign warriors to help defend Leeander.

A tale of romance and battle, and of course, humor.

---

1. https://books2read.com/u/bMny05

2. https://books2read.com/u/bMny05

Also by A. J. Gallant

Braeden the Barbarian
Forbidden City: Braeden the Barbarian
King of the Castle

Dracula Hearts
Dracula: Hearts of Stone
Dracula Hearts of Fire
Dracula Hearts of Glory

of Kingdoms and Magic
A Dragon Named Koontz

"of Knights and Wizards"
Knights of the Dragon
Knights of the Wizard

Olivia Brown Mysteries

I Was Murdered Last Night
Five minutes after Midnight
Dead Man Talking
Murdered Last Night

Paranormal Detective
Killer Detective

Young Adorok
Young Adorok

Standalone
A Christmas Carol A New Version
Garden Star The Awakening
Moon Diamond The Cat Detective

.